Finding Fran

A MIDLIFE MOXIE NOVEL

NANCY CHRISTIE

Praise for Finding Fran

"I loved the premise of the romance writer floundering in a relationship herself and then finding her way. And I always enjoy reading about the lives of writers, even fictional ones. As a writer myself—and as a woman—I could so relate to Fran's indecision, lack of confidence and self-doubt as well as be inspired by her pushing ahead despite it all."

-DOROTHY ROSBY, AWARD-WINNING AUTHOR OF
'TIS THE SEASON TO FEEL INADEQUATE

"Nancy Christie is an author who has made a career of writing about women's lives, and as a women's fiction reader, I'm glad to have discovered her work. Christie's strength is in her ability to thoroughly insert you into the life of her heroine, Fran. In *Finding Fran*, you learn about Fran's floundering writing career and her relationship troubles. Fran is relatable, and I found myself rooting for her to pursue and earn the life she deserves."

-MONIC DUCTAN, AWARD-WINNING AUTHOR OF
DAUGHTERS OF MUSCADINE

"With her Midlife Moxie series, author Nancy Christie has tapped into a long-overlooked, yet vital and thriving, world of women in mid-life. Sadly, so many books dealing in romance and achieving life goals only revolve around the younger woman, but Christie has wisely realized that 'women of a certain age'—like her, like you, like me—have been dealing with heartbreak, pursuing true love, and achieving their wildest dreams from time immemorial. Christie realized that it's time to start the conversation, which is why her book, *Reinventing Rita*, was such a success. With her follow-up work, *Finding Fran*, Christie delves into the shock and heartache of learning a so-called life partner has committed the ultimate betrayal that feels like a death, but leads to beauty, fulfillment, and self-awareness. Christie's characters are complete studies of humans with all of their messy, imperfect vulnerabilities, who realize they are ultimately in control of their destinies—they just needed a little push. I highly recommend *Finding Fran* to anyone on the journey of self-discovery, working to tap into their own strengths to create the life they've had at their fingertips all along."

-JENNIFER BOWERS BAHNEY, AWARD-WINNING JOURNALIST
AND AUTHOR OF *STEALING SISI'S STAR*

Other Books by Nancy Christie

Fiction

Finding Fran: A Midlife Moxie Novel (2024)

Reinventing Rita: A Midlife Moxie Novel (2023)

Mistletoe Magic and Other Holiday Tales (2023)

Peripheral Visions and Other Stories (2020)

Traveling Left of Center and Other Stories (2019)

Nonfiction

Rut-Busting Book for Authors—Second Edition (2023)

Rut-Busting Book for Writers—Second Edition (2023)

The Gifts of Change (2004)

Upcoming Books

The Language of Love and Other Stories (coming 2025)

Moving Maggie: A Midlife Moxie Novel (coming 2025)

Scan this code for more information about her current and upcoming books.

A MIDLIFE MOXIE NOVEL

NANCY CHRISTIE

Find your moxie and live your dream!

Cover Design by BookBaby

Printed in the United States of America

First Printing, 2024

Print ISBN: 979-8-35094-224-8
eBook ISBN: 979-8-35094-225-5

https://www.nancychristie.com

Acknowledgements

I OWE A HUGE DEBT OF GRATITUDE TO ALL THOSE WHO HAVE helped me along the way as I wrote this book.

First, to my fellow writers who served as beta readers, including Anita Gorman, Clarissa Markiewicz, Mary Staller, Robin Baum, and Valerie Jones—your comments and insights were more helpful than you know during the writing (and rewriting!) process.

Next, a huge thank you to Ann Henry, my editor *par excellence*— you not only identified what needed fixed but patiently took the time to explain why you made the corrections you did. As always, I couldn't have done it without you.

Much appreciation to Mary Bisbee-Beek—your detailed suggestions and recommendations made the story stronger and the relationships between the characters better developed.

And to all my friends, including Dianne Schwartz, Dawn Reno Langley, Paulette Dockry, Candi Aubuchon, and so many others over the years—thanks for listening to me, encouraging me, and in general, putting up with me throughout this writing process!

Dedication

To those women questioning if they should take charge of their future or let someone else dictate their choices and control their lives.

Your dreams are yours to pursue and your desires are yours to fulfill. Find your inner moxie and go for it!

Chapter 1

"JOHN? JOHN?"

I rolled over in bed and saw that John's pillow was uncreased and still neatly positioned atop the sheet.

"John?" I continued calling as I headed down the stairs. The click of the coffee cup and muted sound of the morning news led me to the kitchen where I found him checking emails as he ate breakfast.

"You didn't come to bed last night," stating the obvious.

"It was late and I didn't want to wake you, so I slept in the guest room," he said, not bothering to look at me.

I wanted to ask why he had been so late or where he had been but held my tongue. Instead, I poured what was left of the coffee into my cup and brought it over to the table.

"What time will you be home tonight? I thought we could go out to dinner. There's a new restaurant in town and—"

But before I could finish, he was already shaking his head. "I have clients to meet. I don't know what time I'll be done."

It was the same answer I'd received so many times before. John *always* had clients to meet. And while initially I accepted that as a facet of his career—he was a sought-after photographer after all—lately it seemed to be more the rule than the exception. Worse, it didn't seem to bother him.

Getting up from the table, he gave me a perfunctory smile. "I've got to go if I'm going to beat the traffic. I'll call you later."

Right, I thought with an inward sigh. We'll see.

He shrugged into his jacket, picked up his equipment bag, and went out to the garage, leaving behind the remnants of his breakfast: the half-filled coffee cup and plate with a few crusts of bread. I waited to see if he would come back, give me a kiss goodbye or at least a hug, but when I heard the garage door go back down, I knew it was just wishful thinking.

"You could have at least put your dirty dishes in the sink," I muttered as I cleaned up after him. I polished off the bread crusts, thinking it a perfect metaphor for our life together: my settling for whatever "crusts" in terms of affection or attention John left me.

But instead of exploring that more deeply—and did I really want to?—I made a note on a scrap of paper: *Have character see the bread crusts as an example of what little she had been receiving from Lover #1.* And as the irony of my using a real-life experience as fodder for my book struck me, I just shook my head.

That's what writers do, I told myself. We add reality to the plot until we come up with a workable story. There's nothing wrong with that, conveniently overlooking the fact that while it added a potential element to Book Four, my current novel-in-progress, it did nothing to resolve the lack of interaction in my relationship with John.

Knowing that with the work I had ahead of me this would be a multi-cup day, I set a fresh pot to brew before going upstairs to change. Then, armed with a fifteen-ounce mug of caffeine, I headed into my office. There was mail to open, voice mail messages to listen to, emails to read, and a manuscript to work on—none of which I wanted to do but all of which I had to deal with.

And it was the last item on the list that was the most troubling. Usually, I like the writing process: making up characters, developing plotlines, figuring out the motives that drove the choices made by the heroine. But this book was going nowhere fast. I had run smack into writer's block and couldn't see my way around, over, or through it. So instead, I focused on the administrative side of being an author, which included a hefty outgo of money to pay for all the marketing and promotional activities.

I had just finished writing my quarterly check to Uncle Sam, trying unsuccessfully to ignore the steadily dwindling balance in my bank account, when my office phone rang.

"*Now* who's calling?" I asked aloud, as I eyed the telephone with distaste. I was unwilling to hear from yet another telemarketer how XYZ insurance would save me big money or from another political supporter explaining why Candidate A was better than Candidate B for California's economy.

Not now. Not when my publisher was waiting for a synopsis, the first three chapters, or at the very least, a working title for my next book—none of which I had.

Sighing, I picked up the receiver and offered an unenthusiastic, "Hello?"

"Is this Fran Carter?"

"Yes. Who's calling, please?"

I held the phone with my chin and started riffling through the stack of envelopes on my desk.

"My name is Ben. Ben McCallister. You don't know me, but we need to talk. It's about John Robbins—*your* John Robbins," followed by a pause that stopped my hands from moving, "and my wife."

Variations of that kind of sentence often surface in romance novels when the woman (wife or lover, it really doesn't matter) first learns of her partner's infidelity. I should know, having published a few of them myself. And when that happens, her world reels and nothing is ever the same again.

But the reality was I didn't initially understand the import of the caller's words. Along with his professional clients, which included Wilson-Morrow, my publisher, John had quite a few private ones: women who wanted to present their husbands or lovers with sexy photos of them wearing little more than revealing lingerie or skimpy swimsuits. Aside from taking the publicity photos of me that my publisher required, his business had nothing to do with me.

"If you want to discuss something about his work, you'll have to call Mr. Robbins at his office."

I took a fast gulp of coffee from my half-full cup before returning to hunt through the mail, hoping my answer would satisfy the caller and allow me to get back to what I was doing. But no such luck.

"I did, but he hasn't returned my messages," he said impatiently. "You don't understand. It's not about work. It's about what's been going on between the two of them. They're having an affair."

"An affair?" I repeated. "Are you sure? How do you know?" wondering why I was more likely to believe what this stranger said rather than whatever John would claim when I questioned him.

If I questioned him. Because that's the thing with asking questions—sometimes, you get answers you'd rather not receive. Sometimes, ignorance, if not bliss, is at least a coping strategy. Sometimes, silence may not be golden, only cheap gold plating, yet it was still better than the clear crystal of truthful words.

"I've read the emails and text messages. I've overheard the phone calls. I even have hotel receipts. What else do I need?"

"Nothing else," I said. "I have to go." And with that I ended the call—and my life as I knew it.

I sat at the desk, my fingers playing aimlessly with treasured objects that were mementos of my writing life—the engraved pen from my very first book signing, the stack of bookmarks for my current book, *Love in Unexpected Places*, the crystal paperweight shaped like a heart.

Uncomfortable recollections flashed through my mind, like the time I found a jeweler's box in John's dresser drawer. He took it away from me before I could open it, mumbling something about its being a surprise for later—a "later" that never came.

The fact that lately John had been spending more nights at his San Francisco studio instead of coming home. And all those weekend trips he'd been taking, ostensibly to meet with prospective clients—trips that never seemed to result in signed contracts.

"It's the economy, you know," John explained when I asked about it last month. "People want to talk, but they don't want to commit."

Commit. An odd choice of words from a man who, if this caller could be trusted, paid the verb only lip service when it came to a more than half-decade-long relationship.

In my novels, there is always that scene when the heroine gets the worst news she can imagine, and she wonders how she missed all those little hints that should have alerted her to what had been going on. First, she cries and blames herself for what happened. Then she gets angry and considers some form of revenge. Finally, she moves on to a better, happier, more fulfilling life, shedding a few pounds and gaining a few lovers along the way.

But this wasn't a scene in one of my books. This was reality. *My* reality. Unlike my heroines though, I couldn't cry. At least, not right now.

Maybe I was in shock. Maybe I was in denial. Whatever it was, I did what I always did when confronted with a situation that I wanted to avoid: I shifted into my author mode. Not that it was a more comforting place to be, given that Alix, my project editor at Wilson-Morrow (aka W-M), wasn't happy with me. I was close to a month behind schedule and had to come up with something acceptable to turn in soon if only to avoid another "How is the new book coming, Fran?" call.

To make matters worse, my semi-annual statement and royalty check from my publisher still hadn't arrived, and I needed that money to pay for my planned two-week book tour. Not that I wanted to head back out on the road—those promotion trips could be grueling affairs—but I had to do what I could to boost the sales figures for my latest book, which weren't anywhere near what my first two books had achieved. Yet another reason why I couldn't afford to alienate the people whose contract I had signed.

I made a note to call my publisher's accounting department and then double-checked the schedule for my upcoming appearance on *Los Gatos Live*, a local television show where I was to talk about writing, romance, and real life.

Real life. The interview was likely to include the story of my own "fairy-tale love affair" and how John and I had met when Wilson-Morrow assigned him to do my publicity photos. It was a great hook and one that Vanessa, W-M's PR person, played up in every release. She'd use phrases like "Fran Carter's own magical love affair" and "The author's books demonstrate that love can be found at any stage of life." And she always included "Ms. Carter shares her California home with celebrated photographer John Robbins" in the bio section.

That was the focus of many of my interviews: how love had turned my life into a veritable fairy tale of excitement and fulfillment. It was what readers—or at least, *my* readers—wanted to hear about and believe in.

All the things *I* had believed in until the phone call that signaled the next chapter of this particular story. The evil witch (in the guise of a stranger's voice at the other end of the line) had arrived, and now it was time for the heroine to suffer. But in my case, I didn't know if there would be a "happily ever after."

What to do next… I opened the file of my latest manuscript and looked at the few notes I had made: a sketchy plot outline along with a few ideas for character names and locations. For the next hour or so, I gave it my best shot, playing with ideas for conflicts and resolutions, setbacks and successes, but to no avail.

Frustrated, I closed my laptop and shut off the desk lamp. The writing just wasn't happening, and there was nothing else to distract me from addressing the crisis at hand.

I carried my now cold coffee into the living room to slump down in the corner of the black leather sofa. Like many of the furnishings in the house, it was John's choice.

"It's modern, contemporary," he had said, running his fingers across the smooth surface. "It'll look great. Trust me."

And it did *look* great. The trouble was that the surface had a nasty habit of sticking to any exposed piece of skin. That didn't *feel* great— another perfect metaphor for our relationship.

Appearances can be deceiving, both to outsiders as well as to those right in the thick of things. But now, thanks to that phone call, I could no longer deceive myself. So, what to do next?

Throw his belongings out onto the front lawn and have the locks changed? Maybe.

Cry until my eyes are sore and swollen? Possibly.

Mentally shove the details into a box, operating on the "out of sight, out of mind" premise? Most likely.

Opting for the last, I pushed myself off the couch and headed to the kitchen, figuring a healthy dose of ice cream would help with the process.

"After all," I said as I pulled the carton of chocolate-cherry-crunch from the freezer, "until John gets home and we talk, there's really nothing I can do about the situation."

A great delaying tactic that unfortunately lasted less than five minutes. Before I could even fill my dessert bowl, I heard the front door open.

"Fran? Are you home?"

John's voice echoed through the house, and I toyed with the idea of not responding, of pretending to be deaf, of not caring whether he found me or not. But I couldn't. There was a part of me that hoped the phone call was a mistake, that John would come into the kitchen and suggest we go away together because he missed me and wanted me all to himself.

I shoved the ice cream back into the freezer and turned to face him.

"You didn't answer," he said. "I thought you were out."

He stood in the doorway, the same man I'd thought I knew so well. I looked in vain for some evidence that he'd been with *her*. Oh, nothing as obvious as lipstick on his collar or the faint scent of a woman's cologne. But something—something that would tell me conclusively that he had been unfaithful. *Something*—but there was nothing. Just his blue eyes looking straight at me, his camera bag hung over his left shoulder, his shoes scuffed from all the stooping and crouching he did to get the right angles on his subject.

It wasn't until I went to him and put my arms around him that I knew—the way you know, even before the test results are back, that there is something wrong. I knew it and couldn't deny it.

I pulled away and said the first thing that came into my mind. "How could you *do* this to me? My book has just come out and I have all those interviews when I'm supposed to talk about romance and real life! How *could* you?"

The absolutely wrong thing to say—I knew that as soon as the words left my mouth, but my pride was hurt. I had to say *something* instead of all the questions that were colliding in my mind: *Have you slept with her? Did you do it here? Is she better than me in bed? Is she thinner, sexier, younger than me?*

And of course, the really big question that I was too afraid to ask: *Do you love her?*

John looked at me, and I could almost see the wheels turning in his mind as he debated how to play it. Admit it and ask my forgiveness? Deny it and accuse me of being unreasonably suspicious?

He came into the kitchen, set his bag on the floor, and rubbed his shoulder. He always complained that by the end of the day, it ached from the weight of the bag. But it was his own fault. Although he kept most of his equipment at the studio, he refused to let his beloved Nikon out of his sight, carrying it on every shoot as well as back and forth from San Francisco to our home in Los Gatos.

I used to rub his back and neck for him, massaging the tight muscles until they relaxed under my fingertips. I hadn't done that for a while though, I realized. How long had it been? Weeks? Months? Maybe *she* was playing masseuse now.

That image drove my next words. "And don't bother to deny it! Her husband called and told me all about the affair. How long has it been going on? Is she the first, or have there been others?"

For a moment he was silent. Then he shrugged, a tacit admission of guilt, and said, "Look, it's been a long day. I'm tired. You're tired. Let's not talk about this now."

He turned to leave the room, but I planted myself right in front of him, turning into the angry shrew I'd promised myself I wouldn't be.

"I trusted you, for God's sake, and you have abused that trust! And I would *never* have done that to you!" My voice shaking, I went on. "I thought we had made a commitment to each other! How could you destroy that, destroy what we've built together, what we've planned—"

I ran out of breath and stared at him, my chest heaving, willing him to say something, *anything*, that could turn things around.

Instead, in that maddening way he had, he began to talk slowly, quietly, as if I were some crazed animal or suicidal jumper who needed to be talked back from the edge.

"This isn't the way I wanted you to find out," he started—so something *did* happen, my mind registered. "And it really doesn't mean anything. It's just the reality of the situation. We've been together for a few years now, Fran, and let's face it, it's not as exciting as it was in the beginning. And with your books, well, you're so busy that you don't have time to spend with me—at least not as much as you used to. And you can't blame me for being tempted, especially when many of my clients are gorgeous women with great bodies and beautiful faces. That's what I see, day in and day out. Beautiful, young, sexy women...."

And then I come home to you. He didn't say that part out loud, but I knew that was what he was thinking. And it was true in a way. I wasn't young or beautiful, skinny or sexy. I was just me: average-looking, fifty-five-year-old Fran with a few extra pounds and gray roots in need of a good color job. Not that my readers cared what I looked like. They were more interested in the women in my books: what happened to them, how they coped with setbacks and breakups, when and where they found their "happily ever after."

As for not giving him enough attention, with all the publicity appearances and book promotion events I had to attend and the necessity to write a second book and then a third to keep both my publisher and my fans happy, I didn't have any extra time or energy.

Now, when John came home, he found the real Fran, the working Fran: a middle-aged woman who worked hard and wanted to end her day with two aspirins and a hot pack on her cramped neck muscles instead of having a glass of wine and sex by the fireplace.

It was a bad thought, a dangerous realization, and one I wasn't ready to deal with, so I latched onto his other words instead.

"So, because I have to write and promote what I write, it's *my* fault you cheated on me? Am I supposed to be *competing* with your models? And what about you? You're always off on some shoot, and it *always* seems to be women—young women—that you're photographing. *I* didn't complain when you missed my birthday to do that photo spread for *Napa Live*. I didn't cheat on *you* when last year's planned weekend trip to Las Vegas was cancelled because you had to spend two weeks in Portland looking for the just-right vineyard for your latest assignment while I stayed home!"

I paused as much to catch my breath as to recollect the details of that specific incident. "Or maybe it wasn't the vineyards you were exploring but one of your models. Maybe it wasn't the right setting but the right *woman* who kept you there. You were cheating on me even then, weren't you? You've been doing it all along, and I've been too stupid to see it."

I stood there thinking, remembering, while he stepped around me, the way you would step around an obstacle in your path, and headed up the stairs.

"I have a photo shoot in Dallas next week, so I'm leaving tonight to scout locations," he said over his shoulder. "I'll call you."

And less than half an hour later, he was out of the house, his gear in one hand, his suitcase in the other.

Chapter 2

I wasn't sure if I should be comforted by the knowledge that, since he only took his carry-on, most of his clothes were still upstairs or angry that he thought he could take off and leave me here wondering and waiting. *Now* what was I to do?

I didn't know, so I did the one thing I could think of: I went back into my office. At least there I felt like I knew who I was and what my tasks were—even if I was struggling with the latter. With each book, the creative process had become harder instead of easier.

I had enjoyed writing my first book, *Love in the Moonlight*: creating the characters, developing the plotlines, figuring out how the crisis would be resolved to my satisfaction. But once the book was published and sales skyrocketed, Wilson-Morrow offered me a contract for the following three, and that gradually turned what had once been a satisfying creative experience into a job with deadlines to meet and expectations to fulfill.

There was the tracking process, as I tried my best not to repeat descriptions, dialogue, or plotlines from one book to the next. There was the editing stage with my publisher's team weighing in on what I wrote, how I wrote it, and where improvements could be made.

And above all, the sheer task of creating the aura of romance, of imagining a whole new set of characters and new ways to find love and lose love and find it again. Not to mention the research trips to unfamiliar locations to capture telling details: the rocky beaches, the romantic hideaways, the crowded city streets. Each book had to have a strong sense of place so readers would feel they were right there with the heroine.

My readers, Vanessa often reminded me, were not likely to ever spend a week on Cabo, ten days on New York's Upper East Side, or a weekend in Santa Fe.

"And they expect—they *deserve*," she emphasized, "to read a narrative that at least allows them to visualize themselves at those places, walking alongside Victoria or Rebecca or Alexandra or whatever your heroine's name may be in whichever book of yours they happen to be reading."

And Wilson-Morrow's latest marketing ploy made that kind of research even more critical.

"We're planning something special for your fourth book," Vanessa told me before I'd even finished the third, let alone come up with plotlines for the one after that. "Every reader who preorders your book will be entered in a drawing, and the winner will be selected on the date the book is released to the stores. The prize"—she paused dramatically—"is a five-night stay at the very same location where the heroine meets the hero. It will cost a fortune, but the sales and publicity will be well worth it. Of course, it takes time to set it up, so you need to give me the locale for that book as quickly as possible."

I had to admit it sounded like a great plan that should result in more sales *and* heftier royalty checks. *If* Book Four ever got written. And *if* my contract with Wilson-Morrow and my image with my reading public survived my personal romantic disaster.

Too many *ifs* to consider, especially now.

There was no point in staying in my office, trying to figure out what I would do regarding all the problems confronting me: John's infidelity, my latest book's less-than-stellar sales figures, and the fact that I had gained ten pounds in the past six months, which would be embarrassingly obvious on television.

"Not that it matters now," I grumbled. "The way things are going, who knows when I'll be in front of the cameras again anyway!"

It was late, but I didn't want to go upstairs, up to that king-size bed that was far too large for one person, to our bedroom where I'd be surrounded by all John's personal items, like his favorite book on photography or his prized camera: a 1930s Leica that he never used anymore but had earned him his first international photography award.

All those bits and pieces of his life that had always stayed behind when he left to go on shoots and that I took comfort in seeing last thing at night and first thing in the morning.

But now the sight of them would bring me pain. No, better to stay downstairs, watch old movies, and sleep on the sofa. Reality could wait until tomorrow.

But the next morning I was in no better condition emotionally or physically to face the truth than I'd been the night before. I had fallen asleep watching Bette Davis in *Watch on the Rhine* and awoke to find crease lines on my face from the corduroy throw pillow and puffy eyes from the three bags of airline peanuts I had devoured well after midnight.

And my knotted stomach told me the combined stress of John's unfaithfulness and the ongoing writer's block was still having an impact.

"What time *is* it, anyway?" I shoved myself upright as I heard the unmistakable whine of the weed trimmer and roar of the mower outside my windows. The lawn service. That must mean it was already eight in the morning. In three hours, they would be at my door, presenting me with the bill, yet another economic drawback to living here. One more expense that, if my downward sales continued, I could ill afford.

I checked my voice mail, hoping there was one from John. There wasn't, but there *was* one from Madison MacArthur of *Los Gatos Live* delivering unwanted news.

"Good morning, Ms. Carter. I hope this won't be too inconvenient, but we need to reschedule your appearance on our show. Of course, we *still* want you on," in a falsely reassuring tone. "We know what a great draw it will be for our viewing audience—a best-selling author right here in our hometown! I'll call you in a week or two to set up a new date. Okay?"

"No, it's *not* okay," I said, resisting the urge to throw my phone across the room. I had counted on that interview to generate more interest in my books. But now it had been pushed back to some undefined time, one that I suspected would never materialize.

Worse, I'd have to let Isabella, my literary agent, know about the cancellation—but *not* about my personal situation. I was no fool. As long as I was making money, my agent loved me, but should something happen to slow the income, that love would definitely cool. And the information that my "mid-life romance" was in trouble, coupled with the low sales figures for my latest book, would hardly reassure Izzie, let alone my publisher.

"Well, there's nothing I can do about that now," I said as I opened my calendar app to delete the *Los Gatos Live* entry. That was when I realized that, in less than one hour, I was due at yet another event at a nearby bookstore to give a talk on "Writing the Romance Novel: How to Integrate Reality into Your Work."

How had it slipped my mind? I raced upstairs to take a shower in record time before rummaging through my closet for something to wear that said "famous author" instead of "betrayed lover."

Then, I pulled my hair up into a pearl clip and hit it with a cloud of hairspray, hoping the strands would stay in place until the event ended. John had once told me wearing it up looked better than having it hanging down around my shoulders, adding (unnecessarily, I thought at the time), "It tightens up your face a bit and makes your jowls less apparent."

Maybe he was just being professional, the photographer telling his subject what flaws needed to be addressed and how to fix them. But thinking back, I wondered: did he really have to say "jowls"? Couldn't he have said it more tactfully, like "improves your profile"? What *was* he seeing when he took those pictures: his successful author-slash-lover or a middle-aged woman complete with sags, bags, and droops?

The camera never lies, they say. But just once, couldn't *he*? Couldn't he have told me I looked beautiful?

"Damn it! Stop thinking about him!"

I took a final glance in the mirror before heading downstairs to pick up my stack of bright pink bookmarks—one side adorned with hearts and flowers and a list of my books and the other with "Five ways to keep romance alive" tips—and headed out.

I turned onto the freeway, hoping traffic would be light. But everyone, it seemed, was heading toward Scotts Valley, and what should have been a thirty-minute commute was stretching closer to an hour, which would make me late for the dreaded event.

How different this was from those signings I did when my first book came out. Then, I couldn't wait to meet my readers, share excerpts from *Love in the Moonlight*, hear their comments (all positive, I recalled) about my book, and then spend an hour or two signing copies. Even though most of my sales came from online retailers, it was the one-on-one contact with readers that I most loved and drew encouragement from as I worked on my second book.

With *Love in the Islands*, the experience was still somewhat enjoyable even though the crowds were smaller and the sales fewer. But by the time *Love in Unexpected Places* came out, sales (both in brick-and-mortar stores and online) had dropped and reader feedback was more "meh" than "yay" when any bothered to comment at all.

As for in-person publicity events, they were more of a chore than a celebration, something I did because I had to, not because I wanted to. The days spent traveling on what people who didn't know any better enviously referred to as my "exciting book tours." They didn't know what it was really like: on and off planes followed by hours standing in the mall, bookstores, and coffee shops.

And smiling. Always smiling—a lesson I learned the hard way when a Chicago newspaper photographer took a candid shot of me leaning wearily against a bookshelf, eyes closed, mouth drawn down. The fact that I had been traveling across the country for six days straight was no excuse for looking like that, Vanessa scolded me.

"You're supposed to look like a woman who's living the life of romance, and if you *must* look worn out, it should be from a night of passion, not a night of traveling. You should have a satisfied, satiated look about you instead of the exhausted appearance of a woman in her fifties who just finished washing ten loads of laundry!"

But I *am* in my fifties and I *am* exhausted, I wanted to retort. But I kept my mouth shut. No one likes a whiner, and no one, especially not a company that had a vested interest in keeping the "Fran Carter" brand alive and strong and selling, wanted to hear anything other than enthusiasm from its product. Or that its carefully created image *for* that product had developed a serious crack.

And today's event would be even more challenging, given the current state of my relationship with John. How could I provide my audience with ways to keep their romance alive when my own was in its death throes?

These were hardly the thoughts that would put me in the right frame of mind for meeting whatever fans might be there. And to make it worse, I was nearly fifteen minutes late when I pulled into the parking lot.

"Sorry, sorry," I said to Elise, the community relations manager who had arranged the event. She smiled tightly then led me to where my audience waited, more than a little restive. Not a good start to the event, I knew, and I apologized as I took my place at the podium.

"I am *so* sorry," I said. (*Smile, smile.* I could hear Vanessa's voice in my head and obediently smiled brightly at them.) "I had every intention to be here on time, but John had a surprise for me, and you know the cardinal rule of romance: put your lover first!"

That at least got a laugh from my audience, some of them no doubt imagining a sexual tryst in the morning hours. I took advantage of the lightening of the atmosphere and started my talk.

"We all want more romance in our lives," I began, my standard opening since there ought to be few women who disagreed, at least among my readership. "But we don't know where to find it, or once we do, how to keep it alive. And in my latest book, *Love in Unexpected Places*, that's the situation Caroline finds herself in."

I opened to the first chapter and began to read a few paragraphs— enough, I hoped, to whet their appetite for the book:

> *Caroline opened the door of her condo, wishing as she*
> *often did that there were someone to greet her. But no one was*

home—not unless you counted Sammy, the gray-and-white kitten she had rescued the month before. Most cats were loners who regarded humans more as their servants than as their masters—obligated to provide them with food, shelter, and clean litter without expecting any sign of affection in return.

But Sammy was different. From the very beginning, she stayed right by Caroline, sitting on her lap while Caroline watched the evening news and curling up alongside her in her bed. But while Caroline was grateful for the affection the tiny animal gave her, she wished there were someone else in her life as well. She wanted a man to watch television with, to share the day's events, to cuddle up with under the oversized patchwork comforter she had bought on a recent singles trip to Branson.

As it turned out, the comforter was the sole item from the trip that would keep her warm at night. Most of the unattached men she met wanted a woman a decade or two younger than Caroline or had reached the level where their idea of physical activity was playing pinochle for hours at a stretch. It had been a waste of money and time, leaving Caroline with a firm resolution to never again be taken in by advertisements for activities for singles, all promising desire under the sun and passion under the stars. But it didn't stop her from wanting excitement, romance, love.

I stopped for a moment and looked up to gauge their interest. Usually at this stage of the reading, the women sat still and silent with a faraway look on their faces as they imagined themselves in the heroine's shoes, identifying with her longing, her hopes, her dreams.

But this time, I saw more than a few with slightly impatient looks on their faces, like they were waiting for something more to come along: something better, something more interesting, something new. Worse, I caught several women glancing surreptitiously at their watches as though they wanted to know how much longer they had to stay there before they could politely take their leave. It was a warning sign that I had better acknowledge.

Chapter 3

I CLOSED THE BOOK, DECIDING TO SHIFT GEARS FROM READING mode to interactive session.

"Well, enough about Caroline for now," I said. "To find out what happens next, you'll have to buy the book!" and was glad to see at least a few smiles in response. "But let's talk about you. How many of *you* want more romance in your lives?"

A few women tentatively raised their hands. "Come on, I know there are more of you out there who are starved for the excitement of being pursued, for roses and candlelight and slow dancing under the stars! Let's see those hands go up!" and to encourage them, I raised my own.

More arms drifted upward until most of the women in the audience had raised their hands.

"So, what's stopping us from finding it, getting it, and when it comes our way, holding on to it? Where does the romance go and why does it leave? And once it departs, how can we get it back again?"

Under the circumstances, this wasn't a rhetorical inquiry. I really wanted to know, perhaps even more than my audience did.

"I'll tell you why we can't find it," said one woman, stiffly getting to her feet. "I'm seventy-eight and I've been waiting my whole life for a man to sweep me off my feet. And it's been a long wait, for sure! First, they wanted to sow their wild oats. Then, they were married but wanted someone on the side or they were divorced and just wanted to have a good time and didn't care about love. Now, men my age are alone and want someone to take care of them: make their doctor's appointments and clean up after them and cook dinners for them like their mothers used to do. They spent their whole lives getting what they wanted and still aren't willing to do something for someone else—and they certainly don't want to be romantic! You younger ones have it easier than we do. Romance hasn't passed *you* by. You still have time."

Her companions nodded vigorously, but then a soft-looking woman timidly raised her hand. "It's not any easier for women in their fifties," she said, looking down at the floor as though ashamed to admit the truth. "Romance is something the young can have: the women whose figures look terrific in beautiful clothes or when wearing nothing at all. But what about us? We look the way we look: a few wrinkles here, a bit saggy there."

I could hear the murmurs of agreement, and as if in response, her voice grew stronger. "And why is it that men in their fifties and sixties are called 'distinguished' or 'silver foxes' while women that age are referred to as 'mature' or even 'elderly'? Men who date women a decade or more younger than them are admired while women who do the same are called 'cougars.' We can't win!" she finished in frustration. "As for romance, it's gone the way of roses and candy—out the door! And no offense, Ms. Carter," she said, looking directly at me, "but isn't it a bit of a cliché: the single fifty-something woman with a stray cat who finds love in the arms of her veterinarian?"

I started. How did she know that was the way my novel ended? Had she read the reviews—not that there were that many—or sneaked a peek while she waited for me to arrive? Or was it what my agent had said: I was writing "the same old story"?

The rest of the audience stirred uncomfortably, not necessarily disagreeing with her but possibly thinking it might be bad form to criticize the author to her face. But with a forced smile, I held up my hand. "Well, I have to say that, in my case, for all the years I *did* live alone, I didn't have a cat. Or dog. Or even a goldfish! But I think we've gotten a little off track here. Who or what *is* to blame when the sparks stop sparking? Is it our fault? The fault of our mates? Or just life in general?"

The room was quiet as they contemplated my questions. Then another woman who at first glance might pass for being in her thirties stood up. "The reality is that we are all trying to get through the day. Everyone expects so much of us. If we're stay-at-home moms, we had better be active community members while raising perfect kids. If we're career women, we had better be fast-tracking our way to the executive seat. And whatever path we choose, we'd better look damn good while we're doing it!"

She stopped for a moment as though considering whether she should go on. Then, taking a deep breath, she continued. "I'm over forty-five, and already I've spent more than I thought I would on face-lifts and tummy tucks, makeup and hair treatments, gym memberships and workout gear—just so my husband will be proud of me and find me desirable. Now I'm looking at breast implants! Why? Because my *husband* has decided that being seen with an 'older woman' isn't helping his career. He's fighting to hold his vice-president position at the company he works for, but he's been told that he has to fit in with the younger clientele. And that means looking the part at all those social engagements we have to attend. So, *I* have to fit in as well. There's no romance in our life because every time he looks at me, he's reminded of his real age. So, he's stopped looking. At me, anyway," and she sat down, staring at her hands and biting her lower lip.

"Okay, it's clear that we aren't happy. Or at least most of us aren't," said another woman in the front row. "You're the romance expert, Ms. Carter. You write all these books about love and romance for women who are no longer 'sweet young things.' And you found your man," pointing to the inside back cover shot of John and me on the beach where we met, "when you were what, turning fifty? How do *you* keep the romance alive?"

I took a swig from the glass of water on the podium, wishing it were something stronger. Or that the fire alarm would go off and we would have to evacuate the store. Or that I was anywhere else but here, facing a question that I felt no longer qualified to answer. Of course, once news got out regarding the demise of my relationship, no one would be asking *me* how to keep the romance alive since clearly I had failed.

And it *would* get out. If there was one fact I knew, it was this: the only thing that would beat out good news in the PR world was bad news. The information that a best-selling (okay, former best-selling) romance author's *own* love life was coming to an end would be fodder for social media posts and incentive for my up-and-coming competitors, a double whammy I didn't need.

If the news got out... or could I change John's mind? Could I seduce him back into our bed and into our relationship? *Could* I? Did I even *want* to?

This line of thought surprised me. Of *course,* I did! I didn't want our life together to end. I *loved* him. I loved *being* with him. Didn't I?

The shuffling of feet brought me back to the room. I realized I'd been caught up in my thoughts much longer than I should have been. I smiled, hoping to finesse my way out of dangerous territory.

"Oh, I don't think of myself as a romance expert," I said lightly. "As a matter of fact, I started writing my first book because I was living a life where romance didn't even have a place. I was single and had lost my position as a copywriter when the advertising firm I worked for shut down. I had no choice but to take on a series of part-time jobs to bring in enough money to pay the bills while I considered my options."

That certainly sounded better than what the reality had been: long nights crying over my steadily decreasing bank account balance and a steadily increasing number of unpaid bills. But that would be too much information, or in literary terms, too much backstory. Instead, I stayed on point.

"As for my choice of genre, it was triggered by the last job I held. Shall I tell you the story?" and without waiting for their response, I launched into a slightly edited version of my past as an inventory counter by day and would-be novelist by night.

I told them how frustrated I'd become when counting greeting cards in store after store, looking at endless racks of love and engagement and wedding selections and wondering if I would ever have the occasion to receive any such cards myself...

How I started imagining scenarios where I would meet that special someone—in the checkout line, at the car wash, while picking up parts at the hardware store—and our eyes would meet and fate would intervene and we would live blissfully ever after. And how, as I counted pieces and entered data, I started fleshing out the story and, at night, began drafting what would become *Love in the Moonlight.*

And how eventually fantasy became reality when I found my "special someone," and we fell in love and had plenty of great sex (not necessarily in that order) and lived "happily ever after."

Needless to say, I omitted the epilogue to my story: how "happily ever after" had turned into "unhappily at the moment and potentially forever."

I had caught their attention—a good thing, too because I wanted to avoid any more questions about how to keep romance alive. With any luck at all, this part would soon be over. Elise would come over to break up the presentation and move it into the next and, from the store's perspective, more important part: the book signings and sales.

So much for luck. I looked up, hoping to catch Elise's eye, only to realize she had left the area. Worse, there were still one or two upraised hands.

"Um, yes, you had a question?" looking at a woman whom I estimated was in my age bracket. I was hoping that it would be something along the lines of what did I wear while I worked (my standard and untruthful response: a silky negligee), what did I do to relax (drink champagne in a bubble-filled bath—another lie I often used), or what my upcoming book was about.

The last one would be the easiest to address because I would just shake my head, explaining I was "under orders from my publisher not to divulge details about future projects."

"Ms. Carter, I started reading romance novels when I was in my teens," the woman began. "I bought into the whole 'a white knight will come and sweep you off your feet' myth. That's what I was waiting for, and that's what I thought I married. And I kept reading the books and doing everything they said to keep the romance alive. I served romantic dinners by candlelight—*after* feeding the kids, of course. I made sure my hair was done and my makeup was perfect, even after spending the whole day cleaning the house or running to pediatrician appointments or school meetings. And I never, not *once*," she emphasized, "said 'no' regardless of how I felt physically or emotionally. Nope, I was the perfect little wife that romance books said I had to be. I did it all, but it didn't make a bit of difference. The kids grew up and left home, and pretty soon, he left, too."

She raised her hand to forestall any sympathetic outpouring. "Hey, don't feel sorry for me! That was the best thing that could have happened. I don't regret having my children, but looking back, I realize our marriage never gave me what I wanted. I'd been so caught up in the fantasy that books like yours create that I never asked myself what kind of life I really wanted. So, I hung on a lot longer than I should have. My whole life was focused first on finding a man and then on keeping him. These days I'm concentrating on *me*—and I'm a damned sight happier than I've ever been! There *are* no 'white knights,' Ms. Carter. So why do you keep writing about them? Why don't you write about *real* life?"

I started to take another sip of water but saw the glass was empty. Unfortunately, so was my brain. I didn't know how to answer or what to say. I was publicly forced to justify my books' existence—*my* existence—at a time when I was wrestling with the very questions she had raised.

Surprisingly, another audience member came to my rescue. "Now, don't be too hard on her," she said. "I'm sure Ms. Carter knows that reading her books is our way of taking a break from our real lives, right?" looking up at me.

"Yes, of course," I said, so grateful to have someone on my side that I didn't stop to analyze my words. "I mean, these books," waving at the shelves behind me stocked with novels featuring women with heaving bosoms and half-dressed muscular men on their covers, "they are *fiction* after all! No one *really* believes life is like that. It's like in the movies when the lovers wake up in the morning and start kissing each other. Did the directors never hear of morning breath? It's all make-believe, all of it! A fantasy! Escapist literature! And if you try to turn your life into a romance novel, you are bound to be disappointed."

My words echoed in the sudden silence, and I realized too late what I had said. I had trashed not only my own books, but the entire genre. Worse, in so many words, I had told them that if they were looking for information on how to rejuvenate their lives, they were wasting their money buying my novels.

What had Vanessa said to me—that my readers wanted to believe that life and love *hadn't* passed them by? And now I had told them that it was all a load of crap.

"Thanks for coming here today, Ms. Carter," said Elise, pushing me none too gently from the podium and toward the stack of as-yet unsigned and unsold books.

When had *she* arrived? Obviously, by the force of her shove, soon enough to hear my last bit.

"Let's give her a warm round of applause," and she started clapping, with the rest of the audience following suit while I smiled. And smiled.

"And now," she continued, "Ms. Carter will be happy to autograph books for all her loyal fans. We've even set up a sales area right here," no doubt to avoid the sticky situation of books being signed but never quite making it to the cash register, "so you can purchase your book and have it autographed quickly and easily."

She pulled out a chair and motioned for me to take my seat, and I continued to smile as I prepared to go through the familiar line of conversation: "Shall I autograph the book to you? Your name? And how do you spell it?" Then signing my name with a note above it wishing Mary Jane or Dorothy or Kelly a life of romance.

I could have saved the effort, since it soon became obvious the women were more interested in talking among themselves than buying my books. Finally, a few of them came my way, probably more out of politeness than any desire to read my book. But while they waited for me to sign my name, they kept glancing back at the happily single woman holding court and sharing what she was doing now that she was on her own. Snatches of her words drifted my way—"my last trip to Italy" and "turned my spare bedroom into an art studio"—and I found myself envious of the life she had created. Which was ridiculous because wasn't I already living the life I wanted, the life I had created? Well, *wasn't* I?

"*She* should write a book," the first one said to the others in line. "Her life is incredibly interesting and exciting!" before grabbing my book and heading back to the growing cluster of listeners.

It took less than half an hour to finish the sales part of my event. This was not a good outcome, considering that signings for previous books had stretched to two hours or more. And when the crowd faded away, there was still an embarrassingly large stack of novels left on the table—unsigned, unsold, unwanted. Like me.

"Well, that went well, don't you think?" I said to Elise, still smiling although my cheeks ached from the effort. "Shall I sign these?" looking at the books.

"Um, yes, just a few," she said, pushing half a dozen my way.

"A few," not "the whole stack," I noted, which meant that, in a month or less, the unsold and unsigned ones would be shipped back to my publisher, ultimately to be listed on my royalty statement under the "returns" heading.

"Just a few" also meant she didn't expect them to sell, even with the "Signed by the author" sticker on the front cover.

But I smiled and signed my name and then, still smiling, picked up my belongings and headed for my car. Time to go home and lick my wounds and prepare for the call from Vanessa (who always checked in with the store after an event) asking me what in hell I'd been thinking when I opened my mouth.

As for the can of worms this day's event had triggered, I'd use Scarlett O'Hara's approach and think about it tomorrow. God knows I wasn't ready to deal with it after today's debacle.

Chapter 4

OLD HABITS DIE HARD, AND AS IS OFTEN THE CASE, THE OLD HAB-
its tend to be bad ones at that. My remedy for handling life disasters was
food—in this case, an eight-inch pizza loaded with everything: extra
cheese, anchovies, mushrooms and, to get some actual nutrition into it,
peppers, broccoli, and cauliflower. I carried my dinner into the house, on
the way removing the lawn maintenance bill wedged in the front door.

It was only four o'clock and I wasn't really hungry, but the aroma
of melted cheese worked on my mind like the smell of a lit cigarette to a
smoker. I polished off a slice before I even made it to my office and started
on the second while I checked for messages on my business line and cell.

No message from John. Not that I really thought there would be,
but I *had* hoped. I realized that all day I'd been figuratively holding my
breath, waiting for his call when he would tell me that *of course* he loved
me and *of course* he would be coming back and *of course* he wanted to stay
with me.

Knowing this, my emotions made a sharp right turn from self-pity
to anger—not at John but at myself.

"How could I have been so stupid?" I said aloud. "How could I
even *think* that this would work? I should have known he would find

someone else! All those models, all those gorgeous bodies he sees through the camera lens. And then he comes home to me!"

I stared at myself in the mirror on the wall across from my desk, a feng shui correction that was there to warn me if an enemy were sneaking up from behind. Well, the mirror hadn't done what it was supposed to do. Or it had, and I hadn't wanted to see what it reflected.

I took a bite of pizza, chewing slowly while I thought about it all—what might happen and what I really wanted to happen. And the questions that had come unbidden into my mind at the signing: Could I bring him back to me? And if I did, would he stay or would he stray again? And even more telling, did I actually *want* him back?

And that leapfrogged to the next point of contention: When did it stop mattering *what* I wanted? While I had envisioned a romantic relationship with the two of us building a life together, the reality was that my life wasn't all that different *with* John than it had been *before* him. I wrote my novels and only left home for the necessary book marketing appearances.

And John? John did essentially what he had done before he met me. He either went to work at his studio or traveled to locations picked by his clients. Or he took time off to, as he put it, "recharge his creative vision" (though I now wondered how he had been recharging it—and with whom).

Or he was out late attending numerous social events—necessary, according to John, to enable him to network with prospective clients. Our first year together I went with him, but it wasn't long before he stopped inviting me.

"You know you hate being out late at night," he had said. "And these are work events, which means I have to schmooze with all kinds of people and you'd be on your own with no one to talk to."

It all sounded reasonable. But gradually it became clear that John was spending more time *away* from me than *with* me, and what was worse, he didn't seem to mind it. As for me—well, I had become one of my own heroines *before* the Great Romance came her way and changed her life forever: the neglected wife, the unloved middle-aged woman, the career professional who came home to an empty house.

But in my case, this happened *after* the love affair began, not before, leaving me to wonder what would happen next.

It was like being stuck at a literary impasse: my heroine (in this case, *me*) was standing on the edge of a cliff, and the hero, who was to appear in time to save her, had instead been the one who had left her there before riding off into the sunset without her.

A piece of green pepper cascaded off the pizza slice to land on yesterday's mail, recalling me to my senses. There may not have been messages from John, but the caller ID on the landline showed two other calls had come in while I was out. I started with the one from my agent.

"Fran, it's Izzie. I hope the signing went well and you sold lots of books!"

Of course you hoped that. If my sales dropped, so would my value to Wilson-Morrow and the potential for future publishing contracts. And that would have a negative impact on *your* income as well.

"But I *am* a little troubled after my conversation with Alix. She said you have yet to send in anything regarding your upcoming book, not even a title or synopsis, and she's concerned about how this might affect the overall timeline. I know you needed a bit of a break after the last project," and here her voice took on the soothing tone that was aimed to convince me that all she cared about was my state of mind, "but you really must get back on the horse and start writing."

There was a pause, then she went on, a touch of warning in her tone. "You have a deadline, you know. You wouldn't want to break the contract. Besides," and here it came again, the encouraging words that were supposed to get me all revved up and back to work, "I just *know* you could be another Jacqueline Susann or Danielle Steele or Stephenie Meyer, cranking out best sellers year after year. Call me and let's talk."

The next message was no better. It was not from Alix but from one of her underlings—a bad sign that even a blind man could see. Before this book, my calls had come directly from Alix, congratulating me on exceeding sales projections, telling me how great the latest book was, and promising even more incentives to keep me happy and productive: a book-tour assistant in each city, a nicer hotel, a limousine at the airport instead of taxi service.

But she had been ominously quiet since *Love in Unexpected Places* had hit the bookshelves and the numbers had hit a wall, with sales not even matching those of my previous books, let alone of my nearest competitor.

"Ms. Carter, this is Janet from Wilson-Morrow. We had a meeting involving your fourth book, and Alix wanted me to tell you that the timetable has been moved up. She'll need your synopsis and the first three chapters by the end of this month, not next month as originally planned. Please call me back to confirm you received this update."

A pause, and then, almost as an afterthought, "I love your books! You have a nice day!" *Click.*

By the end of the month... less than thirty days away. I could, of course, call them back and say that the deadline was outrageous, that there was no way I could meet it, but that didn't seem like a prudent move. I might have gotten away with it if the sales from my current book were better than anyone had anticipated, but unfortunately, the reverse was true.

Sales were down, interest in *me* was down (if the cancellation of the TV interview was any indication), and this was no time to rock the publishing boat. It didn't matter that I was originally given two months to turn in this material. I couldn't risk alienating my publisher, especially after what had happened today.

I needed to get writing and fast—get something down on paper: a few chapters, a synopsis, even a title, for God's sake!—despite the fact that I was beginning to doubt my own creative expertise. Despite the fact that things were not "all right in the world" between me and my agent, let alone between me and Wilson-Morrow. Despite the fact that my own romance had hit the skids and might even be sliding down that slippery slope to a cataclysmic finale.

How would it end? I wondered as I shifted around the papers on my desk. Would John change his mind after spending time away from me, from our home and our life together? Or would he finish packing up his belongings after telling me that he wanted out, that the relationship just wasn't working for him anymore, as Robert, the low-life spouse, had said to the heroine in the final scene of Part One of my second book, *Love in the Islands*?

I thought back to that plotline: how Melanie's marriage had turned into a disaster when her husband refused to stop seeing other women. How she tried everything she could think of to bring him back: sexy lingerie, romantic weekends, even counseling—all to no avail. How the last straw was when she found her spouse and his lover together in the very place where he used to take *her*, sharing the same romantic dinner and, from what Melanie could tell in the dim light, the same type of wine.

How pathetic she was—and *I* could say that since I was the one who created that character. She confronted Robert, eyes tearing and voice quavering, and asked him what his plans were—although anyone else would know he had already told her, just not in actual words.

But now he did: he stood up, all six-foot-three handsome body of him, and said, "Sorry, Melanie, but this marriage just isn't working for me anymore," and sat down again to go back to eating his dinner.

When I wrote that book, my life was so much better than that of my heroines, at least during their "I've been dumped and I'm all alone and no one will ever love me again" phase. John and I were together at that point, and as I'd read over the breakup scene, I'd think to myself how glad I was that I was out of that stage and finally had someone who loved me.

And I really thought John *did* love me. After all, he'd moved in with me even though he passed on the idea of legalizing our arrangement with an "I do."

"Marriage is for people who want to have kids, and we're past that stage," he said when I broached the idea. "Plus, if we got married, our combined income would put us in a higher tax bracket, and who wants to give more money to Uncle Sam? Living together as an unmarried couple makes more sense. And think of the time and gas you'll save," he added persuasively.

I had to admit he was right. After all, I was the one who had been making the nearly two-hour commute each weekend from my home to John's San Francisco apartment.

But it was worth it, I'd tell myself each weekend as I drove north on Route 85 until I picked up Route 101, all while trying to ignore the soreness in my shoulders and the crick in my neck from working all day at the computer. We would have dinner together, followed by an evening making love.

Unless he was tired from shooting all day. Or if he had an early morning appointment and needed his sleep. Or if he just didn't feel like it.

All his reasons for not getting married sounded valid, and if some part of my mind wondered why he had them right at his fingertips, I dismissed it and agreed with his decision. And I did think that living in the same house would be better. John would be happier, more attentive, more available, I thought. We would spend more time together and really build a life as a couple. Basically, I told myself all the things we women tell ourselves when we want to believe our decision is the right one.

We were in love, I thought as I started working on Part Two of my book when my poor lonely heroine finds true love and lives "happily ever after." This was my fairy-tale ending.

Well, now I was back in Part One—in writing and in real life. And while I hadn't figured out what I wanted to do with our relationship, I could at least take the reins where my career was concerned.

But not here. I couldn't sit in this house trying to write while waiting for John to call. Or to send a bouquet of flowers with a heartfelt apology. Or to pull in the driveway, take me in his arms, and tell me it was all a big mistake.

No, I would have to go somewhere—*anywhere*—to a place where I could work and not think about John. That's what I would do. And by the time I came back home, everything would be clearer, and I would have made some progress—at least on my novel.

I finished off the last bite of pizza, then headed upstairs, too exhausted by the day's events to care that the bed was only half occupied. But if I hoped things would look better the next morning, I was quickly disabused of that notion. Even a third cup of coffee didn't help. I sat in my desk chair and looked at the framed book covers on the wall: *Love in the Moonlight, Love in the Islands,* and *Love in Unexpected Places.*

Once the sight of them had filled me with pride and satisfaction, but now all they did was add to my overwhelming sense of trepidation. While my first book had been a runaway best seller to everyone's surprise, including mine, the subsequent two hadn't reached that status in terms of sales.

And there was that conversation with Isabella after Book Three came out. While *Love in Unexpected Places* had a respectable number of preorders, it wasn't as many as the first or even the second. There were fewer interviews as well and fewer opportunities for signings at major book retailers and in big cities, forcing me to settle for events in smaller stores and less populated towns than had been previously arranged.

"Shake up the storyline a bit," Isabella had said when I called her to complain about the lack of interest from the usual media markets. "Everyone has heard the same old story. They want something fresh, something new."

"But my books basically *are* the 'same old story,'" I pointed out. "That's what Wilson-Morrow asked for, that's the contract I signed, and that's what the reading public wants!"

"Well, obviously, they *don't* want it—at least, not in the numbers they once did," she retorted. "Look, my job as your agent is to keep you marketable, and that means facing facts. The first two books did well, but now there's a formulaic feel to your novels. Even the dialogue has a 'been there, done that' quality to it. I know the world is jumping on the green bandwagon, but that doesn't apply to fiction. You can't recycle old plotlines and 'he said, she said' conversations. Either inject something fresh and new into your books or run the risk of your next book being rejected, if not by Wilson-Morrow, then certainly by your readers!"

But when Izzie said to shake things up a bit, I doubted she meant for me to become a woman whose lover cheated on her. I was to be a role model for the new "midlife woman": a woman who had found love in her post-childbearing years and kept it alive, despite the maturing of her face and body.

That was why my books had struck a chord with my target audience, Vanessa told me right before my second book was released.

"Most of your readers are women in their late forties, fifties, or even older. They want to know that life hasn't passed them by. They want the thrill and the excitement of love. And they want sex—or at the very least, to know that women in their age group are *having* sex—with all the fireworks it entails," she said. "With you and your books, they get the whole package. Not only are your heroines women they can relate to in terms of age *and* appearance, but you represent possibilities for them—even the ones who are married. You've got that great romantic thing going with your handsome photographer lover, and they can see it in the publicity photos."

Come to think of it, I hadn't had that kind of rah-rah conversation with anyone at W-M since... Well, now I couldn't recall. Certainly not when my third book was approaching release and advance sales were less than half of previous numbers. Were my fans tired of reading about sex? Were they tired of being told, however indirectly, that passion could and should be a part of their lives?

Or were they tired of *me*—me-the-author—and my concept of what romance was like, or supposed to be like, for women my age? Was I destined to go from successful author in love to dumped woman and has-been novelist in less than ten years?

This wasn't what I had expected when I became a full-time novelist and John's lover. I had anticipated that both situations would continue forever and I'd live happily ever after, cranking out books by day and making love to John by night.

Not what I expected, but the reality in which I found myself. And I had no idea how the next chapter would turn out.

Chapter 5

LUCKILY, JUST THEN MY CELL PHONE RANG, INTERRUPTING THE downward spiral my thoughts had taken. Or maybe not so luckily, as I saw it was my best friend Diana. It was close to nine. By now I should have been in my car and heading to Los Gatos Creek Trail for our weekly hike.

"Are you on your way?"

"Yes, I'm pulling out of the driveway even as we speak," I lied, heading upstairs to get out of my pajamas and into my workout clothes.

"No, you're not. You probably haven't even brushed your teeth yet. Look, you've got ten minutes to get moving. I'll meet you in the parking lot. Okay?"

"Okay," knowing she wouldn't accept any excuse for me not show-ing up. Ever since John and I moved to the area, Diana and I had formed a routine of meeting every Sunday morning. It was her idea—I wasn't much for exercise—but she said it would help relieve the work stress for both of us.

Although, given how successful her real estate agency was, I couldn't imagine what kind of stress she could be under. Since she opened her firm more than ten years ago, she had done remarkably well. But then Diana was one of those people who never let setbacks deter her or fears derail her. The woman exuded confidence—something that was apparent at our first meeting.

She strode into the ad agency where I was working at the time, introduced herself as "Diana Alexander, top Realtor in Santa Cruz," and proceeded to drive a hard bargain with my boss for a comprehensive marketing campaign to get her new business the attention she felt it needed.

That job became my baby, and by the time her website was up and running, her ads developed, and her media releases scheduled, she and I had formed a solid professional and personal relationship.

I envied her "go get 'em" attitude and considered her a role model for what I could become, especially given that she was more than a dozen years my senior. And if sometimes her "quit complaining and get moving" approach was a bit much to take, I accepted it as a facet of her personality.

Besides, I would tell myself, when something she said hit a little too close to home or wasn't exactly what I wanted to hear, she meant well. She just didn't always understand. We were two different people, after all.

I made it there in record time, pulling next to Diana's BMW Z4 with its REALTR1 license plate.

"Took you long enough," she observed, looking pointedly at her watch. "Come on, let's get going." And without even waiting for me to respond, she headed to the trail access point.

I caught up with her, as usual feeling slightly underdressed when compared to Diana's stylish running outfit: this time a canary-yellow tracksuit that set off her gleaming black hair. I, on the other hand, was in my usual t-shirt and leggings, both gray, a color that matched my mood.

"Slow down, will you!" trying to catch my breath.

No one would ever guess that Diana was just a few years shy of her seventieth birthday. With her long legs—she was easily five-foot-eight—and stellar physical condition, she was hard to keep up with on a good day. And today was definitely not one of those.

"What's wrong? Not enough sleep last night?" She turned to look at me. "No, it's something else. Did your signing go badly, or is there another problem?"

She led me over to the side of the trail, out of the way of other hikers. "Okay, out with it. What's up?"

I hesitated to share the phone call I'd received about John's affair. From the beginning, Diana hadn't liked John, and I was afraid of hearing some version of "I told you so" from her. But I needed to talk to *someone*, and Diana was the one person I could trust to give me both comfort and support, even if it came in the form of "pull up your big-girl panties and deal with it."

"It's all a mess," I said and immediately started crying while Diana patiently waited for me to gain control of myself. I blew my nose, took a deep breath, and then gave her the highlights—or more accurately, the low points—of what had transpired, ending with, "How could he *do* that to me? I thought we'd be together *forever*!"

"You sound like you bought into the very stories you've been writing," Diana said bluntly. "Ever since you two started dating, you looked at him as your knight in shining armor, as the prince who would rescue you from a loveless life, as someone who would encourage and support you as you pursued your dream of being a novelist. And why? What exactly did he do, from day one, to give you that impression?"

It was obvious that I wasn't going to receive a full dose of sympathy, comfort, and encouragement. Or advice on how to get John back. Or even reassurance that all romances had their rough patches and problems, and that patience would win out in the end. No, what I was getting was the no-holds-barred, tell-it-like-it-is Diana. And her next words confirmed it.

"Look, Fran, I'm sorry that he cheated on you. I'm sorry that he hurt you. But it's time you faced the truth about your relationship. I warned you in the beginning that you were expecting the unreasonable—remember?"

I did. It was during one of our weekly walks, less than a year after John and I had started seeing each other when he brought up the idea of sharing a place.

"The man has never been married and, by his own admission, has never even *lived* with anyone," Diana had pointed out. "That smacks of failure to commit."

"But I've never been married either," I'd said in defense.

"Yes, but you're always *ready* to commit," she retorted. "You are the antithesis of a commitment-phobe. Every man you get involved with is 'Mr. Perfect' and every relationship is 'the one.' Look, I'm not trying to crush your hopes, but do you really think this is a good idea? I mean, how well do you know this man after all?"

"I know he makes me happy," I said stubbornly, but now I had to ask myself exactly *how* he had made me happy.

Was it just the sex—certainly welcome after the long dry spell I had been experiencing? Was it because I had someone to call after a long, frustrating day of writing, even if my calls often went straight to his voice mail? Was it just because I was happy to have someone—*anyone*—and the fact that he wanted to live with me was reason enough to agree to his arrangement?

I didn't know. Or didn't *want* to know. And that decision not to know was probably how I ended up in the unfortunate situation I was in right now.

"Fran? Are you listening to me?"

Diana's voice brought me back to the present. "Yeah, yeah, I'm listening," I answered irritably.

"I think what would be best would be for you to take some time away from him so you can think things through."

I didn't bother to tell her that John had already beaten her to the punch. Except that if he was "thinking things through," he was doing it with someone else.

"Besides," she added, "aren't you supposed to be working on another book?"

Thank you, Diana, for reminding me of yet another failure on my part, I thought as I chose not to answer.

But I didn't need to. And apparently Diana could tell from my lack of response that her tough talk might have been a little too harsh for me to handle right now because she switched gears.

"Look, do you want to come to my place? I can make some lunch and we can talk—or *not* talk if you'd rather. What do you say?"

"No, no, you're right. Some time away might help. And since I need to finish a couple of chapters to stay on schedule"—*Finish*? I hadn't even started!—"I think spending a few days somewhere else would be a good idea."

Until I said those words, I hadn't understood how much I wanted to get away—from this house, this book, this life I had created that had gone all sideways. So, the walk with Diana, while not quite giving me the comfort I needed, had been useful after all.

I headed back to the parking lot, and she followed along with me.

"Well, okay, if you're sure," she said.

I couldn't blame her for being more than a little suspicious of my sudden about-face from pathetic to determined. "I'm sure. Tell you what, once I get back, we'll get together and I'll tell you what I decided, okay?"

"Sure, sweetie, and in the meantime, if you need to talk, I'm here for you. You know I want you to be happy, right?" She surprised me with an unexpected hug—Diana was usually not the demonstrative type—but then finished it by giving my shoulders a shake.

"Yes, I know. And thanks for listening," getting into my car. But as I drove away, I found myself dwelling on her words, or more accurately, on the concept of being happy. When *was* the last time I'd felt truly happy? Was it when my career as a romance novelist took off? I had submitted *Love in the Moonlight* to more than seventy-five literary agents and was ready to toss the manuscript in the trash, both literally and figuratively, when Isabella signed me as her client. And it didn't take long for her to secure me a contract.

"Your book speaks to all those women who are middle-aged but still want love and romance, or at least the dream of it, in their lives," she told me. "And that's why it will be a success!"

Her confidence pushed her to demand all sorts of terms and conditions from the publisher in addition to the ten-thousand-dollar advance and fifteen percent royalties.

"But, Izzie, what if they change their mind?" I had protested, a little overwhelmed by her hardball tactics.

"Just let me do my job," she answered, pouring herself another glass of Merlot. She was treating me to dinner to celebrate my first offer and to calm my fears. "Don't you trust my judgment?"

I did, but what I didn't trust was my debut novel's sales potential. But as it turned out, she was right. The book practically flew off the shelves, becoming a best seller to everyone's surprise, including mine and Wilson-Morrow's.

I was on my way, I thought at the time. I was heading down the road to author success. But here I was now, working on Book Four, and the road had taken a very ugly turn indeed, landing me at a destination I had neither anticipated nor desired.

I had two choices: stay where I was metaphorically and physically, or head in a different direction.

"Anywhere is better than staying here," I said as I pulled into my driveway and was confronted by the sight of a house that had been too big for the two of us and would seem even bigger and emptier with only me in it.

A house I hadn't even wanted but had agreed to purchase when John suggested we move inland from the small town of St. Lucia to the more upscale (and expensive) town of Los Gatos. And while it was nice to have a bigger office—there hadn't been much room in the twelve-hundred-square-foot Craftsman I'd inherited when my parents died—I missed the sound of the ocean and the comforting sense of being *home*.

But John liked sleek. John liked sophisticated. And John felt that a successful novelist and successful photographer should live in a home befitting their earnings. Although, since we weren't married and the rent on his studio in the Embarcadero area of San Francisco cost a fortune, it was *my* earnings that paid the mortgage each month.

I agreed, hoping that with a shorter commute he would spend more nights here than in San Francisco. And six months later, the house, *my* house, was sold and John and I were ensconced in what was described in the ad as a "4br, 3ba, 3000 sq. ft. house on 1 acre." It was a beautiful home with a fireplace in the master bedroom as well as in the great room, an office with French doors leading out to the teak deck and pool, and a kitchen with more storage space than I had items to store.

"You'll notice that the garden tub in the master bath is jetted and large enough for two," said the real estate agent with a meaningful glance at us. She knew who I was, of course, and probably envisioned us enjoying long intimate soaks amidst chilled champagne bottles and candlelight.

But her fantasy collided with my reality. More often than not, John would be gone doing God knows what with God knows whom, and I would be either in my office working hard to meet my latest deadline or preparing for yet another book signing.

My life wasn't what I'd envisioned when my first book came out and John and I got together. And while I didn't know what the future would hold, I knew that staying here to obsess about it wouldn't fix anything. Before I could change my mind, I quickly packed my overnight bag. Then I loaded my briefcase with my laptop, the scarily thin folder with hand-written notes for the new book, and to satisfy any midnight cravings, two packages of Oreos and the last few chocolate bars from the freezer. That done, I took off.

Chapter 6

NOT THAT I HAD ANY FIRM PLANS OR SPECIFIC DESTINATION IN mind. The best I could come up with was to stay at a hotel in Lexington Hills, about a half hour south of home. I'd be far enough from the house to keep myself from being distracted by John's absence but close enough to rush back should he call me and say he was on his way home.

But once I was on the highway, my subconscious took control and I found myself heading west toward the coast until I picked up Highway One where I carefully navigated around sharp bends with a rocky hillside on one side and the Pacific Ocean on the other. It was my favorite drive and one that I had taken many times when I was writing my first book.

I'd follow the coast road from St. Lucia to San Gregorio, stopping at various places like Greyhound Rock and Bean Hollow State Beach to work out the difficulties in the latest scene or read over chapters that went particularly well. I loved the Pacific Coast Highway. I loved everything about it: the cypress trees that were bent and gnarled from the wind yet still vigorous and alive, the way the ocean changed from light green to azure as its depth increased, the sound of seagulls crying out as they dove toward the surf looking for food.

I was almost sorry when I finished *Love in the Moonlight* because that meant I no longer had an excuse to spend my free time driving in the area I loved best while imagining what my heroine would do next and how her life would turn out. And it seemed like fate when the cover shot was taken there and I fell in love... No, we are not going there, I told myself. No thinking about John. This was a work trip, a writing retreat, and that's where my concentration had to be.

I checked the trip app on my cell and was relieved to see that before long I'd be coming up to one of my favorite places, a restaurant and gift shop south of Pescadero, perched right above the ocean. I required food, coffee, and most crucially, a bathroom. A few miles more and there it was: the familiar Bay Diner sign.

Soon I was seated at the window, watching the waves crash on the rocky beach. I finished my second cup of Arabian Mocha Java while waiting for the house special: a three-egg omelet with smoked salmon, goat cheese, and spinach.

"More coffee?" the server asked when she passed my table and noticed my empty mug.

I gratefully held out my cup and while she refilled it, said, "I'm looking for a place to stay for a week or so, somewhere quiet. A little farther up the coast but not all the way to San Francisco. Any suggestions?"

"The Whale Inn is a good place. It won't be busy this early in the season. The temperature is still on the cool side and not what visitors expect when they come to California. But the inn isn't easy to find," she warned as she added more tiny creamer tubs to the bowl on the table. "It's only a little over seventeen miles from here heading north, right off the highway after you pass the road to Poplar Beach. There's a sign, or at least there *was* a sign the last time I looked. Take a sharp left there and you'll be going down a private road that's more ruts than pavement, so be careful. The inn is right at the end."

It sounded less than promising, and my doubts must have shown on my face because she quickly added, "It may be a bit tricky to get there, but once you're there, you'll love it. There's a small beach area and a deck with a fire pit so you can sit outside and still be warm. And the food is great! Maybe not as great as here," she added loyally, "but the pizza is to die for!"

Pizza. The magic word. It was just what the doctor ordered—or at least the comfort food I most desired. And I could eat it hot or cold, while taking a break or working at the computer: the perfect twenty-four-hour meal. The Whale Inn it would be. Now all I had to do was find it.

But a seventeen-plus-mile drive on Highway One with all the weekend traffic (was *everyone* in California heading north?) slowed me down significantly. After forty-five minutes, I concluded that either I was practically on top of the place or had already passed it.

I had two options: keep going or stop at the next observation point and use my phone's GPS. Choosing the latter, I typed "Whale Inn" in the search bar, but my phone couldn't get a fix on my location and refused to provide any direction—a metaphor for my life if I ever saw one. Aggravated with technology as well as my own inability to follow what should be a simple route, I got back in the car and began to retrace my path.

And then I saw it, perched on the side of the road and visible only to those traveling south: "The Whale Inn—Stay here and have a whale of a good time! Only 5 miles ahead!"

I cringed at what someone assumed was a clever tag line, especially since I wasn't in the mood for a "whale of a good time." I wanted work time, productive writing time, the kind of time that would make my agent and publisher happy and keep my mind off my personal disaster. And just as important, I wanted to feel the joy and creative excitement that had been so strong with my first book but had been fading with my second and third novels.

The truth was, by the time I'd started writing *Love in Unexpected Places*, the excitement had pretty well worn off. Novel-writing had become a formulaic process. First, the two potential lovers would meet, either in a cosmopolitan location or a romantic vacation spot. The protagonist was a lonely widow or lonely single woman or lonely married woman whose marriage was breaking up—being alone with no one to love and no one loving her was the consistent defining aspect of all my heroines.

She was middle-aged, past the menopausal hot flashes but not quite old enough for Social Security and with just enough figure flaws so my readers could connect with her. Not too gray, not too unattractive, not too out of shape—someone my target audience could identify with, feel sorry for, and most importantly, not hate because she was better looking than them. Someone who counteracted the belief that you had to be slim and young and lovely to get and keep a man.

Next came the obligatory romantic conflict. The hero had a wife or money predicament or a health crisis or an emotional conflict—take your pick. He would leave her because he wanted to work it out on his own, while she tearfully faced a future *sans* love. And then, midway through the book, purely by chance they meet again. It was an event full of "will they or won't they" romantic drama, which ends with another parting full of tears and backward looks and promises that "I'll never forget you, darling!"

Finally, the denouement when they would see each other on a crowded subway platform or in a crowded airport or across a crowded restaurant floor. They'd fall into each other's arms and live happily ever after. It was the same old romantic recipe I had followed for three books and one that I was sick to death of writing.

But that realization, far from creating a lightbulb moment for me, only plunged me deeper into the dark hole of writer's block. If this was the problem with my writing in general and my books in particular, what the hell was I supposed to do with Book Four?

After all, my agent had pitched it as "another in the Fran Carter tradition." Wilson-Morrow expected another romance centering around a protagonist in her fifties. And here I was, not only tired of writing the same crap over and over but also in the unenviable position of knowing from firsthand experience what a bunch of crap it was because real life just didn't turn out that way.

Middle-age romance wasn't so easy. Too many men expected that fifty-year-old women would have the bodies of twenty-year-olds, and they also wanted a level of attention that women my age, who often had demanding careers or increasing personal or family obligations (or both), simply couldn't provide.

That was John's complaint: that I was always working.

"But he was, too," I said resentfully. "Or at least, that was what he *said* he was doing all those nights when he came home late or didn't come home at all or went on those trips to find the right spot for his shoot."

But there—I was doing what I swore I wouldn't do during this planned writing time: dwelling on my disastrous personal life and what went wrong rather than on my book-to-be, I realized as the inn's entrance sign came into view. Shaking my head in disgust, I made a sharp right onto the narrow, graveled driveway and followed it down to the office entrance where I parked the car.

I must get my priorities straight, I told myself as I lugged my laptop case and overnight bag from the trunk and bumped my way up to the entrance. Otherwise, I would be left with no Book Four as well as no relationship.

But finding the Whale Inn turned out to be only part of the problem. Finding someone to check me in was the second challenge I faced and one I wasn't much in a mood to contend with. The lobby itself left a lot to be desired: a few vinyl chairs cracking at the seams and a counter with dog-eared brochures touting whale-watching and winery tours piled in one corner. It certainly lacked ambiance—along with someone to take my name and give me a room key.

I looked in vain for a bell, but it appeared that management wasn't given to such extravagances. So, unwilling to go back out on the highway and risk the temptation to return home and stare at the phone like some rejected teenage girl, I left my bags on the floor and walked around the counter to a door that presumably led to an inner office.

"Hello? Is anyone here? I'd like to check in," pitching my voice loud enough to be heard clear out to the parking lot.

But I might as well have saved my breath. No one was there to respond. I went back to the front office, debating what to do next. But then, faintly but unmistakably, came the slightest whiff of an aroma I knew so well: the smell of baking dough. Carbs. Starch. Thick slabs of bread, fresh from the oven, with chunks of butter melting into every nook and cranny.

It was irrelevant that I had eaten little more than an hour ago. This wasn't about physical hunger but oral gratification, and nothing could have forced me to leave without finding the source of that aroma and indulging in a carbfest when I found it.

I pushed through the door on my right and headed down a long hallway, following my nose until I came to the large dining room. The casement windows at the far end were open to the breeze, bringing in the salty tang of ocean air mixed with the fragrance from a row of California lilacs. But I didn't care about the ocean or the shrubbery. It was the bread I sought—and ultimately found after first opening two wrong doors before finding the one that led to the kitchen.

"Hello?" I said tentatively, the irritation in my voice gone and, in its place, the faint supplicating tone that Oliver Twist might have used when asking for more porridge. "Is anyone here?" looking in vain for a cooling loaf, a bread knife, and a dish of fresh creamery butter.

"Oh, there you are!" A short elderly woman came into view, her voice friendly but with a touch of reproof. "I heard you and hustled out to the office area, but all I found were your bags. You know, you shouldn't leave your possessions scattered around like that. It isn't safe and it looks messy," she added disapprovingly while sizing me up—to see if I were a suitable guest for her inn?

"Sorry," wondering at the same time why *I* was the one apologizing when she was the one who had been derelict in her innkeeper duties.

She must have read my thoughts because her face broke into a smile, laugh lines as deep as the Grand Canyon appearing on either side of her mouth. This was not a woman who believed in face-lifts or, for that matter, hiding her age, which I guessed to be well past the seventy-year mark. She wiped her floury hands on her apron before extending her right one.

"I'm Martha Saxs, owner of the Whale Inn. And I'm sorry I wasn't there to greet you, but the bread was ready to—oh, the bread!" and she turned away, our handshake forgotten.

Grabbing rooster-adorned potholders, she opened the door of the commercial oven and pulled out two pans of the most beautiful, golden-brown loaves I had ever seen. Carefully, she flipped them out onto the cooling racks then turned them right-side up before lightly caressing the tops with a pastry brush dipped in melted butter. Then she came back to where I was standing.

"They'll be ready to taste in about fifteen minutes," she said, apparently noticing my longing looks. "Now, where were we?" and she reached out again to shake my hand.

At that point, nothing could have dissuaded me from staying at the inn—not with fresh-baked bread practically within my grasp.

"I'm Fran. Fran Carter," I said, and her smile, if possible, grew even larger.

"I *knew* I knew you from somewhere! Fran Carter, the romance novelist! I am so excited to have you here!"

She dragged me over to the bookcase near the dining room entrance where I saw several copies of each of my first two novels next to books on infamous killers, police procedurals, and a three-inch tome entitled *My Visit to a Body Farm.*

"I do like reading true crime," she said as she flicked a bit of dust from the shelf. "It makes a nice change from romance although in some cases, love and murder can go hand-in-hand, don't you think?"

Under the circumstances, I was inclined to agree with her, but before I could answer, she continued. "Anyway, I didn't buy *Love in Unexpected Places* yet. But when I do, you can autograph it for me. And the other ones as well," looking at me expectantly as though I should whip out my pen and do it right then and there.

I had to admit that her excitement at meeting me was balm to my soul or, more accurately, my wounded pride. Maybe this would turn out to be a good place to spend some time after all: fresh-baked bread and an avid fan in one fell swoop.

"I'd be happy to," I said, smiling. "But what I'd really like, besides a huge slice of that delicious bread, is a room for a week. You see," lowering my voice confidingly, "I'm working on my next book, and I need a place to stay where I can focus on the creative process."

Not for nothing had I spent years as an advertising copywriter. It was all about spin: putting the best face on any product, service, or situation so the public would buy it. If I hadn't been so worried about my reputation, I might have told her the truth: that I was suffering from major writer's block compounded by the knowledge that my love affair was as flat as a failed soufflé.

But I couldn't say that out loud. I hated even admitting it to myself. So, I fell back on what I did best: fiction.

"Oh, of course, of course. I completely understand! The muse and all... And I have the perfect room for you to work in! There's a desk and lamp, a place to plug in your computer—you do work on a computer, don't you? Or are you one of those writers who does everything longhand with a special pen on special paper? I remember reading about Rosabella Robinson..." and she launched into a long story that I only half followed, something about how some now-famous writer had written her first book on paper towels or toilet paper or scraps of boards, using candlelight or an oil lamp or really long fireplace matches to see by—something ridiculous anyway. And how she sold it afterward for a million-dollar advance and ten-book deal to a major publishing house.

I'd heard similar stories before, the details slightly different each time but the gist the same, and I applauded that author's PR machine for churning out such an interesting, eccentric, and highly unlikely version of the creative process. Too bad I didn't use my copywriting background to develop an equally unconventional story for myself. I might have sold more books.

"...and anyway, now Ms. Robinson does three books a year but still writes them longhand. On purple notepaper with a green pen. And her publisher loves it! What about you?"

I realized with a start that Martha was evidently waiting for me to comment on that author's prolific output or share my own creative idiosyncrasies.

"Yes, I use a computer," grasping at the last thing I had heard. "But I do have certain types of music I play when I'm creating, and sometimes I light candles. And then there are the gallons of fresh coffee and the fresh-baked bread I must have every day at mid-morning, my version of the British elevenses," making it up as I went along.

"My lunch is often a fresh green salad of mesclun, arugula, and radicchio, topped with shrimp, avocado, and Kalamata olives. And wine, white of course—a good Pinot Gris or Chenin Blanc will do, but my real preference is for Assyrtiko, a truly wonderful Greek wine."

Like my books, this was mostly fiction. I seldom drank wine when I was working as it made me sleepy. And when I indulged myself with liquor, it was usually something in the chocolate-flavored category: a Black Russian or a Mudslide, dark and sweet with enough alcohol to give me a bit of a buzz.

"Oh, don't you worry," she said, pushing past me and beckoning me to follow. "I can make sure you get everything you need. We have an excellent wine store down the hill from here called Coastal Spirits, and they have everything! Now, let's get your bags," adding with a knowing smile, "We don't want to keep the muse waiting, do we?"

I didn't have the heart to tell her that, far from waiting around, the muse had long since left me. After casting one more yearning look at the bread, I followed Martha back the way I had come to complete the registration paperwork, all the while listening to her discuss her renovation plans for the inn.

"I want to update the office and have lots of ideas: install bamboo flooring and repaint the walls and change out the counter. This one has been here forever! I redid the guest rooms two years ago, and last year I put in a new stove and commercial refrigerator—one of those energy-efficient ones because I know how essential it is to conserve our natural resources."

"How interesting," I said, signing my name and adding my license plate information to the form before handing it back to her. She scrutinized each line before setting the paperwork on a shelf. Then, taking a key from the board behind her, she led me outside and along the building until we came to a smaller structure with windows facing the ocean.

"My guests like their privacy, so I have a separate way for them to go in and out of their rooms," she explained, unlocking the entrance door and holding it open while I went inside, luggage in tow. "In case of rain, there's an enclosed walkway that runs along the back of this building to the dining room. All the doors lock automatically, so make sure you don't leave your room without your key."

We went down the narrow hallway until we reached the last door, which she opened with a flourish.

"*This*," she said dramatically, stepping aside so I could get the full view of the interior, "is your room!"

Chapter 7

AT FIRST I THOUGHT HER EMPHASIS WAS OVERDONE, BUT ONCE I entered, I took back my uncharitable assumption. The room was perfect down to the last detail. A carved oak desk sat in front of the wide casement windows that provided a view of the surf rolling in huge waves toward the shore. The queen-size bed was covered with a thick down comforter topped with huge soft pillows—also down, I noted, when I surreptitiously squeezed one.

And the bath! What could one say about an old-fashioned slipper clawfoot tub, a basket of organic bath products on a nearby wrought iron stand, a separate shower big enough for two complete with dual showerheads and bench seating, and a travertine tile floor topped with handmade braided rugs?

I was taken aback. This was not what I had anticipated, especially after the unprepossessing front office, but Martha was clearly used to such reactions.

"You expected a camp cot, an old dresser, and a mildewed shower stall, didn't you?" she asked and, not waiting for an answer, went on. "This whole building was originally a vacation home owned by the Pierces—of the San Francisco Pierces, you know—one of the richest families in the area. And when they built it, they wanted it to have all the amenities they had in their main residence, all the way down to *that*," gesturing to a small doorway through which I could see a bidet next to the toilet.

"I bought this place after my husband died twenty years ago. Sold my house, cashed in my savings, and chose to make a new life as an inn-keeper. And I haven't regretted it for a moment," she finished, opening the windows to let the ocean air waft in, the lace curtains dancing in the breeze.

"Oh, it's been difficult at times, what with the economy and all. And the rainy season... well, some days I wonder if this whole building will end up floating like the Ark in all that water! But I wouldn't change a thing if I had the chance. Good and bad—this is the life I wanted to lead, and this is where I want to die. But not today!" she added with a laugh. "I still have quite a few years left in me, God willing. I come from good stock—my parents died when they were well into their nineties, and I had two aunts who passed the century mark before they 'shuffled off this mortal coil' as the Bard wrote. I like to read," she added unnecessarily.

"It's perfect," I said truthfully. The only drawback I could see was that I might find it challenging to concentrate on my writing with such a fabulous view, comfortable bed, and a soaker tub temptingly at hand.

"Yes, the inn has everything but satellite and cable TV," she said. "People come here to get away from all that noise and nonsense. Besides, the companies want too much money for the service, and I have to watch my pennies. You never know what's going to happen"—a phrase more apt than she realized, I thought. "There *is* an internet connection though it's a bit iffy at times. And the cell phone reception can be a little dicey, too," clearly believing in full disclosure. "But I do have a landline at the office that you're welcome to use any time as well as intercoms that connect the rooms with the desk and my living quarters, so you won't be completely out of touch."

Dicey cell service... My mind grasped the only fact that was vital to me. What if John called the office line and, when I didn't pick up, tried my cell? Would he worry if I didn't answer?

It was nearly enough to make me change my mind until the more rational side of my brain took over, sounding unmistakably like Diana. *What makes you think he's going to call? You know where he is, and you can guess what he's doing—and with whom! Besides, isn't this why you left your home, to spend time trying to salvage your career with Book Four and not think about John?*

"It's perfect," I said, setting my laptop case on the floor near the desk. "Nothing to keep me from working!"

Nothing except my own bout of creative constipation, I added silently, but Martha beamed.

"I knew you would like it! One of the owner's uncles was a writer, and this was his favorite room. He was quite prolific in his day, too— wrote travel books and articles. Some were even published in the *New York Times* and the *Boston Herald*. Here," handing me a key attached to a large silver medallion imprinted with "Room 10" on both sides before heading to the doorway. "I'll leave you to your unpacking. But I'll be back in half an hour with a pot of coffee, some homemade strawberry-basil jam, and of course, fresh bread!" And with that she gently closed the door behind her.

It didn't take long for me to finish since all I had brought was socks, underwear, pajamas and a robe, and my standard writing uniform: leggings, several long-sleeved flannel shirts, and my favorite black wrap—a combination of fleece throw and baggy sweater complete with pockets. I could wear it, drape it over my legs, or when the writing was really going badly, curl up in it on the bed like a kid with a blankie.

While I changed, I reviewed my plan for the rest of the day. It was simple and straightforward. I'd work on Book Four while enjoying the promised snack Martha was bringing me, then work off the carbs with a walk on the shore. If I was lucky, I could get a draft of the synopsis done by bedtime.

Just a rough draft, I added in case the muse was loitering nearby. That's all I want to write. Tomorrow I can start the outline or develop a character profile or do *something* that looks like writing.

It sounded good: active, creative, and above all else, productive. But the road to hell... well, you know the rest of the quote. When Martha came back thirty minutes later, I was staring out the window, my eyes hypnotized by the movement of the waves crashing on the rocky beach and then receding once more into the ocean. My laptop was still in its case, and my mind was still stuck in Park.

When I wrote my first two books, I couldn't wait to get started. I used to spend my days figuring out plotlines, stealing character descriptions from the people I would see in stores, making up lines of dialogue from bits and pieces of overheard conversations. (When you're a writer, all sorts of minor sins, including eavesdropping, become acceptable.) But now, there was nothing but a big empty space in that part of my brain where I would construct my fiction: no details, no dialogue, no nothing.

"You looked like you could use something a little stronger than coffee, so I also brought you my homemade elderberry wine," she said, setting the tray on the dresser. "Being a bed-and-breakfast, I don't normally do dinner, but since the oven was on anyway, I'm making pizza. If you're hungry, come on over to the kitchen around six or so, and I'll cut you a few slices. How is the writing going?" she finished brightly, her sharp eyes no doubt noticing that the laptop was nowhere in evidence.

"Oh, I'm in the creative, ruminating phase right now," I lied. "I might have a little snack before going for a walk—you know, to get the oxygen flowing to my brain. Then I can buckle down and start cranking it out!"

"Well, in that case, would you rather stay in your room and work?" she asked. "I know how important it is not to interrupt someone when they're inspired. When Rosabella Robinson is writing, she never leaves her office—except to use the bathroom, of course. She eats only fresh fruit and vegetables and poached salmon. She says it's perfect sustenance for a writer: nothing heavy and plenty of nutrition for the brain. And no coffee or alcohol, just water and fruit juice."

"Hmm, is that so," recalling the last photo I had seen of her. Robinson didn't look like someone who was subsisting on fruits, veggies, and fish—not unless they were all battered and deep-fried. Next to her, even *I* would look skinny. "I'll try that sometime, but at this moment the pizza sounds more like what I need."

"Okay," she said doubtfully. "I'll see you then," and closed the door behind her, leaving me with the tools of my trade and no trade to ply, thanks to a dearth of creative ideas.

I poured a cup of coffee from the carafe, adding liberal amounts of cream and sugar before taking a bite of the butter-slathered bread. Martha was one hell of a cook. Maybe I could bring her back to the house and she could cook meals for me every day, and all I would have to do is think about writing.

The house... From there, it was one small step to thinking about John, wondering what he was doing and with whom and if he was coming back home after Dallas—back home to *me*—or if he had other plans. As for my career, well, it was sinking faster than the Titanic with nary a lifeboat in sight to save me.

When I had first proposed the idea of becoming a novelist to Diana after losing my ad agency job, I'm not sure which of us was more surprised: Diana, because I had never before expressed a desire to join the select (and for the most part impoverished) coterie of authors, or me, because the idea of fiction writing had never occurred to me as an occupation.

Granted, I had spent years writing advertising and marketing copy: short, snappy content that was, for the most part, based on fiction, not reality. But whatever made me think I could write something where the word count was in the tens of thousands?

But I had said it, and given that my copywriter position ended when the agency shut its doors, I figured I might as well put my money where my mouth was. And there was always the hope I'd make it big: get my hands on a long-term publishing contract that came with a six-figure advance and never have to worry about money again.

So, each night when I came home from yet another boring part-time job, I would power up my laptop and spend a few hours trying to be creative. I started with murder mysteries—cozies à la Agatha Christie—but I never could work out intriguing plotlines or come up with unusual murder devices.

Science fiction was also a wash—no background in that area and minimal imagination to envision a future of new designs and innovations. Hell, I still wasn't even sure exactly how the microwave worked, just grateful that it cooked my frozen diet dinners. ("All the flavor with half the calories" was the claim on the box, which was fiction writing of another sort.)

It wasn't until February that the idea for a romance novel came to mind. I had been spending weeks counting all the different kinds of Valentine cards for a card shop chain. There were cards from him to her and her to him, as well as from her to her and him to him. Cards from hopeful lovers, from those who'd been left behind, and from those who'd been together for years.

Funny cards, romantic cards, cards that hinted but never promised, cards asking you to wait, and cards announcing now was the time—you name it, and a card was there to cover the situation, desire, or quandary. At first, as I flipped them open and read the messages, I wondered why I wasn't getting any of those and what I needed to do to find the perfect man who would buy me the perfect card.

Then my writer's brain started thinking of the people who bought these cards, envisioning scenarios that fit the choice. Did they long to win back someone or turn up the relationship flame from a low flicker to a raging inferno? Had they been left behind, or were they yearning to move forward? What was the story behind the purchase?

I would go home at night and start writing, making it up as I went along. The protagonist: a not-young woman buying a card for her husband, knowing all along that he wouldn't have one for her. But she hoped… in vain, as it turned out, and that was how *Love in the Moonlight* was born.

And while, in a sense, it was a labor of love, the manuscript was written in a very prosaic, workmanlike fashion: four hours a night on a computer with a ream of twenty-pound bond stacked next to the printer, with good light and a strong pair of bifocals when my eyes were too tired for contact lenses.

The odds were against me, I know that now. But sometimes Fate gives a nod in the direction of some poor lost soul and things happen the way we all want them to. I got an agent, a publishing contract, and met John—all in short order.

"I thought my life was settled," my words echoing in the empty room. "All I had to do was write romance novels and live out my *own* romance with the handsome man that Fate had brought me. So where did it go wrong? Where did *I* go wrong?"

I shook my head. This wasn't the time to do a lengthy post-mortem on the choices and decisions that led me to where I was today. *This* time was for concentrating on my career, my livelihood, my obligation to produce something that would satisfy my agent and publisher and redeem me in the eyes of my readers. This was about writing my next novel, not rewriting my current relationship, hoping for a different and better conclusion.

Fired as much by my newfound determination as the caffeine, I pulled out my laptop and plugged it in, comforted by the familiar hum and whirring when I pushed the power button. I would skip the walk and get started right now. And only eat my pizza if I had something to show for my efforts.

That was my plan. That was my intention. That was my goal. And if there was one thing I was really good at, it was keeping my promises—even if the only person I was keeping them for was myself.

I grabbed the last slice of bread from the tray, downed the small glass of sweet wine after debating the cost (drowsiness) with the benefits (temporary elevation of my frame of mind) and then faced my computer, ready to redeem my reputation and my pride as a best-selling novelist.

My fingers poised over the keyboard, I stared at the screen. I looked away and back again, hoping that something would have magically appeared in that millisecond. But nothing had. Not only was I *not* writing, I *couldn't* write. I didn't even know *what* to write. How could I possibly draft a synopsis about a middle-aged heroine finding true love with the one she has been waiting for her whole life when I hadn't been able to hold on to my *own* "one-and-only"?

How could I not only write the darn thing but then sell that bill of goods to all those women who would be waiting for it and hoping that my book would unlock the secrets of how to find and keep the "happily ever after" life they desired?

I wasn't buying it—and maybe I hadn't even really bought it while writing my last book, which could explain the modest sales *Love in Unexpected Places* was experiencing. Readers know when the author doesn't believe her own words even when the author herself doesn't realize it.

I pushed back from the desk and stared out the window. When did I start to have doubts about our relationship? When John was gone more and more often, when lovemaking occurred less and less frequently, when we seemed to be drifting away from being lovers and more toward roommate status?

I thought at the time (when I let myself think about it at all) that, of course, sex in your fifties wasn't like sex in your twenties. It was the quality, not the quantity, one should focus on, I'd told myself, ignoring the little voice that said the quality wasn't all that great either.

And was it all John's fault? If I was going to be honest, *I* was just as busy, just as preoccupied with my writing and all the attendant obligations that went along with being a career novelist.

Sometimes, when John and I were in bed together, some portion of my mind would even be busy depicting our love play in words: *His hands gently removed her nightgown while his eyes stared deeply into hers. She felt the satin material fall around her feet and didn't even care that he could see her less-than-firm breasts or the softness around her hips. All she cared about was holding him close to her, feeling his body against hers. And she could see in his eyes that was all he wanted, too...*

I knew that fantasizing was essential for a happy and fulfilling sexual experience. But that wasn't what I was doing on those occasions. I was *writing*—in my head, but writing nonetheless. And for the first time, I wondered if John *knew* that, if he felt some part of me leave the bed and go to work. Because that was what I was doing—working.

Oh, not all of me. There was a part that certainly enjoyed what was happening between the two of us at that moment. But if I was going to be honest, at least with myself, more and more often during the past year or so, I had found myself *writing* during sex instead of focusing on *enjoying* sex.

What was worse, at least from the creative perspective, was that the opportunities to turn life into fiction—at least the lovemaking part of my life—were occurring less and less frequently, which meant that my inspiration was drawn not so much from current activities as from what I had already written. Or imagined. Or desired. While it's true that novels are works of fiction, they should, at least to some extent, be based on reality—and my reality was fast becoming less about living the desired life and more about living a life of desire unfulfilled.

Was it all the fault of my profession? Or had I bought into the very fantasy I wrote about: that the magic of romance could be translated into the day-to-day experience?

Was it John I had really wanted or just a relationship? Did I want *him* or just *someone*? Had I really been committed to finding Mr. Right, or had I opted to settle for Mr. Good Enough, Mr. Someone-Is-Better-Than-No-One?

"Be careful what you wish for" is a familiar adage, but one I had ignored six years ago. But now that I had what I *thought* I wanted—a man in my life on a daily basis—it wasn't quite going according to the plotline I had subconsciously developed. As for my reputation as "a successful romance writer living her own romance," well, *that* was soon to be exposed as no longer the truth of the matter.

Unless I could save our relationship and get John back—back to me and the life I had hoped we would have.

Unless Book Four could turn the tide and bring me back to one of the top spots as a best-selling author.

Unless I could figure out what I really wanted, personally *and* professionally: who I was and who I wanted to be and whether this relationship was a good fit for that person.

Chapter 8

The ringing of the phone broke into my musings.

"Ms. Carter, it's Martha," as though I might not know who would be on the other end of the line even though the intercom light was glowing. "I wanted to let you know the pizza will be ready in fifteen minutes. But if you're busy writing, I can bring it to your room so as not to disturb your work. Rosabella Robinson often goes for hours without eating and—"

I interrupted her, knowing from our previous encounter that if I didn't, she was liable to keep me on the phone for hours.

"No, really, I'm at a good stopping point," I said untruthfully. "I've made great progress, but I don't want to burn myself out on the first day, so I'll be there shortly. Thanks for calling."

It had been only half a lie. This wasn't a "good" stopping point, but it *was* a stopping point, nonetheless. Or, to put it more accurately, a wall.

"Oh well, I can always work after dinner," I said aloud, switching off my computer. "Maybe I'll have a clearer head. Maybe I'll have a better sense of the storyline or come up with an opening bit of dialogue. Or an image of the character. Or a rough outline of the plot. Or something. Or maybe I'll grab the bread knife when Martha isn't looking and slit my wrist and put an end to this disaster."

And on that cheery note, I grabbed my room key and headed out to the dining room.

I had envisioned a lonely meal—just me and melted cheese-and-tomato triangles—but the tray Martha carried in held not only an arugula pizza topped with *ricotta salata* but also plates and cutlery for two. She set it on the table, put one of the wrapped silverware bundles and a plate in front of me, and without asking, took a seat on the other side.

And then, with a flourish, she produced what was clearly the pièce de résistance: a copy of *Love in Unexpected Places*.

"I ran over to Barnaby's Books in Coastside Bay and bought it. They only had one left—I suppose it's been selling like hotcakes—but I plan to read it tonight after I clean up the kitchen. Then tomorrow at breakfast, I'll tell you all the parts I loved in it, which could take us until lunchtime if it's anything like your other books—which it probably is, only better—and you can sign it!"

I smiled weakly and shoved a piece of hot pizza into my mouth to avoid having to say anything. And really, aside from "thank you," what *could* I say? That I probably wouldn't even finish my first cup of coffee before she ran out of positive things to enumerate? That she was bound to find more things wrong than right? That she ought to run, not walk, the book back to where she'd bought it to get a refund on her purchase?

"Ohmigod," I said around a mouthful of 500-degree fontina hiding under the greens. The melted cheese was burning the roof of my mouth and my tongue, and when I swallowed it, no doubt my esophagus as well. I drained my glass of water, but the pain was still there—no doubt a punishment from the writing gods for my having neglected my work.

"Oh, you poor thing! That pizza is hot, you know," she belatedly warned and left the table to return with a bottle of wine. "Here, this will help. It's your favorite. I got it from Coastal Spirits right after I went to the bookstore," pouring some into my empty water glass. "Now take a sip and it will help calm everything down. Or drink more and you won't even remember what happened!" giggling like a young girl.

I drank it all, and when she refilled the glass, finished that as well. And that was how I came to consume half a bottle of Assyrtiko along with four thick slices of pizza and, to finish off the meal, a piece of fresh-baked apple pie with full-fat vanilla ice cream melting on top.

"Hand-churned," Martha said. "The owners of the dairy where I get my milk make their own ice cream—none of that fat-free, synthetic stuff you find in the stores. And they add in strawberries and cherries and pecans. You name it and they have it! That's one of the things I like about living here," she added. "Everyone around here has a unique talent or interest, and we all get to benefit from it. Like Pacific Coast Dairy," gesturing to the ice cream. "They have goat's milk and cow's milk, make their own yogurt and ice cream, and are looking at adding cheese to their product line."

She took a bite of her pie and went on. "The apples are from McKinnon's orchard—it's been in the family for generations—and the eggs come from Sue-Ann's poultry farm. She's got the happiest chickens, probably because she gives them lots of room to roam. All the people around here love what they do, and because of that, they do it really well. Like you writing your novels, right?"

Luckily, I had a mouthful of pie, so I nodded. Otherwise, what would I say? That I used to love what I did but wasn't so sure anymore? Or that I still loved writing, just not the kind of stories I was contracted to write? I mulled that over as I drained my wine glass and watched Martha finish her pie.

"There," she said with satisfaction as she stacked our empty dishes on a tray. "That should hold us until breakfast tomorrow. But now I'd better clean up the kitchen!"

"That was a wonderful meal," I said, regretfully pushing myself back from the table. The elastic in my leggings was feeling the strain from all that food while my brain was buzzing quite pleasantly from the alcohol.

Martha smiled at me. "Well, we can't have you be one of those starving writers, can we? Besides, I'm sure all that thinking uses up a lot of energy!"

"Yes, yes it does," I agreed although judging from my literary output so far, I could have easily subsisted on bread and water. But all that is going to change, I told myself. When I get back to my room, I'm going to be so productive that I'll burn through all the calories I just consumed.

I looked at the last slice of pizza, wondering if I should take it back to my room to sustain me while I worked... Oh, who was I kidding, resisting the impulse. After the long drive and what probably amounted to several pounds' worth of starch and sodium, I was more likely to waddle back to my room, collapse on the bed, and sleep the sleep of, if not the innocent, at least the overindulged and slightly inebriated.

And that's what happened. I managed to take off my shoes and make a half-hearted attempt to brush and floss my teeth. Then, not even bothering to wipe off what little makeup I had on, I fell onto the bed where I sank into a less than restful slumber, punctuated by dreams that had me alternately chasing a taxi that was to drive me to the train station, running madly down the pier while my ship pulled away, or standing in the airport lounge crying while my plane departed.

I didn't need a therapist to tell me what those nightmares meant. Life was passing me by, and it was my own fault. My chance at happiness was getting away from me, and the only thing I didn't know was whether it was emotional fulfillment or career accomplishment (or both) that I was losing—or which one mattered more.

Sometime during the night I awoke, chilled by the ocean breeze coming through the window I'd left open. I crawled from the bed to latch it closed and stood there, watching moonlight sliver through the fog. I remembered the first night John and I slept together. I had awakened and stood by the window at the hotel, looking at the waves and then back at the bed.

How did I get so lucky? I'd wondered. How did someone like me end up with such a sexy, handsome man?

Our first meeting hardly had an auspicious beginning. Isabella had called with details for the photo shoot for *Love in the Moonlight* and said it would be done by John Robbins, who did all the author photos for W-M.

"Not here, I hope," I answered, looking at the small section of the living room that I had converted into a writing space cluttered with stacks of papers, piles of CDs (I always listened to music while I wrote), and at least three half-filled coffee cups. It looked less like the home of a successful writer and more like the "before" shot for a home organizing article.

"No," she assured me. "Wilson-Morrow thinks it would be better to have these taken at some upscale location, the kind of place your readers would imagine your heroine—Serena, right?—ending up in. You'll meet him—" a pause while the sound of papers told me she was flipping pages in her datebook, "this coming Saturday at the Coastal Resort hotel. Bring several outfits—Robbins likes to choose what his subjects will wear—and be prepared to spend the day and probably part of the evening being photographed."

"Fine. Great," I had answered, making a face as I hung up the phone. I hated having my picture taken. I never looked the way I wanted, which is to say I always ended up looking just like me. All day and the evening, too… Well, in that case, I'd blow some of my hard-earned advance and stay the night, or even the whole weekend, rather than make the long drive back home. I deserved it, and I needed it. Hadn't I spent the better part of every night the past twelve months slaving over rewrites and edits to *Love in the Moonlight*?

But it went better than I could have foreseen, despite a somewhat rocky start when John went through my suitcase and discarded the majority of the items I had packed. Once he found something he liked—a black silk halter dress with a plunging neckline—we went down to the hotel's private beach for the shoot. It was all very *From Here to Eternity*, but all I could think of was how cold the ocean breeze was and how much longer it would take.

Then we went back to the hotel's dining room for a celebratory post-photo dinner and wine. A *lot* of wine. More wine than I obviously could handle, resulting in a hazy recollection of subsequent events. Touching, kissing, more touching, more kissing, and much later, me standing by the window, watching the waves, and thinking that I had finally found love and how lucky I was that John wanted me.

And when we continued to see each other—sometimes for more photo shoots, sometimes just for sex—I couldn't get over the fact that he had picked me. But now, as I stood here, I asked myself for the first time: why *did* he pick me?

Or why did I pick *him* and agree to a living arrangement that stopped shy of what I really wanted: a full commitment and the promise of a life together? When did I give up on my own idea of "happily ever after"? For that matter, did I even know what my "happily ever after" was?

Was it love that drove me into John's arms or the fear of being alone? Did I truly believe I was deserving of love, or was I just taken with the idea that someone loved *me*? *Was* it love after all—and did I even know what love was?

And the biggest questions of all: What did I really want, and was a relationship with John under its current terms on that list?

So many questions, and the answers were as concealed from my understanding as the ocean was hidden by the fog. I knew the answers were there, I just couldn't see them through my own emotional murkiness. But they still existed.

I turned from the window, my head aching as much from the questions banging around inside my brain as from the wine I had drunk at dinner. I didn't want to think any more. I wanted to sleep—preferably for the next seven days so that, when I awoke, it would all have been a bad dream. I would pack up my stuff and drive back to our home in Los Gatos, and John would be there, and everything would be as it was before. Because I sure as hell didn't want it to be like it was now.

This wasn't what I had planned, I thought as I left the window and crawled back under the comforter. I was supposed to be past all this: the vision of a life spent alone, of relationship problems, of the kind of pain caused by rejection that hurts as much at fifty-five as it does at fifteen. This was supposed to be a new life, a better life, the life I thought I was getting when I agreed to share my home and my life with John.

It was the modern-day version of "I do" that had turned into a big "he doesn't," and I didn't know what to do about it. And on that unhappy, frustrating train of thought, I fell asleep.

Chapter 9

Normally, I do my best writing first thing in the morning, which made my first book's success all the more amazing, given I wrote it after long days spent counting inventory. But once I gave up that job to concentrate on my novels, I adhered to a regular writing routine. Breakfast (usually coffee and a bagel) at five, followed by several hours at the computer before breaking for a walk—or if I was making terrific progress, no walk at all and a makeshift lunch consisting of whatever was handy and didn't require much effort or time.

And like many other writers, I even had my own good-luck rituals to keep inspiration flowing. There was the candle I ceremoniously lit when I started a new book—neroli to inspire right-brain activity or rosemary for creativity. The music that I played at different stages of the story, starting with Carly Simon's plaintive "It Happens Every Day" when the heroine realized her love life had ended, then switching to Gloria Gaynor's "I Will Survive" when she was finally over the man who had done her wrong. And if he was a real rat, I added "Before He Cheats" by Carrie Underwood.

Finally, as I rounded the corner and headed into the home stretch, I turned up the volume for my compilation of Tina Turner songs, all proclaiming a woman's strength and resolve to be in charge of her love life.

But this time, at the official beginning of my as yet unnamed fourth book, I was off to a bad start. I didn't open my eyes until after nine, and when I did, the light streaming in only made my headache worse. The phone was ringing, and after maneuvering myself higher on the pillows, I picked up the handset.

It was Martha—of *course* it was Martha—sounding bright and cheerful.

"I stopped by your room earlier with coffee on a tray because I thought you'd be getting an early start. Didn't I read in an interview that you begin your work time even before the sun is up? I knocked—quite a few times," and her voice took on the tone of a mother chiding her child for sleeping in on a school day, "but you didn't answer, so I brought it back to the kitchen. I'll be leaving in a quarter hour to go to the market, so if you want breakfast, you had better get a move on. You probably didn't notice the hours when you checked in, but I only serve breakfast from six to nine thirty, so you won't have much time."

"Yes, thanks," I said, scrambling out of bed and into my clothes. I could forgo many things, but my morning coffee wasn't one of them. A quick swipe of the toothbrush to my teeth and an even quicker brush to my hair, and I was out the door and on my way to the dining room.

"Good. You made it," said Martha, setting a pot of coffee and two oatmeal-raisin scones accompanied by twin jars of honey and jam on the table in front of me. "I thought for sure you would have been here already—I was all set to make you an omelet if you wanted one and then while you ate, I'd give you my opinion of your book—but there really isn't time for it now. I have a schedule, even during slow times, and if I want the best romaine and some of Sue-Ann's eggs from her prize layers, I need to get over to the outdoor market right now. If you don't mind, just set your dishes on the counter in the kitchen when you're done, and I'll take care of them when I get back."

"Mind? No, you go right ahead," I said brightly. "And I'll be on time tomorrow, I promise," as though I weren't a paying guest but rather an employee, and a tardy one at that.

And the truth was I didn't mind at all. For one thing, between the pounding in my head and the uncomfortable fullness in my midsection (the result of far too much pizza the night before), the last thing I wanted was to sit through a meal listening to Martha's thoughts about *Love in Unexpected Places*. I had every expectation that the praise would be limited and the criticism liberal. She was definitely the kind of person who didn't mince words but delivered them in big chunks—the better to hit you over the head with.

I drank two mugs of coffee in quick succession and shook the pot hopefully but failed to detect a swishing sound. Clearly, when Martha said the breakfast service was over at nine thirty, that extended to coffee as well. I picked at the second scone but realized I was avoiding the inevitable: my as-yet-undefined novel. It was never going to get written if all I did was sit and think about it.

I went back to my room, trying to maintain a positive attitude. But once inside, looking at the dark monitor screen, I was filled with the kind of fear I rarely experienced as a writer. Oh sure, with past books there had been many times when the word river slowed to a trickle and I was forced to work hard to get the character from Point A to Point B. But it was usually the technical side that hung me up: the details, the facts, the searching for the right name or the right place so readers wouldn't later flood my inbox with corrections.

But this time, not only had my character not *gotten* to Point A, I wasn't even sure where Point A was. Moreover, I wasn't even clear in my mind as to who my heroine was. What kind of person was she? What was happening to her? And even more crucially, what did she really want?

I ignored the little voice in my head that said mockingly, *She sounds like you*, and turned on the computer before reaching for my cell phone to check for messages. There could be a call from my agent with good news regarding the latest sales figures. Or a media rep who wanted to interview me for some national television show.

Or John, said that nasty little voice again.

"Oh, shut up," I muttered as I waited for my cell to wake up. But the screen stayed stubbornly dark, and I realized it was in need of a charge. No problem, I told myself. I'd plug it in and by the time I got a draft of the chapter or the synopsis or even just the title written, the phone should have enough juice to let me check in with the outside world.

I pulled out the little leather zip bag where I usually carried the charger only to find it empty—bare as Mother Hubbard's cupboard.

"Shit!" as the image of the charger on my desk came to mind— sitting there, in my home office, plugged into the wall outlet instead of where it should have been: in its little bag inside my laptop case. Although Martha *had* said the cell service at the inn was less than reliable anyway.

I tossed my phone onto the bed, exasperated with its lack of support in my time of need. What good were electronics if they failed you right when you most required their service? All I wanted was some communication, some connection, some contact—noting with bitter humor the irony of my words since that was also what had been lacking in my relationship for some time, resulting in John getting his "charge" somewhere else.

"But what about me? I needed attention, too. I needed—"

The computer interrupted my whining with its little singsong tone that told me it was ready to work—regardless of whether *I* was. Resolutely pushing my personal issues and worries into the farthest corner of my mind, I applied fingers to keyboard.

"Title TK" I typed, encasing the phrase in brackets and using the standard editorial designation for what was missing—or, in my case, for what had to be figured out before I finally submitted the piece.

"I'll worry about the title once I get some of the story down," I said determinedly. "I can't get hung up on details now."

"Synopsis" I typed before looking longingly out the window. The sun was shining, the breeze was warm, and the shoreline looked so inviting... What I needed was a short walk to get the creative juices flowing.

"Only a few more words or even a paragraph, and then I can go outside," I said aloud. "They say that exercise is good for the brain. It increases the oxygen flow and stimulates the senses and does all kinds of other good things. It's not like I'm avoiding work. I'll actually be enhancing my ability *to* work!"

I started the synopsis the way I started all the others: with a quick recap to place the reader right in the middle of the action. *When Character Name TK* (also in brackets because I didn't know her name but only that she was a woman) *came home from work that Saturday night, she found the house empty except for her little gray kitten, Sammy.*

I stopped there, fixed a few minor typos, and read over what I had written. It sounded fine. Well, okay at least. But there was something I couldn't put my finger on, something familiar about the opening.

I looked at the words and then opened the file for my last novel. No wonder the sentences sounded familiar. That was exactly how I had started my last book!

"Oh my God," I said, dropping my head in my hands. "It's true what Izzie said. I've become a 'rerun' writer, recycling the same story over and over. I'm washed up. Through. No good."

I hit the backspace key with far more force than my computer deserved, eliminating every letter until I got to the unidentified title. Then I took a deep breath and patted the laptop apologetically. After all, it wasn't the equipment's fault that I was stuck. And if I started abusing it, maybe *it* would leave me as well, break down the way my love affair had broken down, go silent the way John did when I asked for reasons, justifications, "I'll never do it again" reassurances.

John... No. I'm here to work. And I started typing again.

Unable to sleep, Serena looked out her bedroom window. The garden she tended lovingly was awash in moonlight, and the fireflies danced like magical creatures through the shadows. Not for the first time, she wished she had someone to share the vision with....

"There, that's a good start," I said with satisfaction. "Enough details to place her in the reader's mind before I go on to... well, wherever it is I'm going."

I read the words again—lyrical, beautiful, evocative... repetitive! It was the opening to *Love in the Moonlight*—my first book that detailed Serena's longing for love (the angst of which made her anything but serene!) and how she found it in, of course, the moonlight.

And for the first time since I'd written it, I wondered what happened to her in the light of day. Was the love still as solid, or had it faded the way shadows do when the light gets too bright?

"What the hell does it matter anyway?" pushing back the chair and getting away from the computer. "Who cares what happened to her or any of those characters? Those books are done, over with, finished. And *I'll* be done, over with, finished if I don't come up with a decent storyline!"

What was the problem here? Was I so stressed by my personal problems that I couldn't put myself in a fictional world? Or had I lost my belief that love was possible—not in general, but certainly for women my age? Did I even know what real love was, or had I confused it with romance: the moonlight-and-roses setup that tricked us into thinking whatever we were experiencing would stand the test of time?

Maybe that's why the first book worked—because I believed it. Likewise, that could have been the problem with the last book because somewhere, hidden in my mind, were those niggling doubts about love: *if* it even existed, or in retrospect, if I had it.

I grabbed my room key and a candy bar from my stash and headed for the beach, hoping the ocean breeze would blow away all this doubt and confusion and leave me with a clear head or that oxygen from the exercise would make my brain work better.

It was worth a try, I thought as I navigated the rocky path until I came to the iron staircase that led down to the beach. I had to do *something*!

And if it didn't work, well, there was always the tried-and-true method of loading my pockets with rocks and wading into the surf until I sank like a stone.

"That would show them!" not sure who "them" was or what I would be showing but finding ridiculous comfort in the idea anyway.

Chapter 10

Once I climbed down what seemed to be a hundred steps to the shore, I made my way over to a piece of driftwood. Forgetting my original plan of taking a healthy walk along the beach, I sat on the limb, pulled out the candy, and let my mind wander while I ate.

Love. My books were about love, the love my heroines wanted and never had, the love they longed for, the love only a man—the *right* man, of course—could bring into their lives. The classic romance story arc— the character needing love, finding love, losing love (her fault, his fault, the fault of the gods—it didn't really matter as long as it was lost, albeit temporarily), and then finding love again: the "happily ever after" ending that left the reader sighing with pleasure.

It worked in all those novels that filled the romance section in the bookstores. It had even worked, at least to some extent, in my first three books. That was why the genre was such a consistent money-generator. Everyone wanted to believe that somewhere out there was the perfect lover who would make the world spin out of control before it settled down to a better, happier, sexier rotation. All you had to do was keep your eyes open and you would find your one-and-only.

"Or was it keep your eyes closed?" I asked aloud, thinking back to the scenarios I had created. "Were the heroines making decisions based on what they saw or on what they *wanted* to see—on what existed or what they *hoped* existed?"

I thought of the female characters I had created, how needy they were, waiting for a lover to make them whole.

"And why *were* they in such need? Why did they feel compelled to search for someone to complete them and make everything perfect? Was that *really* the way to start a relationship and then maintain one?"

My questions were spoken with such force that they startled a nearby gull resting on the shore and sent it swooping back over the water, leaving me alone to contemplate my protagonists' situations as well as my own.

Wasn't it possible for a woman who was "whole unto herself" to enter into a loving relationship with a man who was also whole and complete? While true love should result in a synergistic outcome, with the whole greater than the sum of its parts, shouldn't those two parts be able to function independently as well as synergistically?

But in my novels, the women were all standing around, miserable and unhappy, longing for something instead of making their lives work with or *without* a man. And when they did find one—it *was* a romance novel, after all, so it was a given that Mr. Right should enter the picture— they were so pathetically eager and desperate that they overlooked flaws and warning signs instead of taking an objective look at what was there and how it would fit with their own lives and plans.

"My God, that was *me*," shaking my head in disgust.

While it's a given that many fiction writers bring some element of themselves into the characters they create, I had gone one step further. I had recreated my *own* life in each one of my books, albeit changing a few details here and there. Which would have been fine, I thought as I skipped stones across the water's surface, if I had learned something along the way. But I hadn't.

During my pre-John years, while I had been comparatively successful at what I did, my copywriting work never seemed quite enough for me. I wanted more: a fulfilling career, a committed relationship, possibly even a kid or two. And I thought that future was right around the corner.

But when, in my mid-thirties, I turned that corner, figuratively speaking, I was still all alone like Serena in *Love in the Moonlight*. And while I could accept the idea that motherhood didn't appear to be in the cards for me, I refused to admit the possibility that I was going to spend the rest of my life alone.

And *that* explained a lot, thinking back to Frank, who had entered my life just about that time. He was a former-actor-turned-producer whom I met during my ad agency days when he hired our firm to do some promo pieces for one of his low-budget, artsy films. Assigned to his project, I spent my billable time trying to figure out what he wanted for his project and how to give it to him, and later, after the project was done, how to satisfy his emotional and sexual needs. But while Frank certainly kept me busy (and my loneliness at bay), he spent most of our time together screaming into his phone about the lack of screenwriter competence and actor talent.

We stayed together six months, with Frank "blowing off steam" as he called it on a regular basis, his tantrums steadily increasing in frequency and volume. Looking back, I'd like to claim that it was my own self-esteem that provided the impetus for ending the relationship, but I'd be lying. In truth, he was the one who decided to leave because the investor in his latest production happened to be an Orange County divorcee whose settlement left her with way more money than he could resist. He left, and I spent the next six months beating myself up for not having enough of whatever Frank needed to keep him by my side.

"What an idiot I was," I said now, getting to my feet and pacing along the shoreline, dodging the chilly waves that crept closer and closer to my toes. "Why did I pick such a loser?"

Words that Diana had said to me, I remembered, on more than one occasion when I called her, sobbing how I had "lost the love of my life."

"Lost him?" she snorted. "You never *had* him! He had *you*—oh, I don't mean just in the Biblical sense, but in everyday life. Let me ask you: How many hours did you spend on his project that you *didn't* bill to the agency? How much time did you spend listening to him complain when you had problems of your own that you were trying to resolve? I warned you, but you wouldn't listen. You wanted to live inside that 'Fran and Frank' bubble you created. So be glad he's someone else's problem now and get on with your life!"

Harsh words, but what I needed at the time.

"And what would Diana say now?" I asked as I stood there, watching the waves roll in, slowly but surely obscuring the rocks that were offshore. Eventually, when the tide was high enough, they would be covered. But just because you couldn't see them didn't mean those rocks weren't there. And if you didn't take careful note of their position when they were visible, you ran the risk of banging into them when the tide was high. And that, as any seaman would tell you, was likely to do major, if not permanent, damage to your boat.

The same was true in relationships. Just because you couldn't see the problems *all* the time didn't mean they were gone. That's what Diana was telling me each time I came crying to her, I realized as I climbed the sandy metal steps on my way back to my room. And now that these relationship rocks were clearly in view, I must navigate around them and get to safer, calmer waters.

But first things first. I had to stay on course with my work and deal with my relationship crisis afterward. I couldn't do anything about the mess my life was right now. Not until I go home, I thought. Not until John comes back and we're able to talk.

If he wants to talk. *If* he even comes back. *If* I even want him back.

I unlocked the door to my room where the computer waited, sat at the desk, and faced the blank screen. This was not the time to be afraid of writer's block or my public's response to my love problems or the problems themselves. This was work time, writing time, and I had better buckle down if I wanted to have something to show for my time at the Whale Inn besides (thanks to the carbs and chocolate) a whale-size body. Otherwise, my professional as well as my personal life would be destroyed.

I pictured myself walking amongst toppled-over piles of books bearing my name, the "best-seller" sign torn in two and fragments of bookmarks littering the streets. Or my house: grass uncut, curtains hanging haphazardly from their rods, the rusty "Foreclosure" sign swinging in the wind. If I didn't stay on track, *that* would be my future, and all that would be left would be the ruined remains of a promising romance novelist.

Ruined. *Ruins...* The barest hint of an idea swam through the swirling chaos in my mind. Roman ruins, Greek ruins, Stonehenge...

I woke up the computer (no sleeping on the job now!) and typed *Love in the Ruins*, imagining a heroine who goes on a dig to Mayan ruins and finds love.

When Cassandra traveled to the recently discovered Mayan city of— typing "Name TK" in brackets since I didn't have a name yet for this imaginary place—*to sketch the ruins, she had no idea that among the arti-facts of a civilization long past she would find the love on which she could build her future.*

I closed my eyes to visualize the character more clearly: her medium-length brown hair (slightly streaked with gray) pulled back with a scrunchy, her five-foot frame with its few extra post-menopause pounds concealed under the standard-issue archeological costume of khaki shirt and shorts.

Then I was stuck. I had to imagine the scene, the setting, the place where Cassandra would not only recreate the past but also create a new future for herself, courtesy of the handsome mid-fifties professor in charge of the dig. *Or* the handsome mid-fifties executive who was funding the excavation. *Or* the handsome mid-fifties "man of muscle" who was wielding the shovel. Whatever he turned out to be, I knew he had to be good-looking, available, and in the same age range as Cassandra.

But creating my hero's identity would be easier than picturing the country itself. I had never been to Mexico. For that matter, the closest I had come to traveling outside the country was when I crossed over Niagara Falls into Canada on a weekend away with Richard just after we started dating.

Richard... I hadn't thought of him in years. He was a welcome change from Frank. He bought me gifts: little things like a single red rose, a favorite book from a second-hand shop, a single-serving size of my dietary addiction: chocolate-and-pretzel ice cream. At first, I was thrilled by his attention. And there *was* a lot of it—attention, I mean—in and out of the bedroom. In retrospect, Richard seemed to have an endless amount of time to spend with me—a fact I willingly overlooked at the time.

And this attention was always delivered in intimate settings with only the two of us. There were dinners by candlelight at my place—I prepared the meals and bought the wine, of course. (It was nice to be cooking for someone else, I'd told myself.)

Or the picnics in the park, the basket packed with gourmet foodstuffs on which I had blown my food budget: expensive cheeses and fruit, artisan crackers, and imported wine.

Or the popcorn-and-movie nights, the two of us snuggled up in front of my TV watching the newest releases from the streaming service I subscribed to.

But each time I mentioned that it would be nice to go out among people, Richard would put his arm around me and whisper in my ear, "Fran, you work hard at your job. You need some quiet time. Besides, I want you all to myself."

And while it was flattering to hear, there were times when what *I* wanted was a real vacation: a cruise to the Bahamas, a weekend in Vegas, or a trip to New York City to take in a Broadway play and eat cheesecake at Sardi's.

But I didn't want to rock the boat, didn't want to be demanding, didn't want to seem ungrateful. So, I went along with what Diana said were "unbelievably cheap" dates. "My God, girl, you two might as well be teenagers trying to have fun on an allowance! Doesn't that man want to take you *anywhere*? And why is it always your car you use, your home you eat in? Doesn't he have a job?"

"Of course he does! He has his own contracting business!" I had retorted, stung by her words. She was jealous, I told myself. Richard was handsome. Richard was attentive. Richard was... well, Richard was *there*, and that was good enough for me.

But not good enough for Diana, who took it upon herself to check court records and his construction company's listing with the Better Business Bureau and bring the results to me, saying simply, "I thought you should know." She handed me an alarmingly thick sheaf of papers: numerous complaints from dissatisfied customers along with a Chapter 7 bankruptcy filing a year prior.

I looked at her, stunned—not as much by the information as by my own blindness—and waited for the reassuring words everyone wants to hear under the circumstances: "It's not your fault."

But Diana only stated flatly, "You, girl, are a bad picker. You don't look before you leap, and that's how you end up landing in a mess like this. And if you don't start using the brains God gave you, you're going to make a huge mistake someday that will cost you dearly."

I thanked her, put the papers away and, a few days later, loaned Richard five grand from my savings, supposedly for a new piece of equipment. (Not only was I a bad picker, I was also a slow learner.) He gladly took it before closing the business and departing with my money but without a goodbye.

Diana was right, but that didn't make me feel any better. It was several months before she and I spoke again and when we did, there was something there, a strain that made it difficult to return to the friendship we'd had. And that was entirely my fault. I was unreasonably angry at Diana for not giving me a graceful out, for not putting the blame anywhere but where it belonged: on my shoulders.

Because while it was true that I hadn't *created* Richard's problems, I *had* turned a blind eye to the warning signs—a regrettable habit of mine and one that I hadn't yet overcome. I consistently made relationship decisions that I regretted in the end. I could try to excuse my own stupidity as naïveté, but the truth was, when life offered me a choice—turn right or left, go up or down, pick this one or that one—I made the selection with my eyes deliberately closed. I didn't want to see the reality that *was*, preferring instead the fantasy that existed only in my mind.

"No wonder I write romance novels," I said now, staring at the screen. "I want to give my characters a chance to make choices and see if they're better at doing it than I am!"

And were they? How could I know? After all, I never followed them past the "happily ever after" part. Take Cassandra, for example. While I knew the story's outcome was that she would ride off into the sunset with whomever she met on the dig, would the one she picked be the right choice? And what were her options? Only Lover One or Lover Two? Or should I break with tradition and make the choice be either having a less-than-ideal lover or no lover at all?

"Nope. I'd better not make *that* drastic a change," I said aloud. "My readers expect the heroine to find love ever after in the arms of a man. If I don't give her *that*, they'll really be pissed! Besides, I obviously don't know how to write that kind of an ending since, in *my* life, it's always the guy, not me, who makes the decision!"

I went back to my synopsis, fleshing it out a bit more as I sketched out the storyline:

> She had been marking time since she retired from her university position, not sure what she wanted to do, only knowing that her life was lacking some indefinable something. And when the chance came to document with drawings what the team uncovered, Cassandra thought a few weeks in the sun would be the perfect change from Ohio's dreary February weather.

I opened the program where I had my writing playlist saved and looked for the right song to fit the scene: a woman whose life has been filled with disappointment and doesn't know what to do or where to go. There it was: Joni Mitchell's "Both Sides Now." Perfect! I went back to writing as the song filled the air.

She packed the clothes she had bought for the dig as well as some warm pajamas—it would be cool at night at that altitude, and they would be sleeping in tents after all. As for cosmetics—the blush she rarely used, the concealer that didn't hide her dark under-eye circles, the night cream that, instead of making her look ten years younger, left a greasy film on her face and pillowcase—why would she need them? After all, she was going there to work, not to find love. Who would care what she looked like?

I pushed back from the desk and stretched my fingers. Good. I finally had something down on paper—well, technically, on the screen. So, what comes next? Cassandra needs to make the obligatory "two steps forward, one step back" progress: success followed by setback, followed by more success, followed by more predictable ups and downs.

"I could have the lover married or so involved with his work that he doesn't even see Cassandra except as a willing pair of hands," I mused aloud. "Or have him bitten by some mysterious insect and put her in the classic 'wiping his fevered brow' situation so that, once he recovered, he would love her forever in gratitude for saving his life."

I made a few notes, knowing from experience how quickly ideas could disappear, then thought some more. What about a rival for his affections—like the bored wife of the wealthy benefactor who was funding the expedition? Victoria—the perfect name for the Other Woman. She'd come on the scene, dripping in diamonds, her long silky hair always flawlessly coiffed (how she managed to keep it clean and styled in that environment I didn't know, and my readers probably wouldn't care), wearing impeccably tailored yet archeologically appropriate clothing during the day and silky, slit-to-the-thigh gowns at night.

And there would stand poor Cassandra, sweaty, dirty, her hair growing grayer by the minute, unable to compete in any way other than with her sketching tools. But finally, her long hours spent alone in her apartment studying ancient civilizations while other women were out on dates and having sex—lots and *lots* of sex, I thought enviously, forgetting that this was about my heroine and not me—would pay off.

She would uncover the secret meaning of the intricate designs carved on a piece of pottery. And voilà! Her lover's reputation is secured, the funding is guaranteed, and the bored wife departs because now all he cares about is his new discovery. When he expresses his appreciation to Cassandra (in the moonlight, of course), she'll respond adoringly, "But I did it all for you!" and they'll kiss. End of story.

"Wonderful! Great! I can write this!" I said with satisfaction. "And it's not like my other books! I mean, I never put a heroine in Mexico. Or on a dig anywhere. And she *has* to get the man in the end—otherwise, what's the point?"

The point of what? my mind asked in a voice that sounded uncomfortably like Diana's. *The point of* her *life? The point of* your *life? Was that what drove you into all those totally inappropriate arms—the belief that your life only had a purpose if it included a man?*

"Oh, shut the hell up!" I said, grabbing my purse. It was nearly four o'clock, close enough to dinnertime to justify leaving my work in favor of food. Or at least, that's what I told myself.

Chapter 11

MARTHA HADN'T EXTENDED A MEAL INVITATION—JUST AS WELL because the last thing I wanted to hear was any negative feedback on *Love in Unexpected Places*, not when I finally had made some progress, however small, on my next project. I drove up the gravel driveway to the highway and turned north, intending to find the town that had provided Martha with the wine and a copy of my current book.

I would eat something quick yet healthful then head over to Barnaby's Books to check out some of the competition. No one would connect me with my jacket photo. *That* had been the result of a new haircut and an expensive color job as well as John's photographic magic.

John. Had he called? I needed to buy a charger cord for my phone so I'd be able to check my texts and voice mail. There might be a message. Maybe he realized the mistake he'd made. Maybe he wanted a second chance. Maybe—

"Oh, shit!"

The blare of a horn brought me back to the highway and a curve that I had overshot, putting me a tad too close to the driver's side bumper of an oncoming SUV. I yanked the steering wheel to the right, barely avoiding a collision that could have resulted in sending my car (and me in it) several hundred feet to the rocks below.

I could read the headlines: *Failing Novelist Crashes Vehicle. Suicide Suspected.* I had better pay attention if I didn't want to end up as a brief entry in the obit section. Resolutely putting all thoughts of John as far back in my mind as I could, I slowed to a crawl and started watching for signs that indicated civilization: specifically, a town where I could find food and drink.

And there it was, or at least the sign directing me to the exit for Coastside Bay. I took it, and after stopping at the closest gas station to fill up and get a charger cord for my phone, I drove on into the town.

Coastside Bay was one of those quaint little places filled with shops and eateries: lots and lots of them, from fast food joints to Asian, French, and Italian restaurants. I settled on Burger Boy where I ordered a hamburger (virtuously eschewing the cheese) and fries (so much for virtue), washing it all down with hot coffee whose bitter undertones indicated the pot had been left too long on the warmer—like me.

But it didn't matter. This had been a good day, a productive day, I told myself as I crossed the street to the bookstore. And now I would browse among the stacks and see what my fellow romance novelists were up to—and how many of my own books were on the shelves.

I walked in, smiled at the clerk who was ringing up a couple of kids' books, and looked for the romance area, finding it cheek by jowl with the section full of travelogues and maps. An appropriate location since both categories were designed to transport readers to some place strange and new and full of opportunities.

I scanned the selection, mentally taking inventory. There was the obligatory row of Rosabella Robinson's books followed by a cluster of Alexandra Graystone's best sellers. Why did romance novelists all have such romantic names? I wondered. Maybe I should change mine from the prosaic "Fran Carter" to "Francesca Caterina." Maybe *that* would increase sales!

I moved farther down the aisle in search of my books. But where my three-piece grouping should be was just *Love in the Moonlight*—the one that had zoomed straight to the number one spot on the best-seller list, the one the *LA Times* reviewer had said "provided millions of female readers with the promise that post-menopause didn't have to mean post-sex."

Maybe they're sold out, I thought hopefully. I could find out from the bookseller if my books were on order. Or do a little market research: ask what romance novels were hot-selling items in the store. Deciding on the latter approach, I went over to the information desk.

"I was hoping you could help me find a book," I said in my most ingratiating tone to the woman behind the counter. "I have a friend who needs a good read, something to take her mind off her troubles. She's recovering from a broken leg and can't go anywhere or do anything," unable to resist embroidering what should have been a simple request for a recommendation. "What are some of the best sellers in the romance category? I don't read them myself, but she just loves them."

She left her post and led me back to the section where I'd been. "Oh, I know, romance novels are wonderful!" she said, pushing back her gray hair that had slipped free of its side comb. "They take you away and make you think that anything is possible. I've been married forty-five years, and the romance went out of my marriage more than a few years ago. But sometimes, after I read one of the books by Danielle Steele or Fern Michaels, I can remember what it was like when my husband and I first started dating. *He* likes it when I read them, too," blushing a bit.

She ran her fingers along the row.

"Now this one by Alexandra Graystone is wonderful—not too much sex but plenty of romance and wine and roses. And then there's *this* one by Victorina Andromisi," pointing to a second novel.

There we are again, I noted. A mellifluous name that even *sounds* romantic!

"She always has the most exotic settings: Paris, Spain, the Greek islands... I feel like I've been on a vacation after I've read one of her books!"

"What about the books by... what was her name... Fran Catter? No, Carter," I interrupted, unwilling to hear any more praise for my competition.

"Oh yes, *her* books," and the enthusiasm in her voice slightly dampened. "Well, to tell you the truth, although the first one was very popular, the last two didn't seem as good. Kind of repetitive if you know what I mean. Especially the last one—what was it called? *Love in—*"

"*Love in Unexpected Places,*" I said without thinking and then could have kicked myself. I was supposed to be unfamiliar with the genre and especially with my own books, and here I was, unable to resist spouting off the title.

"Yes, that's it," giving me a puzzled look before going back to her unasked-for critique. "Like the bit with the cat in the opening. I think she had used a cat in one of her other books, too. Let me think... Oh yes, in her second book, *Love in the Islands*. I'm sure the character had a cat in *that* one. And the whole cat business—why do writers always give single women cats? If you think about it, dogs would be a better choice. For one thing, dogs can protect them if somebody breaks in. And there is something so masculine, so strong about a dog. I mean, having a cat is one step away from calling these poor women spinsters!"

"What about this one?" and I pulled a book at random from the shelf, anything to change the current line of conversation. But when I looked at it, it was the latest from that ubiquitous Robinson. That woman was going to haunt me through this whole trip, I thought gloomily.

She took it from my hand as though it were a chunk of gourmet chocolate she couldn't bear to share.

"Ah, *this* one," she said reverently. "I think this is Rosabella's best book to date. I read it last year when it first came out and loved it so much I gave it as gifts to all my girlfriends at Christmas. *And* recommended it to my book club. *And* wrote a fan letter to Ms. Robinson. And when she came to San Francisco for a book signing, we all rented a van and drove together to stand in line for three hours so that she could sign our books. Can you imagine how many people were there for it to take that long?"

I could and knew well from my own experience. I remembered my very first book signing. There were so many purchasers lined up outside the store waiting to buy *Love in the Moonlight* that management started handing out free drinks so they wouldn't wilt in the heat, a turnout that hadn't happened for me since, I realized.

"And when we got to her, she was so gracious and sweet. She smiled and told us never to give up on love. That was the book title, you know: *Never Give Up on Love.*"

I smiled and took the book from her hand. "Thanks. I'll certainly consider it. But I really don't want to keep you," hoping she would go back to the information counter.

But as luck would have it, there was no one waiting in line and no way to deflect her from her impromptu literary critique of the genre.

"You know, I always had the feeling Rosabella must have a great marriage, one with all the bells and whistles if you know what I mean. Otherwise, how could she write about love the way she does? It's not like you can research it like Ms. Grafton did with her mystery novels, to make sure she got all the crime details and murder investigations right. I'm no writer"—a phrase that, in my experience, usually preceded nonwriters' opinions about how to write—"but when it comes to writing romance novels, you have to be writing from what you know. Otherwise, you're stuck either stealing from other writers or making it up. Kind of like what *you* would want if you could have it, but because you don't, you don't really know what it would be like, if you know what I mean."

A convoluted sentence, but I got the gist of it nonetheless, in large part because it echoed my thoughts regarding my own books—the last one at least. I started to worry about *Love in the Ruins*. Maybe it was a repeat, too. Had I already written all there was to write about romance and love and relationships—at least from my own experience? Was I taking the same characters and just sticking them in different settings, like when I was a little girl playing with my Barbie doll? First, Barbie was in her pink bedroom and then she was in her pink dorm room and then she was on her way to the beach in her pink Cadillac while wearing her pink bikini.

But she was always the same old Barbie, and there was always the same old Ken by her side. And Midge, too, which made me wonder for the first time if the alleged best friend harbored some amorous feelings for Barbie's guy. I mean, she *was* always hanging around.

But Barbie herself never changed. Didn't she want something more than her cool convertible, cool college lifestyle, cool boyfriend? And what the hell was wrong with *me*, spending valuable work time analyzing the life of an eleven-inch plastic figure with body measurements that were not only unrealistic but downright unhealthy?

I was so caught up in my thoughts that I never noticed when the clerk moved farther down the section. I flipped through the books on the shelf, my frustration and fear growing in leaps and bounds. Why couldn't I write what women wanted to buy? I did it before, twice to be precise, even if the second book didn't do as well as the first. But the third one—well, I had clearly missed the mark if my royalty statements were any indication.

What had changed? Had I lost my capacity to write? Or was it my belief in romance?

I thought back to when I was writing *Love in the Moonlight*. The novel was all about the kind of love affair I wanted to have—hadn't had so far but still dreamed was possible. And when I met John, it seemed like I had all the right ingredients: sexy, romantic love with a sexy, romantic man.

After that, writing *Love in the Islands* was relatively easy. I started, of course, with the "woman in jeopardy" premise: poor Melanie (a wishy-washy name that made me think of the nauseatingly forgiving heroine in *Gone with the Wind*), who was dumped by her cheating husband right in front of his current lover and found herself all alone except for the obligatory feline.

If she had been a little smarter, she would have caught on earlier. But there you are, we women never want to see the truth of the matter. Oh, not all of us. There *are* those who have self-confidence and self-esteem and all those other "self" traits that mean they are psychologically healthy. But the rest of us, well, we aren't willing to look too closely at the fabric of the relationship in case we might find a loose thread.

And that's the thing with loose threads: when you find one, you have an irresistible urge to pull it. And before you know it, everything starts to unravel.

But in Melanie's case, after a fair bit of waffling back and forth when he came back to her asking to be forgiven, she finally came to her senses. Women loved it—not as much as *Love in the Moonlight* based on the sales, but enough to satisfy my publisher. They loved that she finally told off that SOB, loved that she fell into the arms and heart of a rich guy who "took her away" into his upscale condo where all the kitchen accoutrements were from Williams-Sonoma and all the bed linens from Pottery Barn. They clipped coupons and perused sales fliers from their local big-box stores while fantasizing about those romantic dinners à deux the two fictional characters would be sharing.

Then came *Love in Unexpected Places.* Was that where it all started to fall apart? With Caroline, the feline-owning single woman who had to get a pet because she couldn't find a real human to love and to love her back?

She falls for the vet because he has "gentle hands that delicately stroked the kitten's head," imagining, no doubt, those same fingers stroking *her* head—or somewhere else. A vet who was already involved with his office manager, one of those professional women who could run an office and cook gourmet meals and still have perfectly manicured nails.

The predictable romantic conflict: meek-and-mild Caroline versus cool-yet-determined Rebecca, with the stupid vet just standing there. Caroline gives up and goes home to her cat, the vet realizes he loves her, and Rebecca leaves the practice to work for (and sleep her way into the house of) a rich plastic surgeon. And then the de rigueur ending: Caroline and the vet live happily ever after, with Caroline taking over as office manager, of course. (Interesting how none of my heroines to date had their own successful careers *or* identities.)

"Did you find what you wanted?" The saleswoman's question interrupted my musings, which was just as well since I didn't like the path my thoughts were traveling down.

"Yes, I think I'll take this one," and I grabbed *Love in the Moonlight* along with two of my competitors' best sellers.

"Those ought to keep her happy while her leg heals," she said approvingly, and for a moment I was confused. Then I remembered the lie I had concocted involving my imaginary friend with a broken leg. Great. Not only was my talent fading but my memory as well.

Once at the register, I started digging in my wallet for my credit card. But as I realized the name on the card would give me away as the author of one of the books I was buying, she said, "Sorry, no credit cards. It's the store policy," pointing to a sign large as life on which was written "If you can't pay cash, you can't afford it. Buy responsibly."

Thank God, I thought, as I hunted for some bills. But I had avoided one embarrassment to be faced with another. I had been so upset when I left the house Sunday morning that I never checked for cash and now found only six crumpled ones.

"Then I'm afraid I'll have to pass on these after all," setting the books off to one side as I made a mental note to find the nearest ATM and replenish my cash reserves. "But at least I can buy a couple of candy bars!" and I grabbed a few from the stack by the register: two with almonds and one with pecans.

She smiled politely, rang up my purchase, and said, "Have a wonderful day" while handing me a pitifully small bag holding three days' worth of calories and fat grams.

"Um, thanks, and you, too," I mumbled and quickly left the store. All I wanted now was to head back to the B&B where I could soothe my sorrows with chocolate. I went out to my car and, after stopping at a nearby ATM, got back on the highway.

Chapter 12

ONE WOULD THINK THAT AFTER HEARING MY BOOKS CRITIQUED by a small-town reader (I could hardly call her a fan, considering her opinion of my novels) and consuming three jumbo-size candy bars in short order (I had started the first one even before I left Coastside Bay), I would suffer through an evening filled with despair and sorrow followed by a night of bad dreams and frequent awakenings.

One would think, but one would be wrong. In reality, I felt pretty darned good by the time I finished my last piece of chocolate. After parking my car at the inn, I had taken my goodies down to the shore, parked my bottom on my driftwood "bench," and proceeded to nibble my way through the remaining twenty-four ounces of chocolate with a resultant sensual satisfaction one normally associates with great sex. It was quite restorative, which made me wonder if there weren't even more to the health benefits of chocolate than the scientists were telling us.

When I finished, I sat a bit longer, watching the waves roll in and back out again. I loved being by the water: the sound of the surf, the smell of salt air, the feeling of sand squishing between my toes. That was one of the reasons I'd moved back to my childhood home after my parents died instead of putting it on the market as Diana had suggested.

"Property values have really started to go up and sales are strong, especially for lower-priced single-family homes with no mortgage like this one," she'd said when she came to help me clear out the detritus of my parents' sixty-year marriage. "But you still need to take care of all this stuff," indicating the piles of odds and ends that represented their life.

And there was a lot of it. My mother had never met an item she couldn't keep "just in case." As for my dad, he was a "collector's collector": stamps, coins, baseball cards, cigarette boxes—you name it and he had it, catalogued, boxed, and stacked along the walls in the family room as well as up the stairs to the second floor and in odd corners throughout the house.

It all had to go. I knew that, but I found myself unable to make a decision on what to keep and what to discard, sentiment and some sense of disrespecting their past clouding my judgment.

Fortunately, Diana had no such compunctions, and once I made it clear that I wasn't selling, she began winnowing down the decades of stuff to a manageable amount.

"This way, if you do change your mind, you'll have less to get rid of. Although the house will need substantial updating before you can put it on the market," she'd added, looking critically at the interior that had remained pretty much the same ever since my parents bought it right after they married. "And that takes money—money you don't have. But if you're determined to move out of your apartment and back here, you'll be able to save on rent and put it toward renovations. Now, let's get started, okay?"

But I couldn't seem to do it. So, Diana did what she did best. She took charge and started the packing-up process while telling me, in her own fashion, to "suck it up and quit bawling like a baby" each time my tears started when I picked up another memento.

"I know it's hard," she said as she filled boxes with china and glassware, taped them shut, and marked them for the shop run by the local rescue mission while I, still sniffling, turned the pages of yet another photo album from the stack by the chair. "But you're a grown woman— you're in your forties, for God's sake—and you had to know this day was coming."

She came over, took the album from my hand, and added it to a box she had marked "spare bedroom."

"Your parents lived a good, long life, and you should be grateful that they both went peacefully. Think about it. Would your father have wanted to live after his stroke, depending on your mother to take care of him and do everything for him? As for your mom... well, let's face it, after your father died, she didn't want to be here anymore. He was the center of her world. The heart attack was a physical symptom of how she felt emotionally."

"But I miss them. They were my parents. We were a family, and now I'm alone!"

"I know. And I'm not trying to downplay your grief. But you have to get a grip. It's been six months since you buried your mother. Are you sure there isn't something more going on here than just the loss of a parent? And if there is, you'd better figure it out so you can move forward. Now," pulling me from the chair, "help me clear out this stack from the linen closet. There must be sixteen sets of bedsheets here!" And she dumped them on the floor for me to sort.

I did as I was told and started sorting and boxing—*and* stopped crying though I was more than a little ticked off at Diana for what I deemed were heartless words. She didn't understand, I told myself, working my way through the linens and towels, silverware and pans. Of *course* all these tears were because I was grieving for my parents. Weren't they?

But in retrospect, I wasn't so sure. I missed my parents, of course, but how much of that grief was because I was all alone? Was that why I ended up with John—because I didn't want to spend the rest of my life with no one to care for me, pay attention to me, love me?

And what did that decision get me almost six years later? Nights spent waiting for John to return to a house that didn't feel like home—*my* home—not like the one I'd been in when John and I met.

As for the life I was living, well, even *that* was far from what I had imagined when he first suggested we buy a bigger house. For one thing, it seemed like John spent more nights away than I would have expected. There was always some party or event he had to attend in San Francisco. According to John, more client networking takes place over dinner and a bottle of Chardonnay than over lunch, which usually meant he spent the night at his studio instead of coming back to Los Gatos.

As for me, I was struggling my way through writing Book Three. I no longer felt excitement or pleasure in the creative act. And, making it worse, I was away from the sound and smell of the ocean that had been a treasured part of my life since childhood. Now, if I wanted to go to the shore, I had to drive at least forty-five miles, find a place to park, and then put up with all the *other* inlanders who also wanted to live by the water but couldn't and so drove to that same beach so they could at least momentarily satisfy that fantasy.

Even if I found a parking place, the shoreline was so crowded it didn't seem worth the trouble and frustration. Which might be why *Love in Unexpected Places* had been more difficult for me to write.

"I've lost my inspiration, my peace, my connection with the water," I said to John one night while he was cataloguing his latest shots on the computer in the family room.

He didn't answer—when he was working, he wouldn't have responded to an earthquake—and so I wandered back to my office where

I obsessed about my inability to write, worrying that it might mean my creative well had dried up.

But looking back, I wondered if the real cause was that I had lost my home—both physically and emotionally—and found myself in a house where I didn't belong with a man who, to be honest, fit into my life as poorly as I fit into his.

Now, here at the Whale Inn, I felt at home for the first time in a long time. And even though the writing wasn't going well and I had reservations about the concept for *Love in the Ruins*, at least I was writing. And wasn't that what I was supposed to be doing? Wasn't this whole time away intended not just to get away from my personal problems but also to get back to my own career and make what I hoped would be a U-turn from future "has-been" to future "successful writer"?

It could happen if I did what I had to do: stay focused, keep writing, and forget about John—at least for now.

As the fog began to roll in, the night air turned chilly. It was time to go back to my room to write, or at least read over what I had written— or maybe take a long, leisurely soak in the tub before crawling into bed to sleep.

It was the third choice that won out, and before nine I was out like the proverbial light, sleeping straight through until five the next morning when I awoke, feeling rested and restored. Wrapped in my terry robe, my feet encased in thick socks, I turned on my laptop. As I waited for it to go through its warm-up exercises, I watched the morning haze gradually thin over the water and hoped that whatever creative fog had been obscuring my mind would soon be gone as well.

The computer chimed, signaling it was ready to go to work. I opened the document labeled *Love in the Ruins* and read through what I had written the day before, nodding at the good parts and frowning at a few poorly constructed paragraphs. And then, without regret or a second thought, I closed and deleted the file.

"This isn't what I want to write," I said decisively. "No more stories about women who feel incomplete without a man. No more women waiting around, wondering what Fate might bring them. No more!"

I knew in my writer's bones that I didn't want to write that story—*my* story—but a different kind of story. One with romance (there was nothing wrong with sex and love after all) yet featuring a strong female lead who already had the life she wanted and was open to sharing it with an equally contented and fulfilled man.

A romance novel about a love that didn't show major flaws when subjected to the closer scrutiny of day-to-day living, that didn't fade away when the soft moonlight was replaced by the less forgiving light of day. A novel that wasn't about a lonely woman with a cat but a woman who had a productive and satisfying life, the kind that my readers—or at least those who voiced their opinions at my last signing—wanted.

I wanted to write... well, I knew what I *wanted* to write but unfortunately didn't have a good model for that kind of story. That would take some imagining—some inspiration that would propel my creativity into new realms. But rather than intimidating me, the prospect filled me with excitement—the excitement that had been missing, I knew now, when I wrote *Love in Unexpected Places*. No wonder my fans hadn't liked it—I hadn't even liked it myself!

That's the thing about having a loyal group of followers. If you've done your job well, the whole time they're reading the story, they believe it's true and, even better, that it's possible for them as well.

But they also know when you've struggled to make it all come together in the end. They can sense when you're unable to effectively resolve the mandatory issues and conflicts that are part and parcel of any novel. And if you labor so hard that even *they* can see the joists and trusses and studs that went into constructing the "structure" that is the story, they realize it's all make-believe. And *that* is where you lose them—sometimes permanently.

When I started writing *Love in the Moonlight*, I still believed in the storyline I was creating. But that belief had started to fade by the time I wrote the last few chapters of *Love in the Islands* and my romance with John was starting to show wear. And it was gone for good by the time my third book hit the shelves. I knew it, and considering the lackluster sales, many of my fans knew it as well.

"They were smarter than me," I said as I stared at the computer screen. "Now, I need to discover what *they* want and what *I* want—and then write about that kind of life: a 'true romance meets real life' kind of book. But before I can write it, I have to figure it out for myself. What do I want in a relationship? Or first, figure out who I am. If I'm going to write a new kind of romance, doesn't the lead character have to be a new kind of woman: confident, proud of herself, happy in her life—with or without a man? And shouldn't *I* be that kind of woman?"

Chapter 13

IT WAS AN INTRIGUING SUPPOSITION, ONE THAT I MULLED OVER AS I headed to the dining room for one of Martha's mouthwatering Whale Inn breakfasts.

Had I ever been a happy, confident woman? Yes, at least as far as my belief in my ability to write was concerned. I *had* to be confident to be able to withstand the heat of the copywriting "kitchen" all those years. But that ended when the agency closed and I found myself settling for temporary work at a fraction of what I'd once made, an unfortunate facet of the job market at the time.

But even though it was no longer how I was making a living, I still had confidence in my ability to write.

"If I hadn't, I would never have spent all those nights writing *Love in the Moonlight*," I said, pushing open the door to where Martha and her fresh-baked bread awaited me, if my nose was any judge of the aroma wafting toward me in almost edible waves. "So where did *that* Fran go? And how can I find her again?"

"Find who, dear?" Martha appeared before me in an apron about two sizes too large, her hands holding a tray laden with a thermal coffee carafe, mug, slices of toasted raisin-cinnamon bread, and a small jar of honey. "I was bringing this to your room in case you were working, but here you are instead!"

She led me over to a table by the window and set down the tray. "So, how is the book going?"

"It's going." I smiled, filled my cup, and took a sip. It was strong enough to wake the dead but probably what would keep my mind running full steam. "Or to be accurate, it's gone. I did some writing yesterday, but this morning I junked it all. Trashed it completely. Hit that old delete button and watched it disappear!"

Martha looked at me sharply, and then, taking a mug from the table behind her, poured herself some coffee before sitting down.

"You sound awfully happy for someone who has nothing to show for her writing time. I read somewhere that when Rosabella Robinson was having trouble writing, she was miserable. She cried all the time and sometimes even drank herself into a stupor. Once, they said, she even set her manuscript on fire out of frustration. You didn't set any fires, did you?" she asked anxiously, as though worried that she might be harboring a closet pyromaniac.

"Nope," I assured her. I took a big bite of bread and chewed it with appreciation. The sweetness of the raisins and streusel topping were just what I needed: a sugar rush that matched the caffeine blast from the coffee.

"I tossed it right into the little electronic trashcan. The fact is," stopping to swallow the mouthful, "I didn't like the story I'd started, didn't like the character I'd created, and didn't want to go any further with it. It seemed too 'been there, done that,'" unconsciously echoing Isabella's words.

"I'm glad you said that," stirring her coffee a little longer than necessary before looking up at me. "I read your book—you know, the last one, *Love in Unexpected Places*. And it wasn't as good as your first two. The character seemed kind of helpless. And whiny, too," warming to her role as literary critic.

I was fated, it seemed, to be surrounded by people who couldn't resist critiquing my work.

"And a cat—why a cat? Didn't you have a cat in one of your earlier books, too? Let me think..."

She paused, clearly searching through her mental list of my previous plotlines. "Yes, it was in *Love in the Islands* with that woman Miranda, Megan—what was her name?—whose husband had cheated on her."

"Melanie," I said, but she plowed right on as though I hadn't spoken.

"Why not a dog? I got Jake, an Alaskan husky, after my husband died. It made me feel safer to have him around. Isn't he a beauty?" and she pointed to a picture hanging by the doorway featuring a *really* large dog with *really* large teeth salivating at the camera.

I looked around nervously, not a huge fan of anything that could potentially tear me limb from limb, but saw no evidence of a canine companion.

"He was a wonderful dog and great company during that time. I really missed my husband—still do, even though I've made a good life without him. We'd been married for thirty years, and I never thought he would leave me—or at least, not until we were both old and gray. But that wasn't how it turned out."

She picked up her mug, took a sip, and went on.

"But by the time Jake died—ten years ago when he was fifteen—I had made it through the roughest spots and felt a lot stronger. Oh, I still missed Fred, but I was able to start over here at the inn."

"You didn't get another dog?" pushing my empty plate a little closer to her, a subtle hint that she was quick to notice. She walked over to the counter where she put another thick slice of bread on my dish and brought it back to the table, setting it in front of me.

"I thought about it, but the truth is, I'm getting old, my arthritis acts up at times, and a dog the size of Jake would need someone who can take him out for his exercise. So, I got a gun instead."

I stopped in mid-reach, surprise arresting my hand. "A gun? You got a *gun*?"

"Well, of course!" as though it were a reasonable choice. "I had to do something, didn't I, if I was going to stay here on my own? You didn't think I would rely on calling 911 in case something happened, did you? Instead, I bought a handgun—a nice little twenty-two with an easy trigger pull. Sometimes my fingers are stiff, so I wanted a gun that didn't need a lot of effort to fire. Want to see it?"

Without waiting for an answer, she went behind the counter, opened a bin marked "Flour," and drew out a weapon that nearly covered the palm of her hand.

She brought it to the table and held it out to me, saying, "If you know how to shoot, I'll let you fire it."

But I shook my head. "No, I don't know how," and in my voice heard regret and envy. The gun looked, well, like a gun. But holding it, Martha no longer looked like your typical senior citizen but a formidable foe. She was a different woman—or the same woman but with a whole new dimension revealed.

"And I took lessons," she said. "Our senior center set up a firing range and brought in a young woman, a firearms expert, as our instructor. You wouldn't *believe* the number of elderly women around here who took to shooting! Why, we even formed a little group—the Bay City

Bullets, we call ourselves—and we meet every week for target practice. Sometimes I even come close to hitting the bull's-eye!"

She smiled, clearly proud of herself. "So, where were we? Oh, that's right, your books. Why do you have to make your women so, I don't know... needy? As if they're missing a part if they don't have a man? Not that there's anything wrong with marriage, but that's only part of a woman's life, not the whole of it. Like kids—not that I had any since Fred and I weren't blessed with a family, but even if we had been, being a mother is just one part of a woman's identity, isn't it? And then the kids grow up and leave home and make their own life. And if being a mother is all that a woman is or *thinks* she is, then she's standing there with nothing to do and no idea how to spend the rest of her life. Do *you* have any children?"

"Nope. No kids, no pets—not even a cat. I guess my books are my kids," I said lightly.

"Well, they certainly aren't behaving very well," she observed tartly. "I read in the *Chronicle's* books section that the last one hadn't even made the top-ten list. The reviews weren't very good either," sounding like a principal recounting the poor test scores of my underperforming child. "I'd hate to think you were going down that same road with *this* book. Or will it be something different? Is that why you got rid of what you wrote last night?"

I nodded and tried to explain to Martha what I had just figured out for myself.

"Yes. It was the same old story, and even though that story worked in the beginning, it wasn't working now—hadn't even worked well with the last one. I guess that's why the sales are down," something I normally wouldn't have admitted to one of my readers but somehow felt safe saying to Martha.

"When I wrote the first book, I really believed in romance, in finding that 'other half' to make me whole. I never asked myself whether it wouldn't be smarter to figure out what was missing in my life to make me feel that way. It's kind of like eating when you're not really hungry," something I certainly knew about. "You think you want food while what you really need is something else. But it's easier to just eat."

"Hmm," said Martha, looking out the window.

She was taking her time before responding, I noticed. And I was more than a little uncomfortable while I waited for what she would say, like a patient waiting for the doctor to disclose the diagnosis and propose a course of treatment.

Well, it's not like *I* had any idea what to do, I told myself. Right now, I had more questions than answers—about my book *and* about my life. Any advice would be welcome.

But advice wasn't forthcoming—at least, not at this moment. Martha stood, slipped the gun in her apron pocket, and stacked the dirty dishes on the tray.

"Well, you're not going to fix it sitting here talking about it," she said, and I wasn't sure whether she meant my life, my writing, or both. "I think you'd better get right back to work. That's what I always do when I'm not sure how to deal with something. I just start working. And pretty soon, it all gets clear and I figure out what to do and how to do it. Talk is fine," she added, moving toward the kitchen, "but it's no substitute for action."

I sat there, disappointed and relieved all at once. If I was hoping for some brilliant analysis of my life followed by recommendations for how to fix it, I was out of luck. Martha was no life coach, holding my hand and taking me step by step as I struggled through the gray cloud of uncertainty. She simply said her piece and left it to me to decide what to do. That was her style and how she'd handled her life after her husband died: plowed right in and did what had to be done without wasting time second-guessing or obsessing over what couldn't be changed.

Unlike me, who had spent hours—okay, let's be honest, *days*—agonizing over what couldn't be altered or debating how to cope with different scenarios: if John came back and wanted out... if John came back and wanted in... if John didn't come back at all...

It's one thing to theorize how a specific character will handle a specific crisis. You evaluate all the angles, make sure the choice matches what the reader has come to expect from that imaginary person, and arrange outcomes in such a way that the conclusion makes sense. And you can do that with fiction because you're in control of everything: the good guys, the bad guys, the crises that occur, the good times that soften the blows.

But in life, you can't rewrite beginnings, middles, or endings. You can't see into other people's minds and understand why they made the choices they did. And unless you're pretty good at being objective and introspective, you might not even be able to fully understand your own behavior or decisions. The best you can do is take it one step at a time, look at what's happening, and figure out where to go from there—and where you want to end up.

Since it looked like Martha was not coming back to rescue me from my lack of understanding, I headed back to my room. There I started a new file, listing the complications facing my heroine as well as what she really wanted in her life.

Who was she—this woman I was creating? What was and wasn't working for her in her life? And how did she propose to address the problems and carry out the needed solutions?

Of course, there *had* to be crises for her to face, challenges to overcome. And I had to fit love into the picture somehow, somewhere. It *was* a romance after all. But I didn't want her metaphorically clinging to a stick of wood like a Titanic survivor, waiting for a man to come along and save her.

No, I wanted her to rescue herself. And *then* find a man who didn't need rescuing either, after which the two of them would get into a boat and together row happily off into the sunset.

I stared out the window, trying to put myself in my heroine's shoes. Unlike my other books, I wanted to open with her feeling happy, contented, satisfied with her life and her accomplishments to date.

I thought back to when I'd felt that way. Was it with my first book when I would spend long hours staring at the computer screen, watching my character's life unfold keystroke by keystroke? The first thing I would do each evening was read through the last few paragraphs to get back in touch with the characters and their lives, the way you do when you haven't spoken to a friend for a few months and want to catch up. And the last thing I would do before I stopped for the night was note the word count to see how far I had progressed.

On a good night, I might average a thousand words while on a night when the writing was slower, perhaps a few hundred, with nearly as much revising and editing as adding fresh content. But it didn't matter because I felt good about what I was doing and how it was progressing.

I didn't have any goals other than to get the story written. I didn't fantasize about finding an agent or publisher or cashing royalty checks or even doing book signings. No, it was all about the act itself, the creative process, and exploring a type of writing that was vastly different from what I had done at the agency. It was challenging but always satisfying.

And when the book was finished and on the shelves and my publisher reported all the numbers that counted—the Amazon rankings, the best-seller lists, the reviews in library journals—I was thrilled yet more than a little bemused by it all. I felt like a batboy who took a swing for fun and hit a homerun out of the park. As exciting as it was to see the ball sail over the fence, I never for a moment expected to duplicate the result. Instead, I looked at it as a fluke, a chance occurrence—something all writers dream of but never really expect to happen.

But that was nothing compared to my low expectations for my personal life, specifically in the romance department. I failed to set the bar high enough, to demand to be treated as someone of value, to establish reasonable expectations from the men I was involved with. And I got exactly what I asked for, which was very little indeed.

"If your standards were any lower, the guys would have to excavate to reach them," Diana had said when my romance with Richard was finally over.

And she was right. So, once I got through the sobbing-while-recounting-the-pain-of-it-all stage, I decided that next time, the man I got involved with would be financially stable with ambition and goals.

"All I want is someone like me," I'd told Diana. "Someone who can pay his own way, who is willing to work, someone who has a career. He's out there *somewhere*," I said. "I know it. And that's the kind of man I want."

And what I wanted was what I got, which should have taught me to be a darned sight more careful about what I was asking Fate (or Cupid) to bring me. Because what that little bow-and-arrow-toting dickens brought was Paul—or "The Switch," as Diana nicknamed him, because he could seemingly turn his interest in me on and off with barely any effort.

Paul came into my life a few years after Richard. He was a sought-after freelance graphic designer whom my agency often used for "special clients" (translation: inconsistent and exacting). He had an income that was twice mine because he demanded exorbitant fees for his creativity—and got them. We often worked together on projects, and I admired his determination to stand up for what he wanted. After a few months, I was thrilled when it seemed he wanted me.

Late-night dinners wrestling with copy and design turned into night-long wrestling of a different sort—sometimes at my place, sometimes at his. But he was always the pure professional in the office, and no one watching us at work could tell by his behavior that we were anything but collaborators on client projects.

"That's the way it has to be," I told Diana. "He doesn't want them thinking that all those hours he's billing are spent not working."

"Uh huh," she said. "But what about outside of work? I mean, you two never really go anywhere besides to bed. And those times when you don't even have that? Didn't you tell me that sometimes you wouldn't hear from him for weeks at a stretch?"

"Well, he's busy," I said, defending his absence though part of me questioned it as well. "He's got a lot of other companies he works for, and he has to stay on top of his projects if he wants to remain successful. You *told* me" raising my voice "that I had to make sure next time I got involved it was with someone who could pay his bills. And I did! Paul makes lots of money, certainly more than me. But he has to work to get it!"

She shook her head as though I were too hopeless a case to deal with.

"Balance, it's all about balance," she said. "You work hard too, but you make time for him, don't you? If you were truly important to him, if he valued the relationship, he would do the same for you. He could at least call you, couldn't he? But one minute he's hot, the next minute he's cold. He's on, then off—why do you think I call him 'The Switch' anyway?"

She was right, I knew now. But back then I was still into my justifying stage—explaining away major character flaws as foibles, quirks, or "just the way he is." In Paul's case, the way he was, ultimately, was gone. Or more accurately, *I* was gone, replaced after six months with a new "breaker" in his emotional circuit box—someone, I heard through the corporate grapevine, who was even more driven than he was.

Once again, I had demonstrated my poor "pick-ability." Once again, I was left holding the pieces of my heart and self-esteem, wondering what was wrong with me that I couldn't find and keep a man, find and keep love. Maybe, I reflected, that's why I started writing romance novels, so I could live vicariously through my characters and give them the happy ending I was never able to find for myself.

And it worked—at least for the first two books. But not anymore and I knew I needed a new plan. If I were going to write this new kind of romance, I couldn't use my past for inspiration. I had to envision a woman who was better, smarter, and more confident than I ever was—a woman who thought enough of herself to *not* settle for anything less than a man who would treat her right.

Someone who wasn't the me I was now but the me I wished I could be. But who was she? Who was this woman I had yet to create?

Chapter 14

COOKIE. COOKIE O'HARE...

The name popped into my head in one of those serendipitous moments that come to writers when the muse finally takes pity on them and tosses a bone their way. *Cookie*—a nickname she earned as a child because she loved cookies and one she kept when she started her own gourmet bakery, the perfect career for my latest heroine to be engaged in, considering my own fondness for desserts.

Cookie O'Hare. I could see her in her commercial kitchen testing her latest recipe, and I could almost smell the aroma from the rows of pecan-and-raisin hermits cooling on the racks. A little on the plump side (one would *have* to distrust a baker who didn't show evidence of enjoying her own products!) but still very attractive, with laugh lines around her eyes and a mere touch of gray in her red-gold hair despite her fifty-five years.

A successful, self-confident woman who never put up with less than what she deserved. And what she deserved was someone at least as strong and confident and loving as she was.

She was the kind of woman I would want as a friend, the kind of woman I wanted to be. But this wasn't *my* story, I reminded myself, but *hers.* And if I were going to tell the tale of Cookie—who she was, where she found love—and include all the essential details that allowed my readers to connect with her, I would have to do basic background research. And that meant visiting a bakery—one or two or even more—to get a real sense of place.

Ah, the sacrifices we writers make on behalf of our readers, smiling to myself as my taste buds started tingling at the thought of all those baked goods I would have to sample for the sake of accuracy.

I felt a sense of excitement about the character herself, something that had been missing in my last two books. I wanted to get to know Cookie, whom I envisioned as a cross between professional Diana and homespun (albeit gun-toting) Martha. She was not going to be the kind of heroine who sat at home moaning about how lonely she was but a woman who had what she wanted and wanted even more—*and* was willing to take chances to get it.

I opened a new document and started typing, trusting whatever was inspiring me to keep me going.

Cookie O'Hare locked the front door of her bakery and double-checked the lock—an unconscious habit formed after fifteen years of owning her business. She paused for a moment to admire the red-and-white checked color scheme, the letters that were emblazoned across the front windows identifying the business as "Cookie's Heaven," and then strode to her car.

She was tired after a long day in the kitchen, but it was a good kind of tired—the exhaustion that comes from time well spent doing what she loved, of knowing that her energy was expended in the right place. Now she had a day and a half ahead of her to relax since the shop closed early Saturday and didn't reopen until bright and early Monday morning.

She wasn't sure how she wanted to spend her free time. Go to a movie with one of her girlfriends? Pick out some new recipes to try on her customers—always willing test subjects since she gave away samples of new varieties? Or should she check out that dance club at the old roller rink?

Gayle had told her that it was crowded every Saturday night. "Not with teenagers or those young career types but with people our age," she'd said, helping herself to a beignet that Cookie had just finished pulling from the fryer before pouring a fresh cup of coffee. "They play our kind of music—from the Beatles to the Bee Gees—slow dances, fast dances, soft rock and hard rock—even disco! And there are plenty of men there waiting for a partner."

Cookie had filed the information away in her mind, intending to go one Saturday when she felt sufficiently energized to get dressed up. Usually, Saturday night was her downtime when she took a long soak in the tub and then relaxed on her sofa, watching old movies featuring Katharine Hepburn or Claudette Colbert while sipping wine and nibbling on cheese and crackers. She loved the movies from the thirties and forties—the strong heroines who kept it all together during the war, the professional women who successfully managed to keep their careers and their men.

But today, the idea of a movie night didn't appeal to her. She was tired, true, but nothing that a short nap wouldn't cure. She felt a need to shake things up a bit, to do something a little different, a bit outside her comfort zone.

Maybe the dance club was the solution. If she went early enough, she could take advantage of the free lessons they gave.

It had been years since she had been on the dance floor. She could wear her favorite chiffon dress with the flouncy skirt and a pair of heels that, despite their height, were incredibly comfortable, and she'd be good to go.

Dancing—now whatever possessed me to send my character out dancing? That was something I knew *nothing* about. Except for the requisite turns about the floor at weddings, I had avoided that activity my entire adult life, firmly convinced that I had two left feet and a sense of rhythm that bore no resemblance to reality. Which didn't mean that I didn't *want* to dance. Quite the contrary. I would watch those couples on the floor and envy how easily they moved together, including the ones who were several decades older than me.

"Now even my character has a better social life than I do," I muttered but then stopped myself.

That was the wrong attitude to take. I couldn't start resenting Cookie for having more than I did, especially since I was the one inventing her life in the first place. Besides, just because I hadn't danced in the past didn't mean I couldn't do so now. I could even look at it as a form of writerly research.

After all, every successful author knows how integral it is to the process to be able to put oneself in the heroine's place and, as far as possible, to experience what she was experiencing. That was the only way to describe it accurately, to give the scenes a true sense of realism. Not to mention that all that physical activity would be a great way to burn off the calories from my bakery forays.

Yep, if dancing were going to be a key element, I needed to boogie on down to a dance club myself and check it out.

"But where?" I wondered aloud. "I don't even know what people, well, women my age, do for fun, let alone where I could go dancing!"

I could start researching, but that would sidetrack me from the actual creative process. No, I needed to keep writing. Get to know Cookie a little better. Create a rough outline of how her story would progress: how she'd gotten to where she was and where she wanted to go next.

And with that in mind, I started my notes, describing Cookie's physical appearance: a little over five-foot-three and around one hundred and thirty pounds, give or take a muffin or two. Her personality was firm but fair, friendly but practical, warm-hearted but with a business sense that kept her from being taken advantage of by bankers, vendors, and the world at large.

Her past... Now, that was a little tricky. By the time a woman reaches her midfifties, she's bound to have some baggage, some history, some decisions that didn't quite turn out as planned. So, to make Cookie believable, she had to have experienced setbacks in her life that would enable readers to relate to her.

Maybe a failed marriage because her husband wanted a woman who stayed at home instead of running her own business. No children of her own—not by choice but just the way things turned out. Perhaps that's why she pursued a career in baking. Every time she watched the yeast donuts rising or pulled a rack of fresh-baked croissants from the oven, she felt like she'd created something out of nothing—had given birth if only in the culinary sense.

"Well, it will come out as I write it," I reassured myself. That was one thing I knew from experience. While I usually started my books with a rough outline—names, ages, and occupations of my main characters—I didn't construct a detailed history for each at the beginning. If I knew everything that early on, the story would feel stale to me. One of the best parts about writing fiction was getting to know these imaginary people the way you get to know a new acquaintance, one conversation or interaction at a time. I liked being surprised by their words and behaviors, their reactions and decisions.

So, while I had some idea of Cookie's appearance and attitude, I would have to let her story unfold before I could learn all there was to know about her. It would take time—and I *had* time, I told myself. All I owed Wilson-Morrow was an outline and a few chapter drafts. And if I made the outline sufficiently engaging, maybe they would give me back the extra month they had so heartlessly taken away.

It wasn't like I had anything else to do. If I wasn't going to be writing, I would be sitting around the house, mulling over where John was, what he was going to do after his Dallas trip, and whom he would be with if he opted not to be with me.

And why was I leaving all the decision-making up to him anyway? Cookie wouldn't do that. If she wanted a man, she'd go after him. And if he did her wrong, she wouldn't sit around and try to make it work. She would dump him in the trash like a flat soufflé and start over because she would know it wasn't *her* ability that was at fault but rather the "ingredients" he brought to the "kitchen," i.e., their relationship.

I needed more Cookie in my life—and if I wrote the story well enough, I could figure out how to channel her into my own existence.

More Cookie... My stomach growled, and I realized it was way past lunchtime. Although breakfast had been substantial—I really didn't need to eat *that* many slices of toast!—it could only carry me for so long. As much as I wanted to keep working (noting with surprise that this was the first time in a long time that I *wanted* to write instead of eat), I required some sustenance.

"But nothing too starchy, too fattening, too sweet," I ordered myself, grabbing my car keys on my way out of the room. "Otherwise, I'll be too sleepy to work. All I want is a big salad with lots of chopped vegetables and a few slices of chicken. And I'll even pass on the butter and breadsticks."

I pulled out of the parking lot and turned right, heading back to the Bay Diner where I'd had lunch Sunday—only two days ago, but now it seemed longer. At the time, I was still reeling from the knowledge that John had been unfaithful. Not that he had come right out and admitted it, but even someone as blind to reality as *I* could recognize the truth, especially when it hit me over the head, symbolically speaking, via a phone call.

Now, although John—the idea of John, the issue with John, the whole "where is our relationship going after this?" ambiguity—was still in my mind, he had gradually shifted from front and center to somewhere slightly behind my work. Just as well since I didn't have any answers. I hadn't even spoken to him since he left our home Friday morning.

"Although, if I wanted to talk to him—*really* wanted to or had to—I could have managed it," I said aloud. "So maybe I don't want to talk with him after all. Maybe I'd rather *think* about him and our problems instead of do anything about the situation!"

Not an altogether pleasant realization since it didn't reflect well on me and how I would come to grips with our current state of affairs. Instead of being the driver in this car known as my life, I was sitting passively and leaving the driving to John—even if it meant he was taking us right over a cliff.

Chapter 15

I PULLED INTO THE DINER'S PARKING LOT AND, ONCE SEATED BY the window, ordered coffee. While I waited for my much-needed caffeine jolt to arrive, I continued my train of thought. This whole business of not being in charge... Obviously, I had a regrettable tendency to sit on the passenger side in the relationship car and let the men drive it wherever they wanted it to go. And then, when it ran out of gas because they didn't bother to put any into the tank, they left it—and me—by the wayside and found a new vehicle to drive away in.

"Cookie wouldn't do that," I said under my breath, looking at the menu. "She wouldn't let anyone else tell her what to do or arrange her life for her. Not *my* Cookie!"

"I'm sorry, did you say you want a cookie?" The server stood there, pot in one hand and coffee mug in the other.

"No, no, I was just talking to myself," I confessed and looked at her more closely. "Didn't you wait on me a few days ago? You told me about the Whale Inn."

She nodded. "I thought you looked familiar, but I'm so bad with faces that I didn't want to say anything. Did you find it?"

"Yes, and it's great! Thanks for the tip, Sandi," I said, noticing her name tag. "And Martha is such a character!"

Sandi set down the pot and pulled out her pen. "Yes, she really is. And who would have thought she'd still be here running the inn after she got the news?"

I looked at her inquiringly, and she took that as an indication that she should go on.

"Well, when the doctors told her five years ago that, with her kind of cancer, she might only have a year or so to live, we all figured she would pack it in and go somewhere where the weather was nicer, like Florida, instead of putting up with the rain and fog that we get around here. My boss even told her he'd be willing to take over the inn and give her a fair price for it. But she said no way! She told him flat out that she had no intention of giving up any time soon and would show those doctors that they were wrong! And so far, she has. The inn is never closed, even when she has to have her treatments, and she just keeps on going! She sure proved *them* wrong! Now, what can I get you?"

I sat there in shock. Nothing in Martha's behavior had indicated that she had been ill, let alone living on borrowed time. If Sandi was telling the truth, the old woman may have beaten the odds but only temporarily. The game was still being played.

"Ma'am, do you know what you want?" Sandi asked again.

"Yes, yes, I'm sorry. It's that, well, I would never have guessed that Martha had cancer," I said hurriedly, opening up the menu. "I'll take a Cobb salad, please, with light dressing. And no breadsticks," handing her the menu.

"Okay, it'll be right out. And hey, when you go back to the inn, don't let on that I told you. If Martha had wanted you to know, she would have mentioned it. Besides, she doesn't think of herself as sick. She said one time that if she took that on as her—what did she call it?—oh yes, as her identity, that's how everyone would think of her and that's how she would think of herself and before you know it, she'd be gone. She says she's still the same Martha and cancer is just one part of her life, 'like taxes,' she told my boss when she turned down his offer. Something she has to cope with on a regular basis but not *her*. Does that make sense to you?"

It did. Martha was not her illness or her widowhood or any other painful or positive occurrences that had happened in her life. All those events—the good ones, the bad ones, the ones in between—were a part of her existence, but the essential Martha-ness was still in charge, still in control.

I could learn a lot from her if I paid attention, I realized. An older version of Cookie O'Hare, Martha was running her life on her own terms, not on anyone else's. And she wasn't letting anything stop her: not widowhood, not financial concerns, not even disease.

When Sandi brought my meal, I was still thinking about Martha and Cookie and how the future might play out for either of them. Martha had already beaten the doctor's prognosis. Was it the unpredictability of the disease, I wondered, crunching my way through the salad, or her own determination to live and die on her own terms?

As for Cookie, well, I hadn't quite figured out what her challenges had been or what obstacles she'd dealt with in the past. But I knew there had to have been some impediments that enabled her to become as strong and focused and positive as I wanted her to be.

"Would you like dessert?"

I looked up. It was Sandi, order pad and pen in hand.

"We have homemade apple pie and cherry cobbler with fresh-churned ice cream. Then there's the 'Diet Destroyer': a brownie sundae with homemade fudge sauce, real whipped cream, caramelized pecans—"

She would have continued, but I held up my hand. For once, I was going to forgo the opportunity to indulge my sweet tooth with one of those decadent offerings.

"I think I've had enough, thank you. The salad was wonderful, but it absolutely filled me up! Now it's back to work."

She looked at me quizzically, and I explained. "I'm a writer, and I'm working on my new book—my next book. It hadn't been going well and I decided a new place might give me a different perspective. That's why I'm here—well, at the inn, I mean."

"And is it working for you?" she asked, setting down the check.

"Yes, it is. It's given me some new insights on a lot of things."

And that was truer than she knew. Being away from home gave me some much-needed mental and emotional distance from my problems. By the time I went back, I felt confident that I would know what I wanted to do: about my writing, about John, about my life. And I would have learned something about myself in the process.

It was an exciting feeling, and I couldn't wait to return to my room. I wanted to get back to writing about Cookie. I was looking forward to figuring her out and learning from her. And that sense of excitement that's integral to the writing process carried me through most of the afternoon.

I made notes, drafted snippets of events, even created conversations between Cookie and those in her life: her friends, her customers, her ex-lover, and a potential love interest. And the more I wrote, the more excited I became as I saw Cookie's story unfold.

It was nearly six o'clock when I stopped, belatedly aware of the tightness in my shoulders that comes after a long spell at the keyboard. I checked my store of snacks, but I had finished the last candy bar on Monday and now had nothing to eat.

I could beg a sandwich from Martha, I thought, although a part of me was a little worried to see her now that I knew about her illness. After all, this was her private life, and it would be best if I kept that knowledge to myself.

But I was never very good at hiding things as a child and obviously still wasn't since Martha's first words to me when I entered the kitchen were "Who's been telling you about my business?"

"No one," I said, but the minute the words left my mouth, I knew they'd given me away. After all, if I hadn't known anything, I would have asked her what she meant.

She smiled, poured me a cup of coffee without asking and then one for herself. Carrying it over to the table, she sat down and nodded for me to do the same.

"Uh huh. Well, let's see. I saw you leave earlier this afternoon and turn down the road. And I'm guessing you went to the Bay Diner. Was the salad good?"

At my surprised look, she said, "You have a piece of lettuce stuck between your teeth. I know that Sandi does the afternoon shift because that's the schedule that works for her, what with the night classes she's taking. And she's a sweet kid but inclined to be a little too talkative. Oh, she doesn't mean anything by it," holding up her hand as I started to speak, "but she can't help herself. The diner doesn't get many customers this time of year, and she can't resist talking to the ones who stop in. So, she told you, didn't she?"

It was less a question than a statement of fact, and I nodded. Then, given that Martha had opened the door, I walked right through it. "So, how do you do it? How do you find out something like that and keep on going?"

I expected her to immediately launch into a long, convoluted answer. But she took her time, first stirring her coffee and taking a few measured sips before setting the cup down and looking at me.

"You're asking me for the secret of how to handle bad news so it doesn't destroy you or turn you into a sniveling wreck? Well, there *is* no secret. Everybody has to figure it out for themselves. Some people turn to God, some turn to their family or friends, and some just put one foot in front of the other and keep walking and eventually get somewhere. Maybe not where they thought they would and not where they'd originally wanted to go, but somewhere anyway. That's what I did. I just kept walking. I walked when Fred died, and I walked when the doctors told me about the cancer. Oh, I don't mean that I literally walked although I *did* do a lot of that when I got Jake. Dogs that size need to be walked or they get antsy and start chewing things. But I mean I kept walking through my life, moving forward, making plans."

She pointed to a row of eight-foot-tall trees fifteen feet from the rear of the dining room. "See those vine maples? I planted them two weeks after I got the news. They said it would take at least ten years for them to get high enough to keep the afternoon sun off the back deck. Well, in another five years, I plan to sit on that deck and have plenty of shade. Matter of fact, I'm thinking of adding a few more along the north side of the building. And I might *still* be here when *they're* a decent height."

"Walking," I repeated, going back to what she had said. It sounded so simple, so basic.

"Yes, walking. And some days it's more like dancing—like when I try a new recipe and it comes out tasting like a food-contest winner. That's a dancing day! But whether you're dancing or walking or, on bad days, barely crawling, you are still moving ahead. Looking forward, not back. Fixing your attention on what you still want to accomplish instead of what did or didn't work out in the past."

She leaned forward, her blue eyes focused on me to make sure I was paying attention.

"Here's the thing. If you live your life looking backward, then you are bound to trip over yourself. Try it—try walking in a strange place while you're looking over your shoulder. It doesn't work. Even if you don't fall, you sure will be moving a lot slower. And you won't know where you're going. But if you keep your eyes front and center, you can see where you're heading and *what* you're heading to. And isn't that the point: to have a goal in mind to go after, a place where you want to be? And then keep going in that direction?"

She got up from the table. "Now I'm going to fix myself a ham and Swiss cheese sandwich. Want one?"

I nodded absently, still caught up in Martha's deceptively simple advice on life. Look ahead and not back. Have a specific goal in mind. And keep moving, even when you don't feel like it, even when you aren't sure if you're going to reach your destination, even when you aren't entirely sure *what* your destination is. Just keep moving.

I thought about how I had lived my life. I was always second-guessing myself and my choices, blaming myself for screwing up my romantic relationships by not being what the men needed, who *they* wanted me to be.

But in retrospect, it was really my *life* I screwed up. And it wasn't because I failed the men I chose but because I failed myself. I hadn't taken myself into account, hadn't even considered what *I* wanted or what would be good for *me*.

And when they—the Franks and Richards and Pauls—had come into my life, all my energy and attention was on what I had to do to keep them, who I needed to be to satisfy *them* instead of asking myself if they were the right men for me.

What an idiot I'd been! No wonder this relationship wasn't working out. No wonder none of them *ever* worked out!

Chapter 16

MY TRAIN OF THOUGHT WAS DERAILED BY THE APPEARANCE OF Martha and a tray holding two of the biggest double-decker sandwiches I had ever seen. Thick slices of homemade bread, plenty of ham and cheese, and if my nose wasn't mistaken, enough horseradish to give the combination a bit of a kick.

"You looked like you were hungry, so I made it extra big. I can get that way sometimes—just famished, I mean—especially when I've had a good day outside in the yard or inside in the kitchen. Something about accomplishing what you wanted makes you want to celebrate. And for me, celebrating is all about food. And eating," taking a huge bite out of her sandwich with the unselfconscious gusto and enjoyment you usually only see in little kids.

I took a bite as well—a smaller one, only because I didn't want to dislocate my jaw—and chewed with appreciation. The best sandwich I had ever eaten on possibly one of the best days of my life. It looked like I was finally past my dry spell, had blown through the writer's block that kept me from doing what I needed to do and maybe even started figuring out what I wanted out of life—and what choices I had with my relationship with John and my future as a novelist.

The decision was mine. I was in control. It was up to me to keep walking, using Martha's metaphor, and if other people didn't want to keep up with me, the hell with them!

I smiled at Martha. "You're quite a woman," I said in admiration, not sure if I meant her approach to cancer or life in general.

She shook her head and smiled back. "Not really. I've just lived long enough to figure some things out. When I was as young as you," making me feel like a teenager instead of a middle-aged woman, "sometimes I would be so confused! I didn't know what to do with myself. Like after Fred died—at first, I wanted to hole up in a corner somewhere and be left alone."

She paused to have another bite of her sandwich and then went on. "But what good would that do? It wouldn't change things. It wouldn't bring Fred back. So, I told myself I'd better knock it off and get off my duff and decide where to go from where I was. And where I went was right to this spot, this place, and a life I wouldn't have thought I'd be living at my age. Taking care of an inn and meeting a lot of strangers. Learning how to shoot a gun and dance... Oh, that reminds me, I'd better get moving," getting up. "I need to get in some practice time."

"Practice?" I asked in alarm. I had planned on taking a walk along the beach before making an early night of it, but the vision of bullets whizzing past my head made that a less than appealing idea. "You mean, target-shooting?"

"Lord, no," she said, laughing. "I only do that Sunday afternoons at the range up the road. No, my seniors group is putting on a musical at our local rep theater Saturday night, and I still don't have the routine down. It's a few simple steps, but every time I do it, I end up off to the right instead of front and center. Are you done?" picking up the tray and waiting expectantly by the table.

Taking the hint, I polished off the last bite of my sandwich and added my empty plate and cup to the tray.

"Thanks," she said, starting toward the kitchen before turning back again. "I have an idea. If you're not doing anything this Saturday, why don't you come to the show? It'll be lots of fun—unless you think it would be boring to watch a bunch of old people dancing their hearts out to World War II songs."

"I'd love to," I said honestly. The forties had always been my favorite era. There was something about the strength of character and determination that generation displayed that put the rest of us to shame. And the music... well, was there anything better than Benny Goodman's clarinet or Tommy Dorsey's trombone?

"Great! We can ride together. I've got to leave a little early to get into my costume. While I'm doing that, you can help with any of those last-minute things that need doing. We can always use another pair of hands."

She smiled at me and then disappeared into the kitchen where the sounds of clattering dishes and running water indicated she was hard at work. Looking out the window, I realized the evening fog was starting to slip in. If I still wanted my walk, I'd better get moving. And after that sandwich, I needed the exercise.

Once outside, I carefully descended the iron staircase to the beach and made my way to my driftwood seat. Once there, I thought how much had changed in my life in just a few days. The writer's block mountain that had been obstructing my path was starting to shrink, little by little. And while I realized the new concept I was exploring was a risky one since I had no assurance my publisher would accept such a sharp deviation from my previous books, I was excited about the direction my imagination was taking.

As for my personal situation, there was some glimmer of light in that darkness as well. Of course, the possibility existed that John and I could make it over this relationship hurdle, but it was far from a sure thing. I had to admit the likelihood that his dalliance wasn't a one-off but a pattern that I, with my usual blindness when it came to matters of the heart, had failed to recognize.

The other possibility I had to face was that it was over. The love affair I thought would last a lifetime—and to be totally honest was also an effective PR tool—might have run its course. That was a far more likely scenario, and if that was the case, there was a considerable amount of heartache I would have to endure.

"But wouldn't that be better than waiting around for the next phone call?" I said, startling a seagull that had landed a few feet away. "It's not like this isn't going to happen again! For that matter," leaving my seat to stride angrily along the shoreline, "it's not like this was the first time either! All those late nights at the studio, all those long work trips—I should have known John was cheating on me. For God's sake, I'd written those plotlines, put my characters through those very situations! How in hell could I have missed it when it happened to me?"

Disgusted with myself, I dropped onto the sand and looked up at the evening sky as though it might hold some answers for me. I remembered my childhood when my parents and I would sit out on the back deck and watch the stars come out. My father would point to the different constellations and tell me their names, and I would struggle to connect those twinkling lights in a pattern so I could see the same people and animals the ancient astronomers had.

I wasn't very good at connecting the dots in the sky, but at least I was good at connecting the dots in my books. If you stood back and looked at the choices my heroines made, you could form a pretty good picture of the kind of women they were—which explained a lot about the kind of men they were drawn to.

Take Serena in *Love in the Moonlight*. Of course, she was both alone *and* lonely (mandatory for this genre), but she was also a diehard romantic, the kind of woman who imagined her lover coming on a white charger, not in a BMW.

Everything in her life had a fairy-tale aspect, from her predilection for long, flowing dresses to her penchant for aromatherapy and healing crystals. So of course, her romantic interests would be bad men in the classic style: lovers who wooed her with flowers and wine yet had evil in their hearts, men who hid their true nature behind a mask of courtly charm.

And it went without saying that her own true love would rescue her in the required fairy-tale manner: he broke down the door of the room where Evil Guy Number Three (whom she met through an online dating site) was attempting to ravage her. With a few well-placed karate chops, the hero dispatched the villain and saved the princess. Dots connected, picture completed, and they lived happily ever after.

With each book, I peppered the story with events and characteristics that illustrated the nature of my heroines. I detailed their needs, their wants, their desires, the tendencies and self-delusions that put them in jeopardy time and again—my heroines *had* to be slow learners, otherwise the novels would have ended up as short stories!—along with the totally inappropriate guys whom they mistakenly fell for and, ultimately, the absolutely right men who won my heroines' hearts and saved them from lives of loneliness and despair.

Yep, I was good at creating my own literary constellations but not so good at identifying the dots that made up the Fran configuration. I still couldn't see the big picture even though I could name each individual star: Richard, Frank, Paul, and John.

"I need better glasses," I said. "Or a telescope. Something, anyway, that would give me a clearer view."

Maybe that was what this time away was supposed to do for me: allow me to take a good look at things, put them in perspective, figure out how all the pieces went together, how all the dots were linked. And, unlike the real constellations, if I didn't like the picture it made, the "Fran" that they formed, I could do something about it. Shake it up like a kaleidoscope to see what the new one would look like. If I liked it better, if it made a better "Fran"—one who knew what she wanted, where she wanted to go, and what she needed to do to get there—then I would stick with it and use it to guide me somewhere better than where I was.

"But where I need to be right now is back in my room," shivering in the damp night air. It was time for bed, to let sleep knit up my "raveled sleeve of care" as Shakespeare put it. I brushed the sand off my behind as I contemplated my plans for the following few days.

Cookie... Yes, I would work on the story about Cookie and her life, what challenges she would face and how she would get through them. I was intrigued by her and, for the first time in a long time, felt like I was on the right track with my writing.

"Of course, there's always the chance that Wilson-Morrow won't like it," I said as I unlocked the door to my room. "After all, it's not at all like the last three. And if they don't, then what?"

I knew what: if Wilson-Morrow rejected this book, the terms of the contract would have been met, and I would be in the unenviable position of being an author with a book but no publisher. And possibly no agent since Izzie, already unhappy with me, might conclude I was no longer a marketable commodity.

Or, I thought as I showered then pulled on my pajamas, I could somehow write the book they wanted—*Love in the Ruins*—and do it so well that its sales would exceed that of *Love in Unexpected Places*.

"Not that it would be all that hard to do," my words echoing in the room as I thought back to the last few royalty statements for my previous book. "And if I could pull that off, maybe they would be willing to let me do Cookie's story next. That way I could make *everybody* happy: Wilson-Morrow *and* Isabella."

Everybody but *me*. I didn't say it out loud, yet the words reverberated in my mind. I had to make a decision. And not just about my literary career but also about my life. Even if the relationship with John was over, if I wasn't careful, there was a good chance I could find myself in the same mess again, writing the same story for myself with the same sad outcome.

"I'm too old for this!" staring at my face in the mirror. This wasn't where I wanted to be at the more than half-century age mark. After the first book, it looked like I was well on my way to my own "happily ever after": a popular author with a handsome man at her side. But now, more than five years later, I was back at Chapter One. Older but not wiser. And as I crawled into bed, I was overwhelmed with feelings of frustration, pain, and fear.

Instead of having "a whale of a good time" like the Inn's motto had promised, I ended up having a whale of a good cry before falling into an exhausted sleep.

Chapter 17

ODDLY ENOUGH, I FELT ENERGIZED WHEN I AWOKE AT TEN THE next morning, and even the realization that I had slept past breakfast and, more critically, my morning infusion of caffeine didn't bother me. I checked outside my door, hoping Martha had left me a pot of coffee, but no such luck.

And when I buzzed the front desk on the intercom, there was no answer. No matter, I decided. I'd make a few more notes and then go out for an early lunch.

I turned on the computer, a little afraid of what I might find. Would I read the notes and realize they were no good? Was the whole story idea about Cookie O'Hare just a distraction, a detour that was taking me away from what I was supposed to be writing? And if it *was* good, what then? I still had to decide what I would do about satisfying my contract.

"Not now," I said as I opened the file. "Right now, I need to concentrate on Cookie."

I reviewed the notes I had made on my protagonist, then began working on the synopsis that would be enough to buy me some time with my publisher. Once that was finished, I went back to what I had drafted the day before, "pantsing" my way through as I added several hundred more words. I wanted to get enough down to build the writing momentum even if I revised it all later.

Then I could switch into plotting mode, highlighting the events and conflicts that Cookie would have to take care of and the characters who would be part of her life. A few friends, an antagonist—another bake shop that sold factory-made goods?—and a love interest.

"Or more than one," I said, looking out the window but in my mind's eye seeing two middle-aged men: one in a banker's suit and a second in casual chinos. "Instead of Cookie having to fight another woman for her man, I'll have two men fight for *her*. That would be a switch!"

I analyzed several possible plot developments. Cookie explores the idea of expanding her business and opening a café, and the meeting with the bank regarding financing will lead to a nonbusiness luncheon to celebrate the loan. As for Love Interest Number Two, he could be the contractor she hires to renovate the storefront adjacent to her bake shop. And that would lead to late dinners reviewing his plans, which could lead to early breakfasts...

Writing about meals, accompanied by the rumblings of my stomach, interrupted my creative flow and reminded me that I hadn't had anything to eat since the night before. Hours ago, and now it was after one. Time for a break.

I'd clean myself up and drive to the Bay Diner for lunch, taking my laptop with me in case inspiration struck. And while I was feeling confident, call Izzie and read her what I had so far to get her feedback—not so much on the draft's literary merit but more about its marketability and whether Wilson-Morrow was likely to go for it.

An hour later, as I crunched my way through a pecan-and-salmon salad, I read over my morning's work. Even in its rough-draft format, I thought it had potential. Even more important, I *liked* it: the concept, the conflicts, the character herself. I could live with her during the long months it would take to finish the first version and then revise and polish the manuscript until it was ready for publication.

What I'd do if my publisher's feelings didn't match my own I didn't know, and right now, I didn't care. All that mattered was how I felt about this book, I reminded myself, since I was the one who had to write it.

But first, I had to call Izzie.

"Well, it's about time I heard from you!"

Not the most encouraging way to start the conversation. Izzie was clearly not happy with me and wasn't making any attempt to hide it. Considering how our last call had gone, I wasn't surprised. It was going to take every bit of skill I had to get this chat moving in the right direction.

"Yes, I know, and I would have called sooner, but I was so busy writing that the past few days just flew by," I said, wondering if she had heard what happened at my last book signing. If so, that might explain her less than friendly tone. "But I've made a lot of progress and wanted to run the concept by you to get your feedback. You know how much I value your judgment."

Silence from the other end of the phone, and I wondered if I had laid it on a bit thick. Well, too late now. "If you have a minute, I'd like to read you what I have."

"Go ahead." Her tone was curt, but she was apparently willing to listen.

I took that as a good sign and started. "This one's a little different from the last three. It's still a romance, but the main character is more in control of her life from the outset," barely stopping myself from saying that she wasn't a wimp like the previous ones.

"I don't have a title yet"—I heard a tiny sigh of exasperation and hurried on—"but I do have a working draft of the synopsis and the opening to the story."

Without waiting for a response, I launched into what I had written earlier that day. But even to my ears, it sounded rough, and the plotline wasn't as clear and compelling as I had hoped. Still, there was no point in stopping now.

"If you want, I can read part of the first chapter," I offered since Izzie was still silent. I took her lack of reply as an affirmative response and started reading, but when I reached a thousand words and there was *still* no feedback of any kind, I stopped.

"Izzie?" I said tentatively, hoping the signal had dropped and that was why she wasn't saying anything. Then I heard it again—louder this time—the sigh that meant this was going over like the proverbial lead balloon.

"What *exactly* are you writing?"

On its face, the question sounded innocuous, but I knew her well enough to understand that I was on shaky ground. When Izzie loved my work, she was excited, with her words tripping over each other. But when she wasn't happy with the work or with me, her tone was deceptively calm and her words measured.

I was in trouble. I knew that. And staring at the laptop screen, I wondered what on earth had possessed me to expose the book so early in the process. *The book...* It wasn't even a book yet, just an idea, a notion, a concept, and a bad one at that.

Not waiting for my answer, which was a good thing since I didn't have one, she continued, "And have you forgotten the PR plans they have for this book? A five-night stay at the same location where the hero and heroine meet? Where is *that* supposed to happen? In a *kitchen?*"

This was bad, very bad. Isabella had moved from cold calmness to angry sarcasm. I couldn't remember the last time that had happened, which told me how terrible things really were.

"Well, I didn't get to that yet, but Cookie is going to go to Paris," I said, making it up on the fly. "She wants to study with a famous French pastry chef, and that's where she'll meet him."

"But you opened with her being happy with her life and career," she said. "There is very little indication that she is lonely and in need of love—not like your other characters. And certainly not what Wilson-Morrow is waiting for!"

She was right. I knew that. Wasn't that what I had worried about even while I was writing this morning? It was all well and good to get excited about a character and a story idea, but not when a deadline was staring me in the face and the expectations were for something quite different. But I wasn't ready to give up without a fight.

"Well, here's what I was thinking. You know the last book didn't sell as well as we had hoped..."

"Yes, I know that," came the tart rejoinder, but I plowed on anyway.

"So, this time, even though it would still be a romance, I might tweak the character a bit. You know, make her a little more self-assured, confident. Somebody the readers would want as a friend."

Someone *I* would want as a friend, I thought, but kept going. "As for the romance, have *her* be the object of desire instead of him. Have *her* be the one they want—I was thinking there would be more than one man in her life—and she has to choose. And they are both great guys, but in different ways. And she also has a dream for her business and..."

I finally stopped because by then I was out of ideas and more than a little afraid that I would have to write *Love in the Ruins* after all if I wanted to keep Isabella as my agent and Wilson-Morrow as my publisher.

I drank my now-cold coffee and signaled for the server to refill the cup while I waited for Izzie to say something. Anything. Preferably that she liked the idea. Or that this was an example of what she had meant when she said my reading public wanted something new. Or that Wilson-Morrow would love the new approach I was taking for my romance novels.

And while I waited—and waited and waited—I remembered this was how I used to feel when I pitched new ideas to my copywriting clients, hoping they wouldn't come back with "Well, it's not exactly what we wanted" without telling me specifically where I'd gone wrong.

Izzie finally spoke. "Anything else?"

"Well, I don't know exactly. I'm working on it," afraid to say any more than that.

"No title, just a story concept that isn't at all like the ones you've written in the past and certainly not what your publisher is waiting for. And *has* been waiting for," she added, "since you are behind schedule." And I knew from her tone that she was more than a little displeased with me.

"And in the meantime, *I've* been getting calls from Alix and Vanessa and almost everybody else at Wilson-Morrow. And not just about the new book either. Vanessa called this morning to tell me what happened at your last signing. She said the store was very unhappy with how you presented the entire romance genre as 'fantasy escapist literature' and that if readers think of those novels as how they might live *their* lives, they are 'bound to be disappointed.' That's what you said, right? That's what *you* told a roomful of your fans. In other words, you said they were wasting their money buying your books!"

"Well, I don't know that I said 'wasting,'" I replied, grabbing onto the sole part of her diatribe that I could truthfully deny since I hadn't actually voiced it, only thought it.

"Don't split hairs. You made your feelings on the subject quite clear—clear enough that you barely sold any books that day and certainly clear enough that the store isn't all that interested in hosting you again. You know it, I know it, and what's worse, Wilson-Morrow knows it. And if this next book—the book they are *expecting* and that you are contractually obligated to write—isn't a success, you can kiss your future with them goodbye."

She didn't add "and with me," but I knew she was thinking it. Agents can't afford to carry deadwood, and that's what I was afraid I had become, at least in her eyes. This was a business and I, along with my books, was a product. If no one wanted to buy me, then it was time for her to move on to a different product, i.e., another author who *would* generate sales.

I heard Izzie take a deep breath, and then, when she spoke, her tone was softer, calmer. But I wasn't reassured.

"Now, I'm not saying that at some later date you can't try out this new idea, but this isn't the right time. You know what they want, and you know you have to deliver it. On time. According to the contract. With no further delays," each phrase gaining in emphasis as Izzie hammered home her point. "Fran, don't you have something, *anything*, I can pitch to them? If it sounds good, I might be able to buy you a little more time."

I stared at the laptop screen, but instead of the synopsis, I saw Cookie O'Hare as I had envisioned her, her image growing dimmer until it vanished altogether. Sighing, I moved the cursor over to the trashcan icon, opened it, highlighted *Love in the Ruins*, and then clicked "restore."

There it was, the story that Isabella and the powers-that-be at Wilson-Morrow wanted. The story that would at least satisfy my contractual obligations even if it didn't satisfy my reading public. The story that I *had* to do whether I wanted to or not.

But why? came that aggravating inner voice. *What's the worst that can happen if you don't write that one?*

I'll be breaking my contract, have to return the advance, and be broke and homeless, I answered it.

And then, the words dragged reluctantly from my mouth, "Well, I did have another idea. I called it *Love in the Ruins*. A woman artist goes on a dig to sketch Mayan ruins and finds love."

"*That's* what I'm talking about!" she said with more enthusiasm than that one-liner deserved. "That's something we can sell! And I know you can write it. And since it takes place in—what country are the ruins in?"

"Mexico," I sighed, and she went on.

"And since it takes place in Mexico, it's reasonable to anticipate that you'll need a little more time to research or even go there. So, if you can at least give me the synopsis by the end of this week and a chapter or two by the end of this month like they want, I might be able to talk them into pushing the manuscript delivery date back a bit. I know you can do it, Fran. What do you say?"

I nodded, then realized she couldn't see me. "Yeah sure. I can do it," wondering if I could, especially since I didn't want to. Really, *really* didn't want to. Well, this was my job, and like any other job, you had to take the bad with the good, even when the good was in woefully short supply.

"Excellent! Get back to work and email me a decent synopsis by Friday morning so I can send it over to them. Okay?"

"Okay." And the call, like my dream of writing about Cookie, was over.

Chapter 18

I MOTIONED TO THE SERVER TO BRING THE CHECK, HANDED OVER enough cash to cover the bill and a tip, and went out to my car. As I backtracked toward the inn, I realized this was a representation of my current career path. Two steps forward (a successful novelist) and one step back (my books aren't selling, and I don't want to write the next one). Then two giant steps forward with the idea about Cookie and a different kind of romance novel, followed by a big slide back when I agreed to write a fourth book like its predecessors.

The only good thing about *this* problem, I thought when I got back to my room, was that it helped take my mind off the one with John. And wasn't that the whole point of this trip—to focus on work and not my relationship?

I opened the *Love in the Ruins* file, read through what I had, and took a deep breath. All I had to do was edit the synopsis and send it to Izzie by Friday. And then start working on the book so I could have ten thousand words or so drafted by the end of the month. Two chapters. That's all I needed to write. I could do it. After all, I'd done it before.

But by the time dusk had fallen, I was no farther ahead than when I started. The character of Cassandra just wouldn't come alive. She was stuck. Or more accurately, *I* was stuck. Against my better judgment, I opened the Cookie file, read the opening, and started writing one line and then the next until, by nine thirty, I had a solid draft of the first chapter.

I stared at the screen. Great. I'm making progress, but it's not on the right book. And I only had two days left *if* I waited until late Friday instead of Friday morning to send the synopsis of the book that Isabella wanted and Wilson-Morrow expected.

"I could try writing them both at the same time," staring out the window where the stars were dotting the night sky. "One day with hopeless, helpless Cassandra and one day with Cookie. Exciting, in-control Cookie. Or," my mind racing, "I could have the two of them meet. Cassandra goes into Cookie's bakery and orders some treats before she leaves. And they start talking. Or the team hires Cookie to come along and supply baked goods for everyone on the dig! Or—" But then I stopped myself.

Unlike Cookie's desserts, these ideas were half-baked at best. I would have to choose between Cookie and Cassandra. And more broadly, between my future with Wilson-Morrow and my future as an author with no publisher and no assurance that the book I wanted to write would have a reading audience.

Decisions, decisions. I was tired of being faced with them, tired of having to deal with them, tired of watching things turn out differently from the way I wanted.

So, what do *you want?* that irritating voice asked.

That was the million-dollar question, and I didn't have a million-dollar answer.

Frustrated with myself and tired of hearing that little voice in my head, I pushed back my chair and got up. Maybe a walk would help. I pulled on my sweater and went outside where the moon provided enough light so I could see my way, if not mentally, at least physically.

What had Diana said? That I was expecting the unreasonable? She meant John and how our relationship had turned out, but I might be expecting the unreasonable in terms of my career, too. After all, I only had three books to my credit so far. Possibly, I hadn't yet hit my stride. And if I made a major change in the type of characters and storyline I created, that could destroy whatever momentum I had.

"Maybe working on *Love in the Ruins* isn't such a bad idea," I said, not really believing my own words. "Izzie is right. After all, she's the expert. She knows what's selling. Why rock the boat?"

Why indeed? The fact that I didn't want to write the same type of story again was, in the greater scheme of things, hardly relevant. I had a contract. If I wanted to continue living the life I had, I needed to fulfill it. And with that realization my heart sank. The truth was, there was nothing I *liked* about my life: not my work and certainly not my relationship. But the prospect of taking a leap into the unknown and starting all over again, especially at my age, was hardly appealing.

"I'm too old to make such a drastic change." But then the words of that woman at my last book event came back to me: how she'd stayed in a bad situation a lot longer than she should have and that now she is happier than she's ever been. And Martha, who started over again after her husband died to make a new life for herself. What did those women know that I didn't? What did they have inside of them that I lacked? How were they able to face the changes that came into their lives and, instead of whining about them or taking the path of least resistance, take control?

"Darned if I know," I said, with one final look at the ocean before heading back toward the inn. But the closer I came to my room, the less I wanted to return to it. Once inside, I'd have to make up my mind about what I was going to do—which path I was going to take—and I was no closer to knowing that than I was when I came outside.

I was getting nowhere fast and, tired of listening to myself, decided to go find Martha. Even though it was close to ten, she might be in the kitchen, and I could get a cup of coffee and some good advice that she was always more than ready to give.

Taking the long way, I went around to the front entrance, but the door was locked and the "Closed" sign was hanging in the window. I backtracked, let myself in through the walkway that linked the rooms with the main building, and went into the dining room. But it too was dark, the only light visible coming from the kitchen. That's where I found Martha, covered up to her elbows in flour.

"What are you doing here?" she asked, pausing her rhythmic kneading of the mound of dough on the board. "Aren't you busy writing?"

There it was, just the slightest reproof. Obviously, I wasn't living up to her expectations or the image she had of successful novelists—one, no doubt, courtesy of Rosabella Robinson's PR machine.

"Um, I was, but it was time to take a break. I was a little stiff"— *You mean stuck*, whispered that little voice I had come to hate, but I chose to ignore it—"so I went outside for a walk in the fresh air. And," I looked around the kitchen hopefully, "get a cup of coffee, too."

"Coffee? At this hour?" From the tone of her voice, you'd think I had asked for an illegal substance instead of a hit of caffeine. "No, that will keep you up and you won't be fit to work tomorrow. You *did* say you were on deadline, right? Give me a minute to get this dough ready and then we'll both have some of my elderberry wine. A glass or two and you'll sleep like a baby and wake up refreshed and ready to work!"

"Sounds great. And maybe I can bounce some ideas off you. You can be my beta reader, so to speak, someone who provides input during the creative process. What do you think?"

She turned the dough into a bowl and covered it with a clean cloth before sliding it into the refrigerator.

"There," she said. "It will be ready to bake tomorrow morning." Then turning to me, "Beta reader, you say? Well, I've never been one, but I'll be happy to give you my opinion on your idea."

She reached into the cabinet for two wineglasses and brought them and the wine into the dining room.

"Take a seat," gesturing to the chair across from her, "and tell me about the story you're working on."

I picked up the glass she had filled and took a sip, debating which one of the ideas I should describe. Or should I tell her the real story, how my love affair and career were both on the ropes: how John wanted a relationship on his terms and if I didn't agree, then he'd leave, and how if I didn't write the book my publisher wanted, my future with W-M would be over?

And would either outcome be such a bad thing after all? came that voice again.

I set my glass down firmly. No. I'd tell her about *Love in the Ruins* and get her feedback. No point in dragging my relationship or Cookie into the conversation, especially when I hadn't made up my mind what to do about either.

That was my plan, but when I opened my mouth, the words that came out had nothing to do with the story about lovelorn Cassandra or even Cookie.

"Before I talk about the book, I wanted to... well, you see, I'm having this problem..." and there I stopped, still not sure how much I should say.

Martha reached across the table and patted my hand. "Look, I know we don't know each other all that well and you probably think I'm just a talkative old lady, but whatever you tell me stays between us. *I* keep confidences—unlike some *other* people we know," and she gave me a look that told me she was thinking of Sandi at the Bay Diner who had told me about her illness.

"I know. It's just that..." and I paused again.

"I have an idea," and something in the way Martha said it made me smile. "You're a writer. What you do is tell stories about your characters. So why don't you tell me whatever it is you want to but do it as though it isn't about *you* but a character you made up. A character named Rosabella," and by the wicked grin she gave me I could tell she knew how I felt about my competition.

"Okay," and I took a deep breath. "Rosabella has been involved with this guy named John for six years, and at first, it all seemed great and exciting. But then she found out he'd been seeing someone else, possibly even more than one person, and when she confronted him, he said he didn't want to talk about it. And then he left. And she didn't know what to do." I stopped and polished off my wine.

"Okay. Then what happened?" asked Martha as she refilled my glass.

"Well, as she saw it, she had two choices: either forgive him and forget what happened or put an end to the relationship. After all, it wasn't entirely his fault. Rosabella is partly to blame for getting into the relationship for the wrong reasons."

"And they were..." prompted Martha when I stopped for another sip.

"Well, she thought it would be like the books she was writing—which, by the way, weren't selling all that well. At least not the last one. It's like I lost my interest or belief in the stories I was creating," forgetting that this was supposed to be about the mythical Rosabella and not me.

"The truth is, I don't even *want* to write that kind of story with that kind of character anymore. I want to write a *different* kind of book. But if I do that, if I follow my heart and write about this new type of woman, I'll be taking a real risk. But why *can't* I do what I want to do?" I finished, and as the words hung in the air, I smiled ruefully. "I sound like a teenager, don't I? But I'm *not* a teenager. I'm a grown woman. The fact is that I have a contract, and like it or not, I have to fulfill it by sending the publisher what they want."

"Or?" she asked, her eyebrow raised. "You know, if I've learned one thing in all my years, it's that there is *always* another option."

"Okay. Or I send them the synopsis for the new book with a character called Cookie instead. But if I do that, they will probably reject it, and that will leave me without a publisher. And my agent might decide she doesn't want to represent me anymore. And any fan base I've built will disappear, and I'll be one of those authors who showed promise initially but then faded away."

Martha was silent. If I expected her to give me a solution to any or all of my problems, it looked like I was going to be sorely disappointed. I drained my glass and pushed it over to her, and still not speaking, she filled it halfway and sent it back to my side of the table.

"Well?" my question coming out almost aggressively as though Martha held the key to the solution and was refusing to hand it over, which was ridiculous. These were my problems to solve.

"Well, what? You've laid out the situation with your career. It comes down to Plan A or Plan B. You have to choose which plan you want to follow."

That was *it*? I bared my soul, shared my fears, and all she could come up with was that I needed to make a *choice*? I knew that already! What I wanted was someone to tell me *which* choice was the right one.

"Now, as far as your personal life..." and here she paused.

I took hope. Even if she had nothing to offer as far as my literary problems were concerned, maybe she could help me with my relationship situation.

But instead of continuing, she took the last swallow of her wine and refilled her glass.

"Yes? As far as my personal life *what*?" and I heard the irritation in my voice.

"I don't see why you are having such a hard time making up your mind. After all, from what you've told me, it's not like you've been happy with him—or at least, not for some time. Or did I miss something? Not that relationships don't have their ups and downs. Lord knows mine did!" and she smiled a bit. "But they need to be based on a solid, strong foundation of support and trust that can only exist between two people who truly love each other. If that's what you have, then it's possible you and John can work this out. If not..." and she didn't finish her sentence but let it hang in the air.

"If not, then *what*?"

"If not, then it *won't* work out and the two of you will go your separate ways and life will go on."

Those were hardly the comforting words I wanted to hear. I wanted her to give me some magic potion to make it all right again, some words of wisdom about how to approach the topic of John's infidelity with him in a way that wouldn't widen the crack that already existed in our relationship.

But I should have known better. If there was one thing that was apparent, given her comments about my previous books, Martha wasn't the kind of person who sugarcoated things. I finished my wine and started to get up, but she put out her hand.

"Now, don't get all huffy," she said, echoing words my mother used to tell me when she didn't give me the response I preferred. "I'm telling you what *I* think. It's up to you to decide how you want to handle it. But let's go back to the book. Tell me more about this Cookie. She sounds like an interesting person."

What did I have to lose? Even if I wasn't going to write this book, or at least not *now*, I could talk about it. It was a more interesting topic than *Love in the Ruins* and the story of hopeless, helpless Cassandra. So, for the next hour I told her everything I knew about Cookie so far: her life, her goals, her plans for the future, plotlines I'd come up with and ones I was kicking around, even the dancing idea I'd planned on integrating into it.

"Not that *I* can dance, but I can go watch others do it and describe it," I added, and Martha nodded.

"And don't forget Saturday's show," she added. "While you're watching us, you can take some notes. The son of one of our members is going to video it, too, so if you want a copy, I can get it for you. Then you'd have something to refer to when you go back home."

"That would be great!" I said enthusiastically and, as the words left my mouth, realized their implication. The only reason I would need that video would be if I were planning to work on the Cookie story. Had I inadvertently made up my mind?

Martha got up, came around to my side of the table and patted me on the shoulder. "Well, I don't know about you, but I'm ready to call it a night. Shut off the lights when you leave, okay?" and she headed out of the room, leaving me alone with an empty wineglass and a mind full of decisions to make.

Write a book about Cookie or about Cassandra? Stay with John or leave? Two major crossroads and I wasn't sure I was any closer to knowing which way to go than when the conversation with Martha had started.

Or maybe I was, I thought when I was back in my room looking at the laptop. I *wanted* to write Cookie's story. That much was clear. So, what I *could* do was write the synopsis of the story Isabella said she wanted by Friday and then revise the one about Cookie and tell her to offer *that* one to Wilson-Morrow first.

If they rejected it, she could still pitch *Love in the Ruins*. The worst that could happen is that I'd have to write that book after all. But just thinking about it made my heart sink.

"Well, the time to worry about that is once I'm home."

Home. Home where John wasn't and might never be again.

Chapter 19

I WENT TO BED THAT NIGHT THINKING I HAD A WORKABLE, IF NOT exactly desirable, plan but woke up in one of my rare "the hell with it" moods. The last time I had been in this frame of mind was when I started writing my first novel, but at that point, I had nothing to lose since there were no expectations. I had no publisher breathing down my neck, no literary agent telling me not only what I *should* do but *had* to do, and no fan base (shrinking though it might be) expecting another in the same vein as my past three books.

This time, however, I was endangering my career and my financial stability at a time of life when I should be more cautious. I had already taken a big risk. Like so many other middle-aged people, I had engaged in a rebirth of sorts when I threw myself into becoming an author. *That* was supposed to be my new life, my new identity, my future.

Instead, I found myself thinking once again of starting over. But how many rebirths must a person go through before she can stay born and move forward?

No answer then and still no answer after one of Martha's filling breakfasts. I polished off the homemade waffles topped with fresh raspberries, drank enough coffee to power me through a full day of writing and then some, and went back to my room. I was fed up with having questions, with being in a situation where I felt powerless, with being more like my Cassandra character than the Cookie persona I wanted to be.

"And whose fault is that?" shutting the door with more force than necessary. "Nobody *made* me do anything. These were all *my* choices. And if I don't like how my life has turned out so far, then it's up to me to change it—do what I want to do and write what I want to write. And if Izzie and Wilson-Morrow don't like it, well, too bad!"

And that's what I did, first writing more notes for the synopsis for my novel about Cookie then doing some editorial tweaks to the opening chapter I had previously drafted before moving on to Chapter Two. The more I wrote, the clearer the persona of Cookie became and the more ideas for plotlines and secondary characters occurred to me. I was on a roll, and it wasn't until my cell phone rang that I realized I'd been writing for six hours straight.

I stood up and stretched and then reached for my phone where the caller ID displayed a number I knew as well as my own. It was John. Of *course,* it was John. The one time I *didn't* want to hear from him, didn't want anything to destroy my sense of confidence, didn't want to have to think about anything other than the book I was writing.

I was tempted to let his call go to voice mail, but old habits are hard to break, and hope was hard to reject. Instead, I tapped the answer button.

"Where *are* you?" he asked. Not quite the greeting I desired. "I stopped at the house, but you weren't here. And the newspapers were piled up in front of the door!"

He came back was what my heart heard. But that spark of hope fizzled with his next words.

"I flew back to meet a client in town, so I came here to sleep before returning to Dallas tomorrow morning. I needed to get a few more things anyway."

Not *I missed you and came back.* Not *I wanted to tell you I'm sorry.* Not even *I thought we should talk.*

I stayed silent, not sure what to say or even what I *wanted* to say.

"Fran?" and I caught the note of hesitation in his voice. "Look, I know you're upset"—not *I know I hurt you,* I noted—"but not talking to me isn't going to help the situation."

Not cheating on me would, but I resisted the urge to say those words to him. Instead, I answered his first question. "I went up the coast to work on my new book and, well, to get away," without specifying what exactly I was getting away from.

"Okay," and there was relief in his voice. "By the way, Vanessa called me. She wants me to set up some new publicity shots and asked if I knew where your book was set so the pictures would match the location. Apparently, you hadn't told her or Alix either. She sounded really irritated—went on about deadlines and chapters they were waiting for. What's going on, Fran?"

"Did you tell them—about us, I mean?"

He sighed. It was that long-suffering exhalation I knew so well. "Of *course* not. This is business, Fran. There's no reason to drag our personal situation into it to complicate things."

And I bet it would, I thought. The PR department at Wilson-Morrow wouldn't be happy that our relationship was on the rocks. Not because they cared about how I felt, but because it would require a whole new angle to replace the one describing "Fran Carter, the successful romance novelist who found true love at middle age."

And since he was the one who had caused the problem, it could have an unfortunate effect on his professional association with them. John's business, like mine, was full of competitors: younger photographers with innovative ideas that clients would love. His relationship with Wilson-Morrow had opened doors to other high-profile contracts. Losing that one could well have a domino effect.

"Anyway," he went on, correctly assuming that I wasn't going to comment, "I wanted to see what you had in mind as far as the book's setting."

I still didn't answer.

"Okay, I get it. You're mad at me. Fine," and the note of exasperation came across clear as a bell. "But I need an answer, Fran."

So do I, I thought, but I won't get it from you. I must find it myself.

"Look, I'm busy now, John. I'll call you later," and I ended the connection.

Now what? I wondered as I stared out the window. The call with John had disturbed that fragile sense of being the one in control, both in terms of my book and my relationship.

I heard a little voice whispering, *Maybe he called because he missed you. Maybe you shouldn't have been so cold. Maybe you ought to call him back.*

"And maybe you ought to shut the hell up!" I said to the empty room. I glanced over at the laptop where the last paragraph was displayed on the screen, the cursor blinking at me like a caution light. The trouble was, I didn't know what it was warning me about. The danger of thinking the relationship might work if I could overlook John's behavior? The hazard of pitching this story instead of the one that Wilson-Morrow wanted? The risk of making the wrong choice in either circumstance? Although *what* the wrong choice would be, I still wasn't certain.

I was edgy and irritated and no longer in the right frame of mind to work on Cookie. I'd go for a drive and, while I was out, pick up some take-out, hoping that by the time I returned, my mind would be clearer and I would know what to do.

But after burning through a quarter tank of gas traveling south on the Pacific Coast Highway, my mind was still as foggy as the early morning horizon before the sun burned away the mist. I turned around, intending to go back to my room, but then my stomach reminded me that I was supposed to get some food. Pizza? Hamburger? A fish taco or two?

"There's bound to be something to eat at Coastside Bay," I said aloud, and passed the Inn entrance to continue north until I reached the exit.

I drove down the main street, debating my choices, when I saw the sign outside the local library: "Romance Readers Book Club Meeting—6 to 8 PM." And then the idea came to me—one I would probably regret but certainly better than going back to my room where I would be faced with questions for which I had no answers.

I'd go to the library and sit close enough to eavesdrop on the meeting and find out what the members thought of my competitors, all in the name of market research. And who knows, I might pick up some valuable information that would help me with my next book—whichever one I ended up writing.

It was a good plan and might have worked if the group sat near a section where I could browse unnoticed. Unfortunately, that wasn't the case. The meeting was in a separate room that was already half-filled with people by the time I arrived, leaving me with two choices: give up the plan or go into the meeting and pretend to be a reader, not a writer, of that genre.

"Damn it," I muttered under my breath but not quietly enough since one of the women gave me a sharp look. I flushed, mumbled "Sorry," and moved to a place near the back, hoping no one would recognize me.

Not that I looked like the author photo on my book covers: the woman with professionally done makeup and hair, wearing a sexy outfit that cost more than I usually spent on a week's worth of groceries. Right now, my hair was pulled back in a scrunchy, my face was devoid of blush or eye shadow, and as for my clothing, no one would mistake my flannel shirt and leggings for anything remotely sexy.

A woman whom I assumed was the leader of the group moved to the front of the gathering and clapped her hands for attention.

"Welcome, ladies and newcomers," she said. "For those of you who don't know me, I'm Debra Adams, the organizer of Romance Readers Book Club. Are we all ready for tonight's discussion?"

Taking everyone's agreement for granted, she continued. "Last month, the topic was the recent best seller by Rosabella Robinson. I think it's safe to say we all really enjoyed that one, right?"

The positive murmurs from the group indicated her assumption was correct. "This evening, for a change of pace, we're going to discuss Fran Carter's latest book, *Love in Unexpected Places*."

I started. Good God, did I hear her right? Was that book going to haunt me all week long? And what did she mean by "a change of pace"?

"How many of you finished the book?"

I took heart that most of those present raised their hands. Maybe this wouldn't be so bad after all.

But then came the next question: "How many of you liked the book?"

In response, approximately half of the hands went down and with them, my heart. This was a nightmare scenario. I would have to sit here and listen to all their negative opinions about a book that I couldn't rewrite anyway.

"Well, this is going to be a lively session since we are more or less evenly split," Debra said, and I swear she licked her lips like a wolf moving in for the kill, which was ridiculous because no one knew who I was.

But that didn't stop me from feeling vulnerable, and I braced myself for what was to come, grateful that it would only last for two hours.

And it was the longest two hours of my life since I was forced to hear how the plotline was unrealistic, the conflict was contrived, and the entire premise was formulaic. Or as one woman put it, "It was as though she was writing the book like it was a paint-by-number exercise. There was no depth, no unexpected twists, no reality," shaking her head before delivering the coup de grâce. "It was certainly a far cry from Rosabella's latest book, *Never Give Up on Love.*"

The other women nodded, but then one of them spoke up. "Well, that's true, but I did like her descriptions of the different locales."

It wasn't much to hold onto, but I took it like a drowning man grabs a rope. At least I did *something* right, I thought gloomily. But aside from a few other marginally positive comments, it looked like the meeting would end with me feeling even worse than when I came in.

Figuring I had nothing to lose, I raised my hand.

"I don't read much in the way of romances," I began when Debra nodded to me. "This was my first one, so I don't have much of a view on whether it's good or bad," mentally crossing my fingers at that lie. "So, how exactly could the author have made the book better? It really seemed like a typical romance novel to me."

"That's exactly the problem with it," said a young woman two rows in front of me. She turned in her seat to address me directly, and something in the look in her eyes made me wonder if she knew who I was. But if so, she kept it to herself and continued with what she had to say. "It's not that we don't want to read about falling in love, and I have to admit, the setting is interesting. It's that, well, in this day and age, the whole 'helpless heroine' thing is a little passé, don't you think?"

She gave me another look before turning back in time for Debra to say, "Well, we're done for the evening, so thank you all for coming. Be sure to read Alexandra Graystone's *If We Meet Again* and be ready to discuss it next month!"

I slipped out of my chair and made a beeline for the door, not wanting to hang around any longer. While the criticisms of my book were well deserved, that didn't stop my author ego from smarting under their judgment. I had almost made it when I felt a tap on my shoulder.

"You're Fran Carter."

I weighed my options. Ignore her? Or admit to my identity? Taking the latter choice, I answered, "Guilty as charged," with a slight smile as I turned around. It was the same woman who had made the last comment about my book. Even if I didn't recognize her voice, there was no way I could have forgotten her hair: short and spiky with shades of blue running through it.

"I was sure that was you!" And then, as the other members started to crowd around us, she took my arm and led me over to a corner outside the room. "Why are you here?"

I didn't want to answer with the truth, so I murmured something about "market research for my next book," hoping that would satisfy her.

"Mmm." Something in her tone told me she wasn't buying it. "I'm Shauna Adams. And I want to apologize for what I said. Well, not really for *what* I said because it was my opinion, after all, but for not saying it as tactfully as I could have. After all, I'm no writer, and I suppose you have a reason for creating those kinds of female characters in your books. They must be what your fans want."

Not really if my sales figures are any indication, I wanted to say, but I held my tongue. This wasn't the time or place for that kind of honesty.

"Anyway, if you're not in a hurry, may I buy you a cup of coffee? The Moon Bake Shop is next door, and their coffee is to die for. Plus, they have terrific desserts, including my personal downfall, Moonlight Cheesecake."

I should say no, I thought. I should get in my car, go back to my room, and sort out the decisions that awaited me. But it was just after eight, and besides, the idea of coffee and cheesecake was more than I could resist. Which was how I found myself sitting across from Shauna, indulging in a larger-than-necessary piece of Moonlight Cheesecake while already planning my exit strategy.

I could blame it on my work, I thought as I washed down the rich silken mouthfuls with coffee. I could explain that I was deep in my creative mode and only came out because I needed to get some dinner. I could tell her that the muse waits for no one, and sitting in on the book club meeting sparked a secondary plotline that I had to get down before I lost it.

But before I could open my mouth, she asked me a question I'd been asked a thousand times before: "What's it like to be a writer?"

Usually, I'd respond with some facile answer like, "It's a wonderful life and every day I wake up excited to get back to my computer and discover what my characters are up to!"

But something in the way she asked it told me she deserved better than a superficial reply.

"Sometimes it's really great, but other times it's hard and frustrating and disappointing. I spend a lot of time writing sections that I later delete and more time than I would like working on the business side of being an author: drafting social media posts and sending out my book for reviews and calling to set up book events and pitching myself to the media and podcast hosts and...well, stuff."

I glanced at her and noted the look of disappointment on her face. One more fan I'd let down, attacking the remaining bit of my cheesecake with more attention than necessary. I had just swallowed it when she hit me with another one.

"Then why do you do it? It doesn't sound like you enjoy it very much. I always thought being an author would be wonderful. Creating characters and stories out of thin air and watching the plots develop and seeing how it all turns out. And the research part—isn't that fun? Isn't *any* of it fun?"

Somehow, I knew she wasn't asking because she wanted to know how *I* felt about writing. There was something more to it, and it was imperative to think very carefully about what my next words should be.

"Yes, there *are* times when it's fun and exciting," I told her, remembering how I felt when I was working on *Love in the Moonlight*. "And it still is, especially when an idea comes out of nowhere that I know has potential. Or when I'm intrigued by the characters and want to spend more time with them. I'm probably explaining it badly," I ended lamely, but she nodded.

"No, I understand. That's how I feel! Oh, not about writing. I'm not a writer," she added. "I'm an artist. Not a real one, I mean. I've never had a show or won any awards or sold any of my paintings. It's something I do for me though sometimes I wonder..."

She stopped for a moment and then continued. "My day job is at Sun and Moon Salon. I'm a colorist"—I barely restrained myself from reaching up to touch my own gray strands—"and I like doing it, too, especially when I get the chance to give someone a whole new look. But painting—well, that's what makes me feel whole. Happy. Fulfilled, I guess. Know what I mean?"

And I did. Even back in my copywriting days, there were moments when all the words came together and I was as thrilled with what resulted as a mother is with her newborn. When *was* the last time I'd felt that way? *When you were writing about Cookie*, came that little voice, and I shook my head to make it stop.

"Excuse me, ladies, but we're getting ready to close, so if there's nothing else?" It was the server, politely letting us know that it was time for us to leave.

"Oh gosh, it's almost nine and I still need to go to the grocery store!" Hurriedly, Shauna stood up and slung her purse over her shoulder. "I really enjoyed talking with you. Thanks so much! And here," she dug in her pocket and pulled out a business card. "If you're interested, why don't you stop by the salon. I'd be happy to do your hair for you—not that you don't look great right now"—a tactful lie if ever I heard one—"but give you a different color. Or style. Or cut," finishing with a reassuring smile, "You'd be surprised at how it can change things!"

The last thing I needed were any more surprises, but I took the card and dropped it in my purse.

"Thanks, Shauna. I'll keep it in mind. And good luck with your artwork, too. You never know what might happen," wondering if I was making a mistake encouraging her.

But it must have been what she wanted to hear because she beamed like I'd given her a gift.

"Thanks again," and before I knew it, she was out the door, leaving me with my list of still unresolved issues.

Chapter 20

I WAS SO ABSORBED IN THINKING ABOUT MY CONVERSATION WITH Shauna that I hardly remembered the trip back to the Whale Inn. I felt *like a ball in a pinball machine* bouncing from side to side but never scoring any points.

"And what points am I trying to score?" unlocking the door to my room. But there was no one waiting inside to answer me.

Was my life to be an endless sequence of writing one book, then another and another, regardless of how I felt about them? While I wasn't naive enough to think that being an author would be one ego-inflating book signing after another interspersed with pleasurable hours spent creating new stories with nary a writer's block in sight, I didn't think that, after only a few books, I should be sick to death of the characters, the storylines, and the theme—in short, the whole damn thing.

A famous author had once been asked in an interview if, after producing almost fifty books, she still enjoyed writing. Her answer was that of *course* she did, and if she didn't, she wouldn't keep doing it.

But I hadn't even written *five* novels, and already I was bored! Was it the books I was tired of? Or was it being a writer? Or simply my life in general?

Uncomfortable questions and ones I was no closer to answering the next morning than I had been the night before. And an answer was sorely needed since it was Friday and I had promised Izzie a synopsis by this very morning. Even after half a pot of coffee and a super-sized fluffy ham-and-cheese omelet topped with fresh chives, courtesy of Martha's culinary talents, I was still struggling with my decision.

"So how is the writing going?" Martha asked, as she stood before me, coffeepot in hand, ready to top off my cup. "I noticed you were gone until late last night," the slight note of rebuke in her voice intended to remind me that I was supposed to be writing, not gallivanting around the countryside.

"I was doing some market research. There was a meeting of the Romance Readers Book Club at the library, and I thought it would be worth attending. You know, to see what readers wanted."

"And?" She took a seat, evidently wanting to hear what I had learned.

I gave her the short version of the comments, not wanting to relive the memory of the trashing of my book that I had received, then switched the subject to my meeting with Shauna.

"I know Shauna," said Martha, who seemed to know everybody within a hundred-mile radius of the inn. "She's the best hair colorist around. You ought to make an appointment with her. It wouldn't hurt, and you'd look great for tomorrow night! You do remember our plans for the show, right?"

I nodded though I had, in fact, forgotten all about it. My mind was caught up with worries about getting the synopsis done to meet Izzie's deadline and, to a greater extent, the decision I had to make about which synopsis I was going to deliver to her, which would ultimately make its way to W-M.

If I submitted the one Izzie asked for, my fate, at least for the next six months, was sealed. If I sent the one about Cookie, I risked ending any future with Wilson-Morrow and probably with Izzie as well. Then what would happen? I certainly couldn't afford to live off my royalties. And John didn't bring in enough to pay for both the house and his studio—assuming that he was even part of the future I was stressing over.

"Fran? The show?"

Martha was still waiting for an answer, but she'd have to take her turn. There were other, more vital decisions I had to make.

I pushed back my chair. "I have to go now. Thanks for the breakfast," and practically ran out of the room. I couldn't take it anymore: the fear, the uncertainty, the frustration—not only with my professional life but with my private life as well.

"I need to make a decision—*any* decision!" my voice drowned by the sound of the waves as I descended the steps that led to the beach. While I knew I ought to be back in my room, pounding away at the keyboard, I just couldn't. Besides, why be so close to the ocean if I spent all my time holed up inside, especially when, in two more days, I'd be back home?

And at that thought, my heart sank. It wasn't only that I didn't want to be away from the sight and sound of the waves. It was that I didn't want to return to the life I'd been living and the problems that were part of it. My unhappiness with my work. My heartbreak over my relationship with John. My worry that, at a time in my life when I had hoped everything would be neatly laid out, the path ahead was nothing but a series of road bumps, one after another, leaving me bruised and shaken.

"I'm an idiot," I said, and a sea tern, picking at the sand nearby, looked up at me before going back to his business. "I had this idealized view of life and love, and now that it's all gone to hell, I can't accept the reality."

The situation would be amusing if it weren't so painful: a writer who expected life to be like the stories she was writing, who thought that when the heroine and hero met and kissed, everything would be rosy even after "The End" was neatly typed.

But that's not how it goes. Life isn't a nice straight line but a series of twists and turns, uphill slogs and downhill slides, with good and bad surprises waiting around each bend. The challenge is to make the right decision at each juncture and if it doesn't turn out like you'd hoped, make another one.

And that's what I'll do, I told myself with determination. I took one final glance at the ocean, waved farewell to the bird, and resolutely returned to my room. There, I spent the balance of the day revising the synopsis for my novel, as yet untitled, about a middle-aged baker whose life is calm and whose career is moving along smoothly—until she decides to shake things up a bit.

In Cookie's case, her desire for something different would lead her down unforeseen paths. What those paths were I had yet to find out, but I knew they would involve conflicts and setbacks, challenges and disappointments that would affect both her personal and professional lives.

"There, it's done," I said with satisfaction after I read through my final draft. While I knew I'd violated the cardinal rule of synopsis writing by not including the ending, I didn't really care. The odds were great that both Isabella and Wilson-Morrow (assuming she even sent it to them) would reject it out of hand since it wasn't what I was supposed to be working on. But at least it was something. I had met the terms of my contract, and the rest was out of my control.

I opened my email program, wrote a short note to Izzie, attached the document labeled "Love in the Light of Day—working title," hit "Send" and powered down my laptop. I felt freer than I had in days, an unseen weight lifted off my shoulders.

"Now what?" I asked, looking around the room. It was nearly dinnertime, but for the first time since I arrived, my mind wasn't focused on food. I caught sight of myself in the bureau mirror, pulled Shauna's card out of my bag, and called the salon.

"Hi, Shauna, it's me, Fran Carter. I know it's last minute, but I was wondering if you might have an opening sometime tomorrow."

"Of course!" she responded. "Cut and color, right?"

And though my initial plan had been for a modest trim, I found myself agreeing.

"Can you come at twelve? I have two clients before that, but then I'll be done," adding, "The salon is just two blocks past the library."

"Perfect. I'll see you tomorrow," and then, after ending the call, I shut off my phone. I was in a good frame of mind and didn't want anything to destroy it: not an angry call from Isabella asking me what the hell I was doing sending her that synopsis, and not a call from John, because no matter what he said, I knew I didn't want to hear it.

I stayed with my plan the rest of the night, opting to spend most of the early evening hours on the beach watching the stars pinprick the night sky. I was well and truly unplugged: from the internet, the cell service, and in a metaphorical way, my life. Every time worries threatened to overwhelm my mind, I blew them away like a night breeze sending clouds scudding into the distance, leaving behind a reassuring vista devoid of any fears. Of the two major problems facing me, I had reached a decision on one, and that was enough for now. The other could wait.

And that mindset was still with me when I awoke late the next morning. Although I had missed yet another gourmet breakfast, Martha had thoughtfully left a tray outside my door with an insulated carafe of coffee along with a few slices of cinnamon bread, which I polished off in short order while I gazed out the window to the ocean beyond.

I filled my cup with what was left in the carafe then reached for the napkin to wipe my mouth. But when I picked it up, a small slip of paper fell out of the folds. It was from Martha, reminding me that tonight was the senior musical. "Be ready at five thirty," she had underlined with three firm strokes.

I contemplated begging off but realized I wanted to go. Not only because of the music—I loved those old wartime melodies—but also because I enjoyed being with Martha and felt I owed her something for the wisdom she had brought into my life.

"Besides, it'll be fun to hang around people who are at least a generation older than me," I said aloud as I rummaged through my small stack of clothing hoping to find something suitable for my night on the town. However, since this stay was intended to be a work trip, not a vacation, I had nothing to fit the event.

I had to do Martha proud, I knew, so there was nothing for it but to go shopping. If I didn't run into too much traffic on my way to Coastside Bay, I'd be able to get it done before my appointment with Shauna. And for a change, luck was with me. I found a small dress shop located conveniently across the street from the salon, and once inside, I started trying on every conceivable combination of skirt, blouse, sweater, and slacks (all in slimming shades of black, of course) that I could find.

"May I help you?" the saleswoman finally asked, undoubtedly noticing my increasing air of desperation. "Is there something specific you're looking for?"

"Actually, yes," I said in relief, putting my body, figuratively speaking, into her capable hands. "I'm going to a show tonight—a performance at your local repertory theater—and I don't want to be too dressed up but dressed up enough since it's a special event."

"Oh, *you're* the woman author staying at Martha's," she said, beaming. "I'm Carol. Welcome to Maxwell's! And you are—wait, don't tell me," as she paused for thought. "I know, you're Fran Carter!" triumphantly, as though she were providing me with the information I needed to complete my day.

"Yes, but how—" I started but she forestalled me.

"Well, Martha was in on Tuesday looking for a pair of shoes for the show and mentioned she had a visitor—kind of unusual since it's still pretty early in the season, and she told me who you were. She said you were working on a new book, and I was hoping you'd come back and do a signing when it comes out. What's the title anyway?"

To my relief, she didn't wait for an answer but rattled on. "I'm so glad I got the chance to meet you because I am such a big fan of romance novels! And writing, too. I'm going to write a book myself. Oh, not your kind of book, but one that is all about the experiences I've gone through and all my problems and how I got through them and everything. You know the kind of book I mean. What do they call it?" and she looked at me questioningly.

"A memoir?" I suggested, which was enough to get her verbal ball rolling again.

"Yes, that's it! Anyway, once I have the time, I'm going to write my memoir! But here I am, talking shop when I ought to be helping you find something for tonight. Come over here," leading me to a row of dresses. "I think one of these would be perfect!"

I looked at them without a lot of optimism, but at least I was grateful that their existence had finally slowed down the overwhelming river of information that had threatened to drown me. But whatever faults Carol had in the conversation department, she more than made up for with her unerring gift for finding two options to satisfy my less than perfect proportions.

She held up her first choice: a sleeveless dress in a shade of sapphire blue with a V-neck that would really show off "my girls," as she put it.

"This will look wonderful on you! The empire waist is so flattering, and the cotton fabric will be perfect for our cool evenings!"

She handed it over to me and reached for another in deep crimson. The bodice cut was flattering and as for the color—"You know," Carol said as she pushed me toward the dressing room, "every woman needs a red dress!"

Holding my breath and sucking in my stomach, I slipped the blue dress over my head and shoulders. I smoothed it down across my mid-section where, wonder of wonders, it didn't get stuck, before I left the cubicle to face the three-way mirror at the end of the dressing area.

"You look wonderful!" Carol said, adjusting the back a bit and then stepping away to get a better look. "What do you think? Is this what you had in mind?"

I twirled a little, feeling the cotton swirl around my thighs. I fantasized how I would look whipping around the floor to the fast paces of the jitterbug or gliding gracefully to a romantic waltz.

I didn't look bad. Really, taking a second glance, I looked surprisingly sharp. Carol was right. The color was great, the fit was divine, and the overall impression was of a woman who looked great and knew she did.

"That's a keeper," Carol declared. "Now try on the red one. *That's* a color that makes a woman feel powerful, in charge. And everyone *else* can feel it, too. That makes it an indispensable wardrobe addition!" she finished.

Obediently, I went back behind the curtain to remove the first dress, hanging it carefully on the padded hanger before putting on the power red one. I wasn't expecting luck to strike again, but it did. The red dress exuded a heady blend of sophistication and success. No one seeing me wearing this could ever imagine that I was plagued with personal or professional self-doubt.

It was a "Look out, world, here I come!" dress and gave me the image I wanted: a famous author who had her work *and* her life under control.

Well, almost the image anyway as I left the cubicle to stand in front of the mirror. While the red dress was exactly the type *that* kind of woman would wear, the hairstyle was the cut and color of a woman who had given up and didn't think she had the right or courage or strength to make a change for the better.

"A woman in a rut, that's what I've become. And I don't like it, not one bit!"

"But it looks wonderful," Carol protested as she came back into the changing area. "You look fabulous in that dress! Why don't you like it?"

"No, it's not the dress," I explained. "You were right. It's the perfect power dress. I was talking about me—the way I look. My hair, I mean. I haven't changed the style in years! And this dress deserves something better than that. I hope Shauna at Sun and Moon Salon can pull off a miracle," my optimism dropping the longer I looked at myself.

"Oh, she will. Not that you don't look perfectly nice right now," Carol added diplomatically. "But maybe a new hairstyle is what you need. And I know Shauna. She'll give you the right color to do justice to the dress *and* to you. Besides, you have all those public appearances: interviews and book signings and all that. You *have* to look great! After all, you're a famous author!"

Well, I might not be quite as famous as Carol thought, but she was right about one thing: I needed a new outer Fran to go with the inner one that was developing. And I still had time, glancing at my watch. Once I bought a new pair of shoes to go with the dress, I'd be ready to unveil the new Fran.

"I'll take them," I said. "Both of them—the blue *and* the red. Could you keep them here until I'm finished at the salon?"

"Absolutely," she said, smiling at me like a mother who'd just witnessed her tomboy daughter turn into a beautiful teen.

"You're a miracle worker," taking one last look at my reflection. "Anybody who could find two perfect dresses that make me feel and look this good is nothing short of a magician—or a fairy godmother!"

"Oh, don't be silly! I'm just doing my job," Carol answered, but I could tell by the way she blushed that my compliment touched her.

"Well, you're darned good at it!" I said as I went back into the cubicle to change. I handed her both dresses and followed her to the register where she totaled my purchases.

"That's $358.95. Will that be cash or charge?"

"Charge, please," wondering how long it had been since I'd spent that much money on clothes. Too long, I concluded. It was time I treated myself.

"Now, you go get your hair done, and I'll see you back here all beautiful and ready for tonight," she said, carefully slipping a dress bag over my purchases. Obediently, I left the shop, filled with newfound optimism and determination.

Chapter 21

MY POSITIVITY WAS REINFORCED WHEN, ON MY WAY TO THE SALON, I spied a shoe store with the perfect pair of high-heeled sandals in the window. I couldn't resist, and in a few minutes I was slipping my feet into a pair of black linen espadrilles. The peep toe would showcase my upcoming pedicure while the jute-wrapped wedge would add three inches to my five-foot-two frame.

This is why we women wear heels despite whatever discomfort they may cause, I thought as I looked at my posture in the mirror. It wasn't only the way they shifted your center of gravity and elongated your legs; it was the height they added, making even a short woman like me feel statuesque. Height equals confidence, and confidence equals a sense of power. As I strode across the floor, I felt like I could walk up one side of Mount Everest and down the other without breaking a sweat—or an ankle.

"I'll take them," I told the saleswoman without even asking the price. "And toss in that matching clutch, too!"

In less than ten minutes, I had paid for the shoes and purse along with a sterling silver bracelet and earrings from the counter display. Then I headed to Sun and Moon where Shauna could work her magic and turn my ho-hum appearance into one that radiated self-assurance and maybe even sexiness.

I was ready for a change, to look different, to *be* different. I was tired of the old Fran, the Fran who settled for whatever was given her, the Fran who agreed to things she *didn't* want because she was afraid to ask for more or demand what she really wanted.

I had taken the first step when I sent the synopsis to Izzie—not the one she wanted to receive but the one I wanted to send. The two dresses—the red one, in particular—represented another step. They made me feel different—not just better looking physically, but stronger psychologically. The old saying "the clothes make the man" certainly applied in this case, except instead it was "the dress that makes the woman."

Now, I was ready and willing to take more drastic measures. I'd let Shauna have her way with my hair. No more same-old, same-old my usual hairdresser would give me: a bit of a trim, a touch-up of the gray roots, and the predictable blow-dry, leaving me looking only marginally better than the way I had when I came in.

No, this time I wanted to look like the kind of woman I now wanted to write about: a mix of Cookie and Diana and Martha, a woman who knew what she wanted and where she was headed and refused to let any obstacles or setbacks or disappointments stop her.

And I maintained that mindset until I pushed open the salon door and was greeted by a receptionist who looked barely out of high school and whose pixie cut was a mix of purple and peach stripes—colors that Mother Nature had never intended for hair. I looked around and saw more of the same: stylists and clientele whose median age was probably twenty-three and hair coloring straight from a box of sixty-four crayons.

"Welcome to Sun and Moon!" she said, smiling. "Do you have an appointment?"

"Um, yes." I hesitated, wondering if it was too late to escape. The dress and shoes were enough for right now. I didn't need to go the whole route. But my thoughts were interrupted by a squeal behind me.

"You're here!" and Shauna gave me a hug. "I was so afraid you'd change your mind! Hey, April, here's Fran Carter!"

As her voice carried across the salon, I saw heads turn in our direction while another stylist set down her scissors and left her station to come over to where I was standing.

"I heard all about you, and we are *so* excited to have you here!" pushing her spring-green strands back from her face. "We never had a celebrity before, did we, Shauna?"

"Not that I can think of. Not unless you count Jackson, but he's just our mayor," Shauna said, summarily dispensing with the town's top official. "Now, what did you have in mind?" running her fingers through her spiky, blue-streaked coiffure until her hair stood straight up.

"Well, I usually have the split ends trimmed and the gray touched up," I said hesitantly. After seeing their hairstyles, I was more than a little worried to let these two do anything more than give me the basics.

There was silence for a moment, and then April took my hand and led me over to her chair, Shauna following behind.

"Well, we *could* do that," she said, and in the mirror I saw her look over at Shauna as she noticeably chose her words with care. "But I don't know if your hairdo does the most for you. It sorta hangs there and doesn't do you justice. And you have such great eyes and a terrific smile! But the hairstyle doesn't emphasize any of your best features."

I looked in the mirror and reached up to touch my shoulder-length hair. Granted, I hadn't styled it before coming out on my shopping trip, but even on the days when I attacked it with a blow dryer and curling iron, it didn't look all that different. Maybe a little wavier, a little less droopy, but basically the same.

"So, what would you suggest?" I asked, feeling like a virgin on her wedding night taking one hesitant step toward the marriage bed.

"Sit down and I'll show you." And in short order, I found myself with a cape draped around my shoulders. "Let's start with a good hair-cut," April said firmly, holding up at least six inches of my hair, "to get rid of a lot of this length and add some shape to it."

"And add some color instead of just highlights," Shauna said. "Real color, a beautiful rich auburn to warm your skin and really catch people's attention." Then, turning to her partner in crime, "I think she'd make a wonderful redhead, don't you, April?" who responded with an oblig-ing nod.

A cut—a real cut, not one of those "an inch off the bottom" trims I generally asked for. And color—red? Me? I almost got out of the chair then and there. But a vision of the red dress came into my mind, and I pictured how I would look with my new cut and red hair and thought, Oh, what the hell. It was only hair. It would grow out if I didn't like it.

And if I did like it, if it looked as great as these two stylists thought it would, it might be just what I needed to complete the rebirth of the new Fran.

"Go for it," I said, closing my eyes and keeping them firmly shut while April's scissors and razor made their way through my hair. It seemed to take forever, but it probably wasn't longer than twenty minutes before she proclaimed that her part of the renovation process was finished.

My initial sense was that my head felt lighter and cooler without the weight of hair I was used to. I looked in the mirror and touched the considerably shorter strands.

"I wanted to give you the 'Tilda Swinton' look," April explained, running her fingers over my scalp, making my hair spike in ways that I never thought it could.

While I knew that I looked nothing like that actress (and what I wouldn't give for her shape and cheekbones!), I was flattered by the idea that April thought I could pull it off. And I had to admit it did look pretty good. Even more significantly, I *felt* pretty good—darned good. Unlike Samson, who lost his strength when he lost his locks, I felt powerful, strong, absolutely overloaded with confidence and determination.

This wasn't the haircut of a woman who didn't know what she was doing or where she was going. This was a style for a woman who was in charge of her life—her career *and* her heart.

I closed my eyes and opened them to look at myself again while April stood by anxiously.

"I love it," I said, emphasizing every word. "It's exactly what I needed!"

"Great!" and she let go of the breath she'd been holding while waiting for my reaction. "I knew it was perfect for you, but I wasn't sure..." and her words trailed off.

"Honey, you *were* sure and that's why you did it," I said, smiling at her in the mirror. "You knew what I wanted even when I didn't. You went with your instincts and the result is nothing short of absolute perfection!"

"Well, that's true as far as the cut goes, but the color, well..." said Shauna, pulling over her tray laden with bowls of hair dye. "You have great skin, but this dishwater shade does nothing to show it off. But if we change it, warm it up, it will make all the difference. I'm telling you, by the time I'm done, you are going to be a fabulous redhead and everyone's eyes will follow you when you enter a room!"

Any doubts I had about such a dramatic color change had been put to rest after that haircut. I was ready to finalize this whole Fran renovation, and if auburn tones were what it would take, so be it.

"I am in your hands, and I mean that both literally and figuratively," I said as I closed my eyes and surrendered.

Two hours later, the cape was off my shoulders and the stylists proclaimed me ready for the world. I looked at myself in the mirror, not quite certain who that woman was but loving her appearance. The dishwater blonde hair interspersed with gray was gone, and in its place were deep tones of auburn and cinnamon, giving a warmth to my skin even in its current minimal makeup state.

And the cut... It was the perfect complement for a woman whose self-esteem was registering full on the confidence meter. I raked my fingers this way and that through the strands. Yes, this would work, I decided, knowing my propensity for using my hair as a stress reliever when I wrote. It was a style that could take messing up. This was a style that *couldn't* be messed up. Regardless of what I did to it or what the elements threw at it—wind, rain, fog, humidity—it would come through looking great. It was perfect for the woman I wanted to be, a woman who could weather the storms of life and still come through looking like a magazine model.

"Well?" said Shauna while April hung over her shoulder, once again holding her breath.

"Breathe," I ordered with a grin, and got out of the chair to hug them both. "I absolutely love it and can't thank you two enough for this transformation! I can't believe it's me," turning again to face the mirror. "I would never have guessed that a cut and color could make such a difference!"

"Now, all you need is some makeup. Not that you don't look beautiful already," April added hastily, "but with that new hair color, you have to change your makeup shades, too. Right, Shauna?" who nodded in agreement.

"Sure, why the hell not?" I said recklessly. "And a manicure and pedicure, too," remembering the remnants of polish that adorned my toenails.

"No problem," said Shauna. "While I was waiting for your color to take, I talked to Donna, and she can take you right away. She's a nail technician and a trained makeup artist. She'll be doing the makeup for the show tonight. She'll get you done, and you can get back to Martha's in time for the performance."

I looked at her in surprise and she answered my unspoken question. "Carol brought your dresses over from the shop on her break. She said you were going to the show and wanted something to wear. I'll be there, too. My grandma's in the show, and I promised I'd come do any last-minute hair fixes for anyone who needs it. Now, come over here where Donna is waiting," and she took me across the salon to a private area where Donna, the last of the little salon elves, was waiting to put the finishing touches on the new Fran.

"Hi, Ms. Carter. I'm Donna and I'm so glad to meet you!" holding out her beringed hand with five perfectly polished nails. "And I love your new cut and color! Now I'll give you your mani-pedi and, while the polish is drying, coordinate your makeup to your new look."

She gestured for me to take the seat on the other side of her table, and then, without even asking, removed my running shoes and socks and placed my feet in a small tub of warm soapy water.

"Now, while your feet soak, I'll do your manicure, and after that, your pedicure. How does that sound?"

How did it sound? It sounded wonderful. It had been a long time since I'd engaged in such self-indulgent activities. I nodded in assent, relaxed in my chair, and let Donna go at it. And in a little less than an hour, the calluses on my heels were sloughed away, my hangnails trimmed, my cuticles well-oiled, and my ten fingers and ten toes French-manicured to perfection.

"I love it," I sighed, stretching out my hands in front of me and flexing my feet to get a better look at my toes.

"Now let's do your makeup," she said, helping me duck-waddle to her makeup chair, my feet encased in disposable sandals with each toe separated by a wad of cotton. "Before I get started, let's see what we have here, okay?" and she proceeded to remove what little makeup I was wearing, leaving my skin exposed in all its middle-aged glory—or lack thereof.

She turned my face this way and that, gently ran her fingers over my cheekbones, and tilted my head up a bit.

"Hmm..." she murmured. "What would be best for you?"

I waited for the words "wrinkle reducer" and "age spot concealer" that would start eating away at my newfound self-esteem. But Donna was good—*really* good, like cosmetic-copywriter good. She used phrases like "enhance your natural beauty," "brighten your blue eyes even more," and "accentuate your cheekbones" instead of "disguise the signs of aging," "combat the droopy eyelid tendency," or "counter your dull, sallow skin tone." She made me feel beautiful even before she started.

And after she flicked the makeup brush across my skin one final time and handed me the mirror to view the results, I had to admit that I did look beautiful. Oh, not Elizabeth Taylor beautiful but beautiful for me. The smoky shadow gave my eyes depth, the artful application of highlighter and blush brought out my cheekbones, and as for my lips... well, in Donna's words, the glossy red lipstick made them "lips waiting to be kissed!"

"What do you think?" she asked.

"I think it's time I junked all that stuff I've been using and use all this instead," I said, waving at the tubes, bottles, and pencils scattered across her counter. "And throw in some of that 'anti-aging' skin cream, too, please!" not even flinching at the term. My skin *was* aging, so why not accept it and do what I could to make it look as good as possible?

She grinned and started ringing up the items one by one and added in the cost of my cut-and-color. And as I handed her my credit card, I didn't even bat a mascaraed eye when the bill totaled nearly three hundred dollars. The way I saw it, this was an investment in my self-esteem as well as my professional appearance. If I felt better, I would write better, and if I wrote better, I would make more money to pay for those things that make me feel better, I reasoned.

It was a nice, neat circle of cause-and-effect and one that I would use every time I felt guilty when styling my hair with these expensive products and doing my face with these top-of-the-line cosmetics.

"Wow, you look marvelous!" exclaimed Shauna, who had come over to view the results.

"I do, don't I?" turning my head to take another look at my hairstyle and then down at my polished toes. From top to bottom, I looked and felt like a new woman. "It all looks fabulous, absolutely perfect!"

And I *felt* fabulous and absolutely perfect. Stunning, successful, sexy even. Walking out of the salon with my dresses in one hand and the bags with my shoes, jewelry, cosmetics, and hair products in the other, I didn't feel like a fraud, like some ugly duckling who had temporarily assumed the guise of a graceful swan, but like a newer, better Fran—or maybe the Fran who had been waiting to be revealed all along.

Chapter 22

BACK AT THE INN, I SNUCK MY PURCHASES INTO MY ROOM, WANT-ing to surprise Martha with the new me. I had less than ten minutes to get ready, but since my hair and makeup were already done, all that was required was to change into my dress and shoes before meeting her in the dining room.

After I slipped on my new jewelry, I surveyed the overall results in the mirror. This was a Fran I had never seen before, one that I didn't know even existed inside me. And I didn't feel like a fraud, didn't feel like I was playing dress-up or that, without warning, the old Fran would suddenly appear and show everyone that it was all PR fakery. No, I felt like this *was* the real me, the me who had been there all along and all I'd had to do was find her.

It wasn't just the hair and clothes and makeup. Granted, all those externals changed my appearance, but I knew the metamorphosis went deeper than that. *I* had changed. I wasn't the same insecure, self-doubting Fran who had arrived at the B&B seven days earlier. This was a new Fran, a better Fran, a Fran who felt that she was on the way to somewhere she had never been before. And even if that destination was still a bit vague, I knew it was an improvement over where I was currently, both profession-ally and personally.

"I want to *be* this new Fran, and by God, I'll do it!" and I gave myself a thumbs-up before heading out the door.

Martha caught sight of me as soon as I walked into the dining room, and her reaction was all I could have hoped for. She beamed, she applauded, she did everything but sound a trumpet and cast rose petals before my feet.

"You look wonderful!" she said, giving me a hug and then anxiously smoothing my dress and touching my hair in case she had done damage to either. "And your hair—I can't believe you cut your hair! But it looks great! You look like a woman ready to take on life!"

She smiled at me, and I smiled back though I wondered how ready I really was. For all the soul-searching I had done the past few days, for all the brilliant realizations that had flooded my mind, I still hadn't reached a decision about John. Oh, I knew I didn't want the relationship we had, and it was incredibly painful to realize that the man I loved (or *thought* I loved since everything was now open to review) had been having an affair—or possibly more than one.

But relationships get past that. Relationships can be fixed, mended, repaired—*if* both parties want that to happen. *If* they know what they want. Which brought up the fundamental question: What *did* I want?

"Fran?" and I realized Martha was looking at me with concern. "Is something wrong?"

"No, nothing," and I smiled again, this time putting more effort into it. What had Martha told me about handling bad times? That the key was to keep moving forward? Well, that's what I had to do—once I figured out what was the right direction for me to move in.

But that was for another time. This was Martha's night and a chance for me to show her how much I appreciated everything she had done for me—even though I doubted she knew what all it was.

"Are you ready?" and I reached out to take the bag that held her dancing shoes. "I'll drive so you can relax and tell me about the people who will be there," not that she needed any coaxing to talk.

And talk she did during the entire fifteen-minute drive to the small playhouse on the other side of town.

"I'm hoping everything is ready to go," she said, frowning a bit. "Charley was supposed to set out the chairs, but his arthritis has been acting up, so they might still be parked along the wall instead of ready for our audience."

She looked over at me, and I responded on cue. "No problem. I can help with that and anything else you need."

"I knew you would," she said, patting my arm. "And once you're done, you can find yourself a seat and relax. You won't have to do another thing until after the show."

"And then?" looking at her suspiciously.

"Oh, didn't I tell you?" she said breezily though she knew full well she hadn't. "I arranged for Barnaby's to bring some of your books over from their stock. I didn't think you'd mind doing a little book signing when the show was over. So many of the women in our senior group love your books, and when I let them know you were staying with me—" there it was, the Coast grapevine in action—"they all wanted to know if you would sign some copies. Some of the women are also bringing books they had already bought since I told them you'd be willing to autograph those, too. After all, they did pay for them. It's just that you weren't there to sign them when they did. And it's all for a good cause. Barnaby's is donating a portion of the sales to our local food bank."

She gave me a sidelong look, like a kid who suspects he might have gone a step too far without checking with his mother. I sighed. All I had wanted to do was go to the show as a way of demonstrating my support and, to be honest, my affection for this elderly woman I had come to know. Instead, I found myself roped into an impromptu book-marketing event—and given how the last one had gone, one I was in no hurry to undertake.

Well, they say that no good deed goes unpunished, and my punishment, it seemed, was to smile and sign books. I hoped the women weren't as chatty as my driving companion or, at the very least, not as likely to provide me with unsolicited criticisms of my work. While I had a pretty good idea of what had gone wrong with the last two books and felt good about the direction the new one was taking, I also knew that a writer's ego was fragile indeed, and the wrong word could send my confidence level right back down to zero.

"Great, we're here!" said Martha, clearly assuming my lack of objection meant that I was fine with her post-show plans. "Turn left at the gate," pointing to a sign half-hidden by climbing roses, "and go around the building. That's where the back entrance is."

Once I parked the car, I followed her into a kitchen filled with women bustling from counter to sink, setting out plates of cookies and stacks of napkins. The rich aroma of brewing coffee filled the air, and I wondered if someone would offer me a cup. But no such luck. I was there to work, and work I did, unfolding chairs and setting them out in rows wide enough apart to accommodate any walkers, wheelchairs, or other types of equipment the audience might be using.

Out of the corner of my eye, I saw Shauna and Donna enter the main room, but before I could wave hello, the two rushed down the corridor that led to the makeshift dressing room where the cast awaited their expertise. Then Martha appeared at my side.

"Now if you wouldn't mind, stay over at the doorway so you can open it if someone is having trouble. But only if it's necessary," she cautioned. "Some people are very sensitive about being assisted. Touchy, you might say. And if you help them when they think they don't need it, they can get a little offended. They don't want to feel like they can't do it themselves, you understand."

I nodded though I wasn't sure how I could tell the difference between those who needed help and those who didn't. But I took my place, unobtrusively pushing the automatic door button when I thought it was called for.

Then, hearing the opening chords of Glenn Miller's "In the Mood," I took my seat, prepared to applaud vigorously like a proud parent whose child stumbles through "Twinkle, Twinkle Little Star" on the piano. But the reality was that the show was darned good, even given the amateur status of the performers. The emcee (playing the part of Bob Hope) knew his lines and his cues, the "Andrews Sisters" were perfectly on pitch all through "Boogie Woogie Bugle Boy," and the "soldiers" managed to stay in step as they marched off the stage and passed through the audience to the tune of "You're in the Army Now."

And the songs... No wonder we won the war with such stirring melodies as "In Apple Blossom Time," "The White Cliffs of Dover," and "When the Lights Go on Again" to keep the spirits up at home and at the front.

Before I knew it, the closing song was played, and the performers and audience made a beeline for the refreshment table like a pack of hungry teens after a football game. Martha came out from behind the curtains still in costume and led me away from the ravenous horde and over to a corner table. There she introduced me to the store manager from Barnaby's who was patiently waiting with several stacks of my titles in front of her.

"Fran, this is Connie. Connie, Fran," said Martha before disappearing in the direction of the food.

"Normally, I would let Cheryl, our customer service rep, take care of this," Connie said, "but I'm such a big fan of yours that I couldn't resist doing it myself!" shaking my hand before leading me behind the table where she had thoughtfully provided a chair. "I brought all the books we had in stock as well as a stack of book plates, so if we run out, you can sign those, and we'll put them in the books when they arrive."

I smiled brightly, not wanting to let my face display my fear that the stack she had brought would be more than sufficient. I wanted to have a good signing—not just for the food bank and my ego but also because I wanted Martha to be proud of me.

And amazingly enough, the signing went better than I would have dreamed. Little by little, the women started heading my way, some still bearing their cups and cookies, lining up to buy not just one but several of my books, and talking the whole time.

"I haven't read this one, so this will be a treat!" "I'm buying this for my daughter-in-law for her birthday." "Oh, good! Connie, you finally got this one in! I've been waiting for it!"

Even Shauna and Donna came over, each buying a book plus one for the salon. "Just wait until I tell our customers you came to the shop!" said Shauna. "That will impress the heck out of them!"

I smiled at them—a real smile, not one of the author-on-duty ones I usually wore at this type of event—and kept wielding my pen, signing book after book. By the time I had autographed the twentieth bookplate (the stack of books having disappeared as fast as the cookies had), it was well after nine thirty and people were starting to drift toward the door.

"What a terrific event!" Connie said, gathering up the last few bookplates. "I can't thank you enough for doing this. I have to tell you, we don't get many authors around here, let alone someone of your caliber. This was really great! You must come back when your next book is out."

"Of course," I said and meant it. Not only because the response had been so heartwarming, but also because, in a way, I felt like I belonged there, that I was part of this little community—a feeling I hadn't had for years.

"When *will* it be out, if you don't mind my asking?" she said, slipping into her sweater before stacking her belongings onto the wheeled cart. "Martha said you've been hard at work on it during your whole stay. What a shame since you probably needed some time off from your busy schedule, but you can't delay—not when you have so many fans waiting for your wonderful books!"

"Well, I *have* made a lot of progress on it," I answered. "Martha's place is the perfect spot for writing. Of course, I need to finish it and do the revisions, which can take even longer than writing the first draft! That's part of the process, you know. But I hope to be out signing copies in a year or so," wondering as I said it who would be publishing my novel if Wilson-Morrow turned it down and whether Izzie would still be willing to represent such an uncooperative client.

"Is it—not to have you give away any secrets—but is it another 'lonely woman rescued by love' story like your other ones?" she asked delicately. "Not that there was anything wrong with them, mind you."

"Not exactly. This one is going to be a little different—still with love and romance, of course, but the heroine won't be one of those female characters who is waiting around for love and happiness to find her. She is already out there enjoying life and happy with who she is. And love is just one more aspect she adds to an already full life. But that's all I'm saying for now," I added with a smile. "You'll have to buy the book to find out the rest!"

"I'm so glad you're going in that direction," Connie said, heading to the door. "Not that I didn't thoroughly enjoy your other books, but sometimes I wanted to shake those women and tell them to get a grip already! And their choices—the Mr. Wrongs they always picked before Mr. Right came along! Honestly, how blind could they *be*?"

Pretty blind, I thought, following her to the exit so I could open the door for her. "Well, I don't think you'll want to shake *this* heroine. I look forward to hearing what you have to say after you read it."

"Oh, good, you're done," said Martha, coming up behind me as I waved a final goodbye to Connie. "I'm exhausted, my corns hurt, and if I don't get this mascara off my eyelashes pretty soon, I'll look like a raccoon!" And indeed, black smudges were already ringing her eyes.

"Yes, and I can't thank you enough for arranging the signing," I said honestly. "I wasn't sure at first how it would go, but it was wonderful—even if all your friends were just being kind to buy the books."

"Don't be silly," she said, pushing open the door and heading to the car. "At our age and with the economy the way it is, we have to watch every penny. So, if they spent money on your books, it was because they wanted them—not to make you feel good! Now, what do you say we go back home and crack open a bottle of Johnnie Walker and have a shot to wind down?"

Chapter 23

THAT ONE SHOT TURNED INTO A SECOND AND THEN A THIRD while Martha, feet propped up on a chair, told me about the trips she and her husband had taken over the years.

"For our honeymoon, we traveled from here to Oklahoma and then down to west Texas," she said, munching on some crackers and cheese she had brought out from the kitchen. "We had a 1950 Pontiac, but not one of the new models with air conditioning, and Lord, it was hot! I took my shoes off and pulled my skirt up until it barely covered my thighs. And when poor Fred saw that, he darned near ran off the road!" laughing at the memory.

She offered me the bottle, but I shook my head. I hadn't even finished the third shot, and I was afraid that one more would mean I'd be sleeping in the dining room instead of in my bed. As it was, I had to fight an overwhelming urge to close my eyes and lay my head on the table while Martha continued her version of what was fast becoming a bedtime story session.

"Fred loved to drive," she said. "One October, he got it into his head to drive to New England to see the trees change colors. But winter came early that year, and we ended up caught in a blizzard that lasted two days! Luckily, we weren't that far from a bed-and-breakfast, so that's where we waited it out. It was wonderful," and her voice softened and drifted off. She looked out the window onto the ocean, but I suspected she was back again at that little B&B.

"You two had such wonderful times," I said softly. "It must be hard for you, being here alone."

"Yes, yes, sometimes it is," she admitted, coming back to the room with an almost visible effort. "I didn't think Fred would go so soon or that I'd be here all by myself for so long. But you know, that's the thing about life. You don't know what's going to happen. You can make plans and promises, but then something happens—people change, things go wrong, whatever—and you have to make the best of it. I did have all those wonderful years with Fred. That's more than a lot of people get. Some people never find the one who's right for them. They keep looking or keep picking the wrong one or give up and crawl in a hole somewhere."

She didn't look at me, but I knew she was thinking about what I had told her a few days ago. I was as well, but unfortunately, I still wasn't sure what my decision would be. I had made my choice about my writing career, but when it came to John, that was another matter.

I smiled at her and then stood. "It's late and you must be exhausted. Let me clean up and we'll call it a night."

I picked up the bottle and my glass, and once Martha drained her last bit of whisky, took hers as well.

Martha got to her feet a bit unsteadily and gave me a hug. "Good night, dear," she said, "and thanks for letting an old woman ramble on about her life. Sleep well, and I'll make us a big breakfast in the morning to celebrate."

She went toward the door at the back of the room, which led to her private quarters, while I left through the back entrance, hearing the lock click behind me. It wasn't a long walk to my room but long enough for me to realize it was time I went back to Los Gatos. I'd been at the inn for a week and gotten more accomplished from a writing standpoint than I could have anticipated. I had a new book to work on, and *that* I could do at home.

Home. Going home also meant going back to the situation I'd left behind: the knowledge that my relationship might be irreparably damaged and the realization that it might have been defective from the beginning.

It was time to make a decision—the same decision I'd been wrestling with since that Friday afternoon phone call that started it all. Stay or go? And while I hadn't quite made up my mind, I knew I didn't want to go back to the type of relationship we had now and was a little clearer about the causes that had made it so fragile.

"Now I need to stop looking back and instead, figure out where to go from here," I said aloud, unlocking my door. I kicked off my heels and slipped off my dress and bra before putting on my pajamas, all the while giving my situation more thought.

"What would Cookie do?" I asked aloud, thinking of my new heroine. "If she were in this position—if she found out things weren't right, never had been right, maybe even couldn't be fixed to *be* right—what would she do?"

I crawled under the covers, still pondering the question, but it wasn't long before the combined effects of the liquor and the rhythmic sound of the waves lulled me to sleep.

The next morning, it wasn't my decision regarding John I was struggling with but whether it would take one aspirin or two to combat the hangover headache that awakened me. Gingerly brushing my teeth (even *they* ached!) before pulling on some clothes, I realized that, not being a whisky drinker, I probably should have stopped at two instead of having that third shot.

But that was water over the dam, I thought as I stumbled to the dining room. Or more accurately, liquor over the lips.

I squinted against the painfully bright morning sunlight and winced when the dining room door slammed behind me. The smell of coffee filled the air, and I hoped that a good dose of caffeine would send the painkiller directly to my brain to silence the drummers who were pounding inside my skull.

"Well, there you are!" Martha bustled out of the kitchen with a coffee pot in one hand and a mug in the other. "How do you feel? Ooh, you look like you had a bad night. I guess you aren't used to spending an evening with Johnnie!" and she laughed.

"Mmm," I mumbled, practically inhaling the coffee. After a few more gulps, I started to feel a little better. The pounding had subsided to a firm tapping, and the sunlight no longer pierced my eyes clean through to my brain.

"I'll have some toast ready for you in no time," she said. "Unless you want an omelet?" and she cocked her head questioningly.

My stomach roiled at the thought of eggs and cheese. "No, toast will be fine," I said, and it was. Or at least fine enough to calm the sour waves that threatened to rise into my throat.

It took nearly an hour before I felt human enough to engage Martha in conversation.

"You were wonderful last night," I said, nibbling on the last bit of crust on my plate while she added more coffee to my cup. "You *all* were! I can't thank you enough for inviting me to the show. It was a great ending to my stay here."

"Ending?" she repeated. "You're leaving? My goodness, the week has gone by so quickly!"

"I know. And in some ways, I feel like I've been here forever. Like it's my home. But it's not, and I need to get back and deal with...well, everything," I finished lamely.

Martha was quiet for a moment and then, in her best hostess-to-guest voice, said "Well, I can't tell you how much I've enjoyed having you here."

Then she set down the carafe and gave me a hug—not a hostess hug but the kind of embrace shared between friends and family.

"And I mean that, dear. I don't often get a chance to talk about my life or Fred, and you were so kind to listen. And I hope you'll come back again because I would love to have you here."

When she pulled back, I saw her eyes looked a bit teary, and I was conscious of a lump in my throat. Suddenly, I would have given anything to stay here, to live in this area and have Martha for a neighbor, to wake up from the bad dream my life had become—or at least, the part of my life that involved John—to a new reality that didn't include heartache and pain.

But you can't wake up from real life, I told myself. You have to live it, and if you don't like the way it is, then you have to change the parts that don't fit. And *that* couldn't be done if you weren't on site, so to speak, any more than a builder could renovate a house without being right there to figure out what wasn't working and where alterations needed to be made.

"Absolutely, I'll come back," I assured her and finished the last mouthful of coffee in my cup. "But now it's time to get back to my room and pack my things. I'll stop in the office right before lunchtime to drop off my key and pay the bill. Okay?" And at her nod, I headed out to have one final short walk along the shoreline.

But if I was hoping that watching the waves would bring me to a decision, I was sadly disappointed. While the past few days had opened my eyes to many things, I still couldn't see my way clearly to what I would do once I was face-to-face with John. The truth was, I wasn't even sure how I felt about him or our relationship anymore. Granted, his own feelings would come into play, and even if I wanted to stay with him, he could still opt to leave and never return.

But what if he decided to stay? What if he regretted his actions and wanted to try again? *Then* what would I do? And who would be making *that* decision: the old Fran who was willing to settle, or the new Fran who would rather have nothing than the wrong thing?

All through the packing up, the two Frans vied for the top spot in my brain, and I didn't know which one would have the upper hand. Maybe I should stay a few more days to be in a better place, emotionally speaking, to face John. Besides, I wasn't sure what Isabella would say regarding the synopsis I sent or what Wilson-Morrow would decide.

Maybe I had made a mistake. Maybe I should have delivered the synopsis for the book they wanted. Maybe... maybe... maybe....

Before I could reconsider, I threw my belongings into the car then stopped at the office to give Martha the room key and my payment and receive a hug and a bag of fresh-baked muffins—"For the road," she said with a smile. But as I reached the top of the driveway, I realized I was stuck in a mental rut, bouncing from one "maybe" to another. What happened to the woman who was ready to write a new future for herself? Where had *she* gone?

I didn't know, but what I did know was that I wasn't quite ready to return to the house John and I shared. So instead, I turned north, and when the exit for Coastside Bay appeared, I took it without thinking.

Once in town, I debated where to go. It wasn't time for lunch and I could hardly spend any more money on clothes, not after my last shopping trip. That left just the bookstore. I looked up at the sign above the entrance: "Barnaby's Books—A Booklover's Heaven." Well, it might be for most customers, but my last visit had been more like a trip to hell than a stay in Paradise. And while I was in a slightly better place, psychologically speaking, than when I'd gone there on Monday, I still wasn't ready to peruse the romance section and see how my books were faring compared to my competition.

I *could* go to a different part of the store though. And I crossed the street as if drawn by some irresistible force. Maybe the home-decorating section... The idea of renovation was appealing to me, considering that I was in a state of psychic transformation myself.

I pushed open the front door and stopped at the counter to ask the clerk for directions to the interior-design section.

"Go past the audiobook display, turn right at the archeology area, and you'll find it on your left," he said, stopping long enough from his task of adding "Signed by the author" labels to a stack of books to point toward the rear of the store. "If you need help, come get me. I have to get these books stickered and shelved before the post-church rush or I'd take you back there myself."

"I think I can find it," and headed in the direction he'd indicated. That's what I'd do, I thought as I approached the relevant bookshelves. Leaf through the books and visualize how I would change things in the house I lived in to make it more what I wanted, to make it fit me better.

Or go one step further and think about the kind of home I wanted to live in now. Maybe it wasn't so much a redecoration but a completely new house that was called for. A whole new house and a whole new life, to go with the whole new Fran I was working on.

When I found the books, I ran my fingers down the row, not sure what I was looking for. Ideas for paint colors? Suggestions for window coverings? Or maybe furniture options since I hated the contemporary style John had chosen.

If you hated it so much, why did you go along with it? that irritating voice asked. *Especially since you were the one paying for it! When you come down to it, why did you buy that house anyway?*

"Oh, shut up!" I said firmly, then quickly looked around, hoping no one was nearby to hear me. But the area was deserted. It was just me, the design books, and the reality that no matter what I chose—whatever paint color I picked or furniture I selected—nothing would change unless *I* changed.

I walked down the row, turned the corner, and saw them on the endcap: book after book on Craftsman-style homes with their low-pitched gable roofs, spacious front porches with tapered columns, and wood exteriors accented by stucco or stone.

The kind of house I loved, the kind of house I grew up in, the kind of house I once owned until John convinced me it wasn't suitable for a successful novelist and equally successful photographer. The kind of house that was *my* kind of house set near the ocean where I could open the windows and hear the soothing sound of the tide rolling in.

My kind of house, and inside, my kind of furniture: handcrafted Mission style. As for the walls, I'd paint them in yellow tones—a perfect counterpoint to the dark oak pieces. Add a few Tiffany lamps and leaded glass for the sidelights on either side of the front door, and it would be exactly the home I wanted. And a far cry from the house I was currently living in.

I picked up a few books from the display, not sure why or what I would do with them once I got back to Los Gatos, and started toward the checkout in the front of the store. But as I passed the kids' area, my eyes were caught by a row of fairy tales, the beautifully colored covers reminding me of my childhood preferences. I had loved those kinds of books, stories with unicorns and magic spells and princesses who were rescued by all those Prince Charmings and ended up living happily ever after.

"No wonder I write romance novels," I said, picking up one after the other to glance at the closing chapters. "I bought into the idea of finding true love and having it all work out and last forever. And it could," thinking of my parents who had loved each other for decades. "But it has to be a good match to start with. And the couple must figure out how to solve all those niggling little disagreements that crop up in the 'happily ever after' part."

That was the trouble with fairy tales. They never took you past the marriage vows to the post-wedding, day-to-day existence. Did Cinderella only marry her prince so she could get out of the fireplace ashes and into a home of her own where someone else could do the cleaning only to find a whole new set of obligations and expectations? Once Sleeping Beauty got over the effects of her "sleeping sickness," did she still feel the same way about her rescuer? Or had his kiss awakened her psychologically as well as physically, energizing her to want to do something more with her life besides being eternally grateful to the guy who gave her the magical equivalent of a cup of super-caffeinated coffee?

Sleeping Beauty... I picked up the Disney version based on Charles Perrault's original story and made my way over to a nearby chair. There, I settled myself comfortably before opening the book to the part where the country was celebrating the birth of Princess Aurora.

That was some christening party, I thought as I read how everyone, from the lowest of the low to the highest of the high, including the young Prince Phillip, came to see the heroine in her diaper and crib.

Of course, it wouldn't be a fairy tale without magical creatures, and in this case, they were fairies—Flora, Fauna, and Merryweather—bringing with them their gifts. One gave beauty, and the second, song. However, after the evil fairy Maleficent placed a curse on baby Aurora, the last good fairy had to do a quick substitution, replacing her original contribution of happiness for Aurora with the far more useful (in retrospect) capacity to recover from a magical slumber after receiving her true love's kiss.

"I wish *I* had three fairies to give me gifts," I said, putting the book down on my lap and leaning my chin on my hand. "Not coffeemakers or toaster ovens, but constructive presents that would have made my adult life a whole lot easier."

But maybe I *did* have a supportive trio of sorts, thinking of Diana, Martha, and my fictional heroine Cookie. They weren't part of my infancy but had waited until I hit the long overdue rebirthing process to smack me with their magic wands as they gave me the gifts I needed.

I smiled as images of the three of them, flitting about with their "tools of the trade" clenched in their hands, came into my mind. What would be the gifts they gave me? Diana's offering would be the ability to do a reality check. I recalled how many times she had stopped me from my incessant complaining to point out my role in the romantic messes I would find myself in.

"What do you mean, you can't believe he did that?" she'd interrupt as I was recounting the latest emotional storm I was weathering. "Are you kidding me? You *knew* it was coming. You're not stupid. You just didn't want to face it."

Harsh words, but wasn't that a good fairy's job after all: to open the princess's eyes to reality?

As for Martha, well, Martha's gift (thinking back to our many conversations) was to learn how to let go of the past, accept what couldn't be changed, and focus on the future. And about knowing what I want, keeping my eyes on it, and moving forward toward that goal. Even Cookie, my imaginary guide, was not without her own magical gift to bestow on me. For one thing, her very existence was a gift of sorts, busting to smithereens the writer's block that had stopped me in my creative tracks. But she also showed me a new kind of woman, giving me a magic mirror (to mix up my fairy tale metaphors) that reflected a new kind of Fran, inspired by the Cookie I had created.

So, I had my three good fairies, but who was my equivalent of the evil Maleficent? Who was responsible for putting me into this psychological sleep state? Was it the men I had allowed into my castle, i.e., my heart? Or was *I* the one to blame for living my life in a semi-somnolent state, for choosing to reduce my awareness of reality to the lowest possible point?

"Huh, great," I said, getting to my feet. "I am my own worst enemy, my own fairy princess and evil witch all rolled up into one!"

Chapter 24

"Did you find the books you wanted?"

It was Matt (I could see his name tag now), the sales associate I had spoken to earlier. He looked at me, then at the book I was still holding, and smiled. "Looking for something for your children?" he asked.

Nice touch, that. He had been well trained not to presuppose that women in my age bracket were grandmothers as well as to throw a compliment my way by implying that I looked young enough to have fairy-tale-aged kids.

"I'm afraid I got sidetracked." I smiled and put the book back where it belonged before picking up my other selections. "I think I'd better pay for these and get going before I get waylaid by any other intriguing categories!"

"Well, stop back if you're looking for something to read. We have all kinds of books: the latest political scandals, murder mysteries, and of course, romance novels." He looked at me more carefully. "You look awfully familiar. Don't I know you from somewhere? No, I recognize you now! You're Fran Carter! I just finished shelving several of your books— the first two as well as your latest that just arrived. Good thing, too, since the ones Connie took to the show last night are all gone. Would you like to autograph them? Then we could put stickers on the cover. They sell even faster when the author has signed them. Not that yours aren't selling," he added hastily.

"Sure," I said, following him to the romance section where I saw far more spines with my name on them than had been there on my last trip.

"Why don't I bring these down to the checkout? Then while I ring up your purchases, you can sign your books," he suggested, and I nodded.

As I scrawled "Enjoy the story! Fran" on each title page, I couldn't help hoping that with those "Signed by the author" stickers on the front, my books would sell faster and satisfy Wilson-Morrow and Isabella and anyone else who expected me to deliver on demand. Then, no matter which book I wrote, I would at least have a more positive track record in terms of sales and a greater number of fans ready and willing to buy it.

"Thank you so much," Matt said, handing me a bag with "Thanks for shopping at Barnaby's Books!" inscribed on the outside. "Perhaps when your next book is out, you could come here for a book signing. We have lots of women who love romance novels, and they would be thrilled to meet you!"

"Thanks," I said as I took my purchases. "I'll definitely add Barnaby's to my list," and went out to my car. I set the shopping bag on the passenger seat where it waited, like a gift I was afraid to unwrap, and got behind the wheel.

Was it just chance or a bit of magic that I came to the bookstore on the very day that my own novels arrived? And did it matter? Not really, I decided. All that counted was that a new opportunity to promote my books had come my way, and it was up to me to take advantage of it when my next book was finished. Then I could introduce my readers to a new kind of woman living a new kind of life, a woman who didn't need a man so much as want a love that fit into her plans for the future. And in the process, they would get to meet a new Fran as well—one I myself was starting to know.

Not quite ready to leave for home, I looked around the shopping center, hoping there would be somewhere I could spend another hour or two. The sign for Moon Over Pasta Restaurant a few spots beyond the bookstore caught my eye.

Now *that* was an option. After all, it was just after one, and my breakfast had been comparatively sparse, thanks to my whisky hangover. I could have lunch before going back to Los Gatos—a good idea since I was pretty sure there wasn't much in the way of food waiting for me in my refrigerator.

Inside, I was greeted by soft music and a thirtysomething server who took me to a corner table with comfortable leather chairs and offered me coffee without even waiting for me to ask.

"Hello, my name is Ellen, and I'll be taking care of you today," she said, her smile reaching all the way to her eyes. "Today's special is cauliflower soup with spicy caramelized cauliflower florets and parsley pesto in a creamy broth, followed by mascarpone ravioli made with artichokes and topped with sage and brown butter sauce. And, of course, rosemary focaccia bread with olive oil and balsamic vinegar on the side for dipping."

A far cry from what I would have been eating at home, I thought. I didn't even bother to look at the menu but put myself in her hands. "Sounds perfect. And a glass of wine, too. What would you suggest?"

She cocked her head to one side and said authoritatively, "I think a Falanghina from Campania. It has nice yellow hues, a grassy and herbaceous palate, and slight oak undertones reminiscent of a lighter Chardonnay."

I had no idea what any of that meant but nodded in agreement. "Falanghina it is!" figuring the carbs would counteract the alcohol, making it safe for me to drive if I stuck to one glass.

The bread and soup appeared like magic on the table, and as I tore, dipped, and munched my way through three slices of bread followed by mouthfuls of the best soup I had ever eaten, I thought about how it would feel to go back to my house and the life I'd left behind a week ago.

I didn't want to go back. I felt like it wouldn't be so much a return to my own home as to a place where I'd once lived but no longer wanted to reside. I didn't want to go back, back to the type of books I had been writing, the type of relationships I had been having, the life itself I had been living.

"No, I want something different," and didn't realize I'd spoken aloud until Ellen stopped in the act of refreshing my coffee cup and asked with concern, "You didn't like your meal?"

"No, no!" I said, noticing with some surprise that my plate was empty. I had been so caught up in my thoughts that I didn't remember eating the ravioli. "In fact, it was absolutely delicious!" figuring that it must have been good or I would have stopped thinking long enough to notice.

"Well, I hope you have room for dessert!" she said, smiling. "You have three choices. There's *affogato* made with espresso, vanilla gelato, and candied orange zest. Or a Meyer-lemon parfait with lemon curd, Italian meringue, passion fruit, caramel sauce, and lemon sorbetto. And last but not least, our best seller: Ghirardelli butterscotch pudding topped with whipped cream."

I debated, but only for a moment. Then, my lust for sugar prevailed. "I'll take the pudding," I said, which I proceeded to enjoy without a second thought for its impact on my waistline. This was, after all, a celebration. I was celebrating the end of writer's block and the release (albeit a potentially expensive one) from the obligation of having to write the kinds of books I didn't want to write anymore.

And maybe, too, having reached a decision regarding my relationship and my future. While there was no guarantee that the road ahead would be a smooth one, I felt I was now in a better place psychologically to handle whatever potholes or detours fate would throw in my way.

What's that saying about pride going before a fall? My self-congratulatory mood lasted until I got to my car, which now was sitting somewhat lopsided in the parking space due to a flat tire on the front passenger side. I'd have to call the auto club, which would delay my return home for at least an hour or two, allowing my resolve enough time to lose its power and giving me the chance to rethink my plans and reconsider my decisions.

And that's how I spent the next sixty minutes, my mind bouncing from the possible outcomes of my email to Isabella to my situation with John and then back again. First, the book. Today was Sunday, which meant the chances were good that Izzie wouldn't even *read* my email until tomorrow morning. I was fairly certain she hadn't opened it already since, if she had, I would have heard from her by now.

While I couldn't cancel *that* email, I could send her another one flagged "high importance" and attach a half-assed version of the other book idea I had mentioned during our call last Wednesday: yet another hapless heroine in an exotic location who goes through the all-too-familiar trials and tribulations on her way to true love. After all, I had time to kill until the auto service guy arrived. I could certainly come up with something in the interim.

Or I could call John. Oh, not to apologize, but to go over the plans for the next photo shoot. I could explain that I hadn't yet formalized the storyline or location (true in its own way) but was working on it. And that as soon as I had it clear in my head, I would let him know.

And that would be it. I wouldn't ask about the affair—or affairs since I was pretty sure this wasn't the first. I wouldn't ask when, or if, he was coming home. This would strictly be a business call.

A business call... which brought me back to my literary conundrum that I'd hoped I had resolved but was now second-guessing. Should I write about Cookie or Cassandra? Would my next novel feature a woman who is in charge of her future? Or one who is sitting around, waiting for her "happily ever after" life, courtesy of Prince Charming?

*Happily ever after...*Would I have that with John? Only if I overlooked what he'd done and what he would most likely continue to do.

"But wouldn't that be better than starting over and trying to create a new life at my age?" I asked as I scanned the road, hoping for a glimpse of the road service vehicle. "It's not like I don't have enough on my plate already!"

I mentally ticked off the items on my To-Do list. Book events for *Love in Unexpected Places.* A publishing contract whose terms I had to meet. And the decision on which story I would write: the one I wanted to do or the one that would make everyone else happy.

I felt like a Ping-Pong ball being batted between players, neither of which cared what I wanted. Satisfy my publisher and agent, or please myself? Resume my life with John, or make a clean break? Fortunately for my poor beleaguered brain, my cell phone rang. It was Diana, and as I answered the call, I realized I hadn't talked to her since our walk last Sunday.

"Just checking in on you," she said, and I knew what she meant. It was her way of asking what decision I had made about John.

"I'm fine," I answered in a falsely upbeat tone. This wasn't the time for another "tell it like it is" session with Diana. I wasn't up to it. Instead, I steered the conversation in another direction.

"I took your advice, spent the week at a bed-and-breakfast up by Coastside Bay, and worked on the book."

Then, before she could ask me about that project, I added, "And I got a whole new look while I was there. A new cut, a new color, new makeup, and even two new dresses!"

There. That should please her. She was always telling me that I was letting myself go and if I weren't careful, I'd end up like one of those frumpy authors whose appearance was in direct contrast to that of the bosom-heaving, hair-flowing, eyes-flashing heroines displayed on their book covers.

"Past time if you ask me," she said. "Now, when are you coming back? I want to see this new, improved Fran."

But before I could answer, I saw a truck with "Bob's Tire Sales and Towing Service" written on the side.

"Later today," I said. "My car got a flat and I had to call for service and—oh, look! There's the truck now! I'll call you when I get back, okay?" and ended the call before she had a chance to ask any more questions since I didn't have any good answers.

I got out of my car and stood beside the offending tire while the young mechanic looked at it from all angles. Then he knelt to run his hands over the sidewall, stopping halfway up the back side.

"Well, that explains it," he said, getting to his feet and wiping his palms on his overalls. "You've got what seems to be a good-sized nail in the tread. It might be able to be repaired, but if I was you, I'd get a new tire. You know," he continued as he checked the other three, "these all look like they should be replaced. The tread has worn down, and your car probably needs an alignment, too." He pointed to the surface of the driver-side front tire. "See how uneven it looks?"

I nodded although I really couldn't tell the difference.

"Yep, you need to do 'em all," he declared.

I had to take him at his word even though I knew I was the perfect road call: someone who didn't want gas or a pull-out from a ditch but a customer who needed four new, and undoubtedly expensive, tires. Not that I had much choice. It wasn't like I could drive home on three tires, and the spare that was to serve as an emergency stopgap was also flat—a fact he ascertained when he opened the trunk and checked it.

"I'll tow you back to the shop, and we can fix it all there. Unless you have another idea?" and he looked at me.

"Fine, fine," I said, retrieving my purse before following him back to his truck and climbing into the passenger seat.

Once he hooked up my car, he pulled out of the parking lot and down a side road, presumably toward his shop. Not that I knew for a fact that was where he was going, recalling news stories of women being attacked by roadside assistance providers who were there ostensibly to fix a car breakdown. He could be going to a deserted stretch of countryside. He could be planning to rob me or worse. He could be—

"Here we are!" and I looked up to see the Bob's Tire Sales and Towing Service sign next to a gleaming red and white building. "You can wait inside the office," he added, pulling up to one of the bay doors in the service section. "My grandma probably has a pot of coffee on. But watch out—she likes to talk!"

Chapter 25

I WALKED IN THE DIRECTION HE POINTED WHERE A WOMAN around Martha's age was waiting, door held open.

"Come on in," she said and then stopped. "Why, you're Fran Carter! I'm Sadie, Sadie Baxter. I was at the show last night. Oh, not as a performer," she added. "I was in the kitchen getting the refreshments ready. But I did buy two of your books, and I overheard you talking to Connie about your next one and it sounded so interesting!"

She grabbed my arm and led me inside, pointing toward a chair across from a desk strewn with invoices and receipts.

"This is my job: keeping the books for my grandson. He took over the business when his father, Bob Jr., passed away, and young Bob decided his old grandma might as well keep doing what she'd been doing for forty years. My husband, Bob Sr., started the business, and when he died, our son took it over. Now it's Bobby's turn. Would you like some coffee? I just made it."

"Yes, please," and she poured it into a beautiful lavender-and-white mug.

"Cream? Sugar?" and when I nodded, she added liberal quantities of both, stirred it, and brought the mug over to me before filling a matching one for herself.

She pulled over a chair to sit by me. "But here, you don't want to hear about my life. It's too boring. Let's talk about you and your books. What's the next one about? Where does it take place? And what's the main character's name?"

Not wanting to get into *that* subject, especially since I couldn't seem to make up my mind, I smiled and fell back on my usual response. "Oh, I'm never allowed to share details about my books until closer to release date! You like reading romance novels?"

"Yes, I do," she answered enthusiastically. "You might think a woman my age wouldn't have much interest in romance and love and even sex, but you'd be wrong there! And this might surprise you, but I'm even dating. Charley and I have been seeing each other for... let's see, how long? Probably since Christmas. He's the one who couldn't do the chairs at the show, which is why Martha had you do it."

"Martha said something about his arthritis. Is he feeling better?"

"Yes, but it'll be a while before he does that again! He's a runner and had been in a race two days before the show, and that's how he got injured. I told him he shouldn't try it, but he was bound and determined since the race only happens once a year. He said it was for a good cause, and he was going to win it for once. And he did! He came in first in the over-seventy age group. *And* he beat last year's time, too!"

She took my cup to top it off, still talking.

"Anyway, like I said, I do like reading romance novels. Jenna— that's young Bob's wife—and I trade books between us. And we talk about them. You know, the plot and characters and settings, what we liked and what we didn't. She's thinking of being a writer herself. Too bad she's not here right now. She'd love to meet you! But she usually goes out with the girls for dinner after target practice."

She stopped long enough for a swig of her coffee before going on. "She's the instructor for the Bay City Bullets. They've got a competition coming up in July, and Martha said everybody had to improve their scores or else! She said she's tired of them losing to Gertie's Gun Group, and this year they have to win."

Good Lord, don't any of these women just sit around rocking on their front porches? "You don't shoot?"

"Heavens, no! I don't have the time. Between doing the books here and volunteering at the hospital and delivering for our local Meals on Wheels—you know a lot of older people can't manage without our help," as though she herself weren't in that same age category. "And then there's my pottery business."

Sadie held up her mug. "I made this one and yours, too. I have a little shop in the back and do custom orders: mugs, vases, pitchers, bowls. When Jenna has her baby in a few months, I'm going to make a set for her: a tiny cup and bowl with the baby's name and birth date on it. Hey, I have an idea! Once you get your story all figured out and know the name of your main character, I'll make you a set of mugs with her name and the book title on it. It'll be a thank-you gift for helping to support our food bank."

I was confused for a minute, then remembered the donation from the sales at the show the night before. Honesty compelled me to set the story straight. "Well, it wasn't really me. I mean, the bookstore made the donation."

"Oh, I know, but Barnaby's wouldn't have had anything to donate if you hadn't done the signing, so in a way it came from you, right? Besides, I love your books, so it's the least I can do for all the enjoyment you've given me."

Her appreciation, welcome though it was, worried me a bit. Would she be as big a fan if I wrote about Cookie instead of Cassandra? Maybe I should stick with what had been working instead of going off in a different direction.

"Although," and I looked up at Sadie, who had paused, "if I might make a small suggestion, can you make this woman a little more, well, proactive? Less dependent? She can fall in love and even make a bad choice or two, but does she have to be so helpless?" unwittingly using the same adjective that Martha and Shauna had applied to my heroines. "I'd like to read about women who are in charge of their lives but still looking for romance. And sex—don't forget sex," she emphasized. "There's nothing wrong with having some steam in the sheets, you know!"

I nodded, although I was pretty sure that she was having more of that than I was these days—and probably would be having in the foreseeable future. But before I could mentally run down the road leading to John and *that* problem, Bob came in, wiping his hands on a rag, and handed the paperwork to his grandmother.

"All done," he said with a smile at me. "I even found a spare that'll do in case you break down again."

"Bob, this can't be right," interrupted Sadie as she scanned the bill.

My heart sank. Did he underestimate the cost or time?

She went over to the desk, punched in a few numbers on the calculator, crossed out the total at the bottom of the invoice, and then handed the bill to me. The amount wasn't higher, but lower, and I looked up at her.

"Don't worry," in answer to my unasked question. "You come back here and do a signing when the next book comes out and give me an autographed copy and we'll call it even, okay?"

I nodded—what else *could* I do?—and handed over my credit card, although in truth, I owed her far more than the cost of a set of new tires and a tow. She had given me something to reflect on, about my book and life in general. Surprisingly, this whole trip had turned out to be quite an education. Now it was up to me to make the most of what I had learned.

I went out to my car, saw the bag of home-design books I'd bought, and went back into the shop.

"Is something wrong?" Sadie asked.

I shook my head and smiled. "No, but I was thinking about the cups you make. Could you make me a set of four in yellow tones like that one?" pointing to a mug on her desk stuffed with pens and pencils. "And matching bowls, too. That would be perfect for breakfast!"

Perfect for breakfast in my new kitchen in my new Craftsman home, but not perfect for the house I lived in now. Was I putting the cart before the horse?

But before I could take back my words, she nodded enthusiastically and pulled out a color chart. "Why don't you pick the exact color you like?"

I had no idea there were so many shades of yellow or, for that matter, so many names: dandelion, butter, ochre, mustard, flax, goldenrod. I looked at the chart, up at her, and back at the chart, bemused and confused. And then I saw it: Tuscan Summer. It was the perfect shade for the kitchen I didn't have in a house I didn't own.

"That one," pointing to the soft yellow with slight undertones of brown. I could imagine drinking my coffee out of that Tuscan Summer mug or eating oatmeal topped with brown sugar out of that Tuscan Summer bowl. "And a pitcher, too, please, to hold my creamer."

"Absolutely." She pulled out an order book labeled Sadie's Pottery Shop, made some notes, then handed me a copy. "Your order ought to be ready by this coming Sunday. But give me a call on Saturday to check. Okay?"

"Perfect!" and clutching my receipt, I left the shop. In a week, my mugs and bowls and pitcher would be ready. The question was, would I be ready, too? Or more accurately, what life would I be ready to live?

No answer during the drive home. And no answer yet by the time I got there, unpacked my suitcase, and took a hot shower. So, when the text came from John saying he wouldn't be back for another week—a text instead of a phone call, which meant he didn't want to continue our last conversation—I was more than a little relieved. That gave me at least seven more days to evaluate my options and make my decision. And not only about John since sometime tomorrow morning I was bound to hear from Izzie relating to the synopsis she had received.

Regarding the latter, it turned out I was wrong. It wasn't until closer to five o'clock Monday afternoon that she called, and for a moment, when I saw her name on my caller ID, I was tempted to let it go to voice mail. Why ruin what had been a great writing day? I was up to five thousand words completed on the third chapter of *Love in the Light of Day* plus a working outline of the plot.

I was at that perfect stopping point that all writers love, and I had looked forward to celebrating with a glass of wine and whatever I could find in my refrigerator. The last thing I wanted was to have someone rain on my literary parade.

Oh, just get it over with, I told myself, and resignedly answered the call.

"You didn't take my advice," Izzie started with, not even bothering to say hello.

That didn't bode well although what she had given me last Wednesday had been a darned sight closer to an order than a suggestion.

I took a deep breath. "No, I didn't."

"So, should I assume you will now be sending me the synopsis for the book we discussed?"

There it was—my last chance to make good on the contract and keep everybody happy. But if I said yes, I would be obligated to work on a book I didn't want to write with a character I didn't care about who would be rescued by a Prince Charming and have a "happily ever after" life I didn't believe in—or at least, not one like that.

"Um, no," I said finally.

"Okay, then. Well, Wilson-Morrow isn't interested in publishing a book that they said was about some boring baker living a boring life. And since the terms of the contract have been met, that's that."

"Her life isn't boring!" I protested, remembering the chapter I had been working on all day. Cookie was entering a competition with the first prize a trip to France and a chance to attend a six-week course at Le Cordon Bleu Paris.

"And I agree with you," she answered.

That was the last thing I expected. I had braced myself to hear that it was time for me to find a new agent, but instead, she seemed to be saying she was on my side. Good thing, too, since there weren't a whole lot of other people standing there.

"To tell you the truth, I've been wondering if the whole 'damsel in distress' narrative isn't getting a bit old. And I must admit, the book idea you presented in the synopsis for... what's it called again?"

"*Love in the Light of Day.*"

"That's right! Anyway, it sounded interesting, especially the Paris angle you had mentioned. And there's a lot that can be done from a marketing standpoint, too: recipe cards with the cover on one side and the directions on the other, tie-ins with popular bakers during book tours, maybe even a cookbook with your fictional heroine on the front!"

Izzie was showing a lot of enthusiasm for someone who had just had her client's book proposal rejected, I thought suspiciously.

"How far along are you on this manuscript? Or, more important, how long will it take for you to give me a working draft?"

This was hardly the way I'd expected this conversation to go. Something was up. I just wasn't sure what it was.

"I don't know," I waffled. "A couple of months or so. Why?"

"Well, I didn't want to say anything yet, but I was on the phone with Carlsbad and Company this afternoon. You know who they are, right?"

That was a rhetorical question. C&C was one of the major houses and a direct competitor of Wilson-Morrow. Isabella pitched my first book to C&C, but they had passed—something about not being interested in genre romances as I recalled.

She took my lack of response as an assent and continued. "My contact there mentioned they are developing a new women's fiction imprint featuring middle-aged female protagonists. It's intended to be a counterpart to their Austen-Alcott line, the one that's geared to young women readers. That way they can hit both demographics: professional women in their early twenties to late thirties and women in, let's see, what did they say? Oh, yes. 'Women in the prime of their lives.' Anyway, I happened to mention that I was shopping a book that would be a good fit for that line, and they were interested—especially after I read them your synopsis. So, if you could have the first draft done in two months or so, that would give me enough time to review it and make some suggestions. That way, we'll be ready to send the manuscript to them when they're open for pitches."

"Which would be when?" I asked.

Her answer had a breezy "this would be no problem for you" tone. "In four months."

"Four months. You want a completed eighty-thousand-or-so-word manuscript in *four months*? A manuscript ready to pitch to C&C, who are notorious for being hard to satisfy. Am I hearing you right?"

"Now calm down, Fran. From what you told me, you already have a lot of ideas for the book. If you buckle down, I'm sure you can get the first draft ready for me in sixty days. And I'll keep my suggestions to a minimum. I don't see why you can't have something ready to send to C&C in four months. That is, if you are truly interested in working on this novel."

She had me there. She knew how much I wanted to work on this book and see it in print. After all, I had risked everything by sending her that synopsis instead of the one Wilson-Morrow wanted. And it wasn't like I had anything else to occupy my time anyway.

"You know, you don't have to go into a lot of depth about the Paris trip either," she added. "I'm sure the advance you'd get would be more than enough to cover your cost of doing some on-site research to flesh out that part. At the same time, we can get some publicity shots to use in prerelease marketing. You know, the 'author doing research in Paris' style photographs. By the way, how's John?"

The rapid, ninety-degree turn in the conversation caught me off guard although I shouldn't have been surprised. He was the one who did my PR images after all.

"Fine. Why?" not wanting to get into the topic of our relationship.

There was silence from the other end as though Izzie were choosing her words carefully. That wasn't like her. She generally plowed right into things regardless of the subject matter. But this time, something was holding her back.

"What's up, Isabella?"

"Has he talked to you yet?"

"About what?" although whatever it was, I could assume it wasn't good.

There was another delay—what is referred to in books as a "pregnant pause"—and then she finally answered.

"Apparently, he made a pass at a model while on a shoot last week, and she turned him down—and not too nicely either. She said he was old enough to be her father and not her type anyway. He didn't take the rejection well and made some vague threat about her future as a model, and *she* countered with references to the Me Too movement. And when she came back to town, she told her uncle what took place, and *he* happened to be the executive editor at Wilson-Morrow. Now John is persona non grata at W-M, and I'm sure, when word gets around, he will be at other houses as well."

I didn't know what to say, so I said nothing.

"Fran?"

Was it my imagination or was there a slight softening in Izzie's voice, maybe even a note of sympathy?

"You might as well know it now. John and I are," and I paused, not sure how to describe the current situation, "well, we're having some issues"—the understatement of the year.

"Will it interfere with your writing?" And there was the Isabella I knew, no-nonsense and professional.

"No, it won't," mentally crossing my fingers. At least it wouldn't for this week since he wouldn't be around to distract me. If I stayed focused, I could get a lot done on the book before he returned and I'd have to write the conclusion to our story. Assuming, of course, that I knew what that conclusion would be.

"Good," she answered briskly. "Well, I won't bother you anymore. You get cracking and I'll touch base in a few weeks to see how the book is coming." And with that, the call I'd been dreading was over.

Chapter 26

I PICKED UP ONE OF THE HOME DESIGN BOOKS I'D BOUGHT AND absently leafed through it while I thought about what Izzie had said. *From a professional standpoint, it was better than I had expected.* While the rejection from Wilson-Morrow did sting a bit, it hadn't come as a complete surprise. And not only did I still have Izzie as my agent, but she might have found me a new publisher.

As for the news about John... well, I'd file that under "to be dealt with later." There wasn't anything I could do about it anyway—at least not until he came back. *If* he came back.

I looked around my office as though I'd see a solution hanging somewhere on the walls, but there wasn't one.

I slammed the book back down on the stack.

"Damn it, I'm doing just what I didn't want to do. I'm thinking about him and what he is or isn't doing instead of my work and my future. If I'm going to get this book done, I've got to sit down and write it!"

And that's what I did for the rest of the week. With no one to distract me and nothing to interrupt me, I plowed right through a few more chapters, rising at dawn to write through the day and then, in the evening, scrolling through the pages while making editorial notes involving changes, additions, and deletions.

"Early to bed, early to rise," the saying goes. In my case, my sleep schedule resulted in a satisfactory amount of work on a book that, one week ago, I wasn't sure I could write or that, if I did, anyone would want to publish. Now, thanks to Isabella, I might have a publisher. But even if that didn't work out, I didn't regret the choice I had made.

By lunchtime Friday, I had completed rough drafts of six chapters, had a workable outline, and had compiled enough notes to keep me busy in the weeks to come. I was getting ready to start chapter seven when my office phone rang—a number I didn't recognize. Remembering what had happened the last time I received a call from an unknown number, I considered not answering.

But I needn't have worried. It was Sadie, letting me know that my order was ready sooner than she had promised.

"If you want to come out sometime tomorrow, I'll be here. I know we talked about Sunday, but there's a shooting competition and I promised the club I'd be there to cheer them on," she explained. "Will that work for you? If not, we can plan for sometime next week."

"No, tomorrow will be fine," I assured her. "I should be there by the afternoon."

I needed to take a break from writing anyway, I thought after the call was over, and if Diana were free, maybe she'd like to go along for the ride. That would give me a chance to bring her up to date on what Izzie had said regarding C&C and a possible book deal. I wasn't sure I wanted to share what else Izzie had told me, the part about John and the model— or at least, not until I knew what I would do when he got back.

"Of course, I'll go with you!" Diana said when I called her. "It works out perfectly since I have to make a trip to that area myself. There are a few houses I'm checking out for a client, so we can kill two birds with one stone. I'll even drive. Pick you up at nine?"

I agreed even though Diana's driving was a little on the wild side. She considered the Pacific Coast Highway an irresistible challenge to her driving expertise, and more than once when I'd been a passenger in her car, I would find myself closing my eyes as she cut a bit too near the edge for my liking. But if I drove a Z4, I'd probably be tempted to floor it myself.

I was ready well before nine, and while I waited for Diana, I had one last cup of coffee—not as good as Martha's, I had to admit. Then, hearing the car horn, I hurried to the front door, stopping to check my appearance in the mirror.

For a moment, I was startled at what I saw. All week long I had been so busy working that the most I would do each morning was brush my teeth and run a comb through my hair. But this morning I had taken the time to apply the blush and eye shadow I had bought last week and even added a bit of styling gel to my newly red strands.

I looked at the woman in the mirror—this new Fran—and tried to recall the old one, the one who looked like "failure Fran," "cheated-on Fran" or "confused-with-no-direction-in-mind Fran" but I couldn't remember how she looked. This Fran looked confident, sure of herself and what she wanted.

And more important, I felt like that, too. The single thing I had to worry about was whether I could hold onto that feeling once John came home. *If* he came home.

And that was a big "if."

There was a second honk of the horn. Diana was waiting, and she was not one known for being patient. I grabbed my purse and, closing the door behind me, rushed to her car, stopping outside the driver's door so she could get a good look at the new me.

"Well?" I said, when she just sat there, silent.

Then she smiled. "For a minute, I wasn't sure who you were! I was waiting for mousy little broken-hearted Fran, and instead, out comes this kick-ass woman!"

I smiled back and walked around to the passenger side. "So, it's okay? I didn't go too far?" I asked, needing one more boost of encouragement.

"Hell, no, girl! You look great!" and she reached over and patted my arm. "Now sit back and relax and tell me all about the book."

I wasn't sure about the relaxing part since I knew how fast Diana drove. But fortunately for me, the morning fog hadn't quite cleared away, so she was forced to maintain a speed closer to the posted sign. But not so fortunately, this meant she didn't have to give all her attention to the road, which would leave her free to play Twenty Questions with me.

Sticking to the topic of my new novel, I shared as much as I could remember about the plot and the character, and when I ran out of those details, shifted into the publishing side of things: being rejected by Wilson-Morrow as well as the interest shown by Carlsbad and Company.

"So anyway, Izzie said I might have a chance with C&C. *If* they like the premise and character and the first few chapters," I said, surreptitiously checking my watch. I had spun out the info relating to the new book and Izzie's call until we were just a few miles from the garage. Once I picked up my pottery order, we'd be on our way to view the houses on Diana's list, and I knew her well enough to know that at that stage of our trip, she'd be totally preoccupied with her real estate business.

"That's great news!" she said, sending gravel flying as she made a sharp right down the road leading to Bob's place. "But four months for a working draft—do you think you can pull it off?"

"I hope so," I said though I was more than a little worried about that myself. But I couldn't afford to blow this chance. I'd simply have to do it.

"There's the garage," I pointed out, and with a flourish, she pulled into the lot.

It didn't take long to pick up my order even though Sadie insisted I inspect every piece before she packed it in a box.

"This is really beautiful," said Diana, picking up a small deep-green vase that was sitting on the window ledge.

"You like that? I started doing vases and flowerpots, just for something different," Sadie said as she ran a strip of tape across the flaps of the box to seal it shut.

"Do you take custom orders?" And at Sadie's nod, Diana set the vase down on the desk. "Tell you what—I'll take a dozen of these if you can do them in the same color I use for my business," and she handed over her card. "And add this down at the base," pointing to her logo. "They will be perfect housewarming gifts for my clients!"

"No problem at all," and Sadie made notes on her pad before tearing off the top copy for Diana. Five minutes later, we were back in Diana's car, the box with my order safely stowed in the trunk and Sadie's order form clipped to the visor.

"Well, shall we go?" and without waiting for an answer, Diana pulled out of the lot and headed toward the first of five houses she was scheduled to see.

Diana was good—thorough yet efficient. At each of the first three houses, it took her less than ten minutes to decide it wasn't the right fit for her client. And when we drove up to house number four on her list, she didn't even bother to go inside.

"He'll hate it," she said, backing out of the driveway. "The last thing he wants is to be more than five minutes from the city. I keep telling him that a condo would be more his style, but he insists on looking at houses. Or more accurately, on having me waste *my* time looking at houses. Oh well, it's all part of the business," and she shook her head in resignation. "Now, where do we go next?"

"Belmont," I answered since I was the designated keeper of the listings for this drive. I held out the form so she could see the address.

"Right, Belmont it is," and she headed south on the highway.

"Well, this one has more promise," Diana said ten minutes later as she drove up the herringbone-patterned brick driveway. "It definitely has the style he wants."

His style maybe, but certainly not mine I thought as we entered the ultra-modern house. I'd never been a fan of the open floor plan since it made me feel like I was on the shop floor of some big factory. As for the interior design, it was all marble finishes and hard edges, and the ubiquitous shades of white gave it a cold, clinical feeling.

I didn't like it, but John would, I thought, then gave myself a mental shake. Don't go there. It isn't relevant *what* John would like. Besides, we already lived in the house he picked out, and that wasn't enough for him.

Or maybe *I* wasn't enough for him.

"I'm heading upstairs. Coming?" Diana interrupted my train of thought—just as well since it was taking me in circles.

"No, I'll wait in the car."

She gave me a sharp look but didn't comment. "Okay, it won't take me long," and tossed me her keys.

And it didn't—less than twenty minutes to finish what she had to do inside. While I waited, I leafed through the other listings she had left on the dash, fantasizing which one of those houses would be the right one for me. And while I didn't find my perfect home, I did see one that looked like the kind of house Cookie would live in: a small cottage on a corner lot with a garden, located in one of those little towns that dotted the coastline.

There was a partly enclosed veranda where she could relax on the porch swing after a long day at the bakery. And, I noticed as I looked at the images and read the accompanying descriptions, a kitchen with a marble-topped counter perfect for rolling out pastry. I closed my eyes, visualizing Cookie living in that house, baking in that house, entertaining friends and lovers in that house...

"Are you *sleeping*?"

Diana's voice startled me.

"No, thinking about this house," and I showed her the listing after she got into the car. "It would be a perfect fit for Cookie—you know, the character in my book."

"Would it help to see it in person?" she asked. "It's down the road a bit and a friend of mine is doing the open house. If we hurry, we can get there before it's over."

"Let's do it!"

And in short order we were parked in front of the nine-hundred-square-foot home. Once inside, while Diana explained to Liz, the listing agent, why we were there, I wandered through the rooms, making notes and taking pictures. If I located the fictional version a few blocks from Cookie's bakery, she could walk home after work, giving her the opportunity to interact with friends and neighbors.

"And that's how she could meet the man who is thinking of buying the empty building next to her shop that she had had her eye on. Only he wants to turn it into a bar or something and he's got the money to outbid her. So, she—"

"Who are you talking to?"

I was so immersed in working out the story points aloud that I hadn't realized Diana had come into the room.

"Myself," I answered. "I was plotting out the story. Look, I'm done. Can we get moving? I'm anxious to get home and put in some time on the book."

"Sure," and Diana handed me some papers. "I got a few more details from Liz that might help," and with a brief wave to the agent who was picking up the Open House signs from the sidewalk, the two of us left what would be Cookie's house forevermore—at least in my mind—and went back to Los Gatos.

"Good luck on the writing," Diana called out her window as I took the box holding my pottery order from the trunk. "And call me if you need to talk, you know, about anything."

I knew what she meant as I waved goodbye and then headed to the front door, stopping long enough to grab the mail from the box. Not about the book—that really wasn't her thing—but about John and the whole relationship problem. But right now, all I wanted to concentrate on was the story that was developing in my head. I dropped the envelopes on the side table and went into my office.

And that's where I spent the next few hours, drafting various scenes and plot points: Cookie in her home, Cookie looking at her finances and wondering how much she could bid, Cookie running into the other buyer at a farmer's market and he ends up asking her out for dinner....

I was so excited about the book that it was well past midnight before I finally went to bed. And I was back at my desk early the next morning, immersing myself in detailing more of Cookie's history and relationships and love affairs.

I started drafting a bedroom scene between Cookie and the man she had been dating. It would take place on a Saturday afternoon, I decided, and in broad daylight. Not for Cookie were dim lights and bed-sheets to hide under. No, she was proud of her body, extra pounds and all, and not averse to showing it off. Not for the first time I found myself envying her self-confidence.

I had just gotten Cookie out of bed and on her way to her kitchen where she would make a delicious après-sex snack when I heard the key turn in the lock and familiar footsteps in the hall.

It was John.

Chapter 27

"IT's ME," HE CALLED, AND HIS VOICE GREW LOUDER AS HE CAME closer to my office. "I wasn't going to make it back until Tuesday, but the client changed the plans so...."

His voice trailed off as I turned to face him. Maybe it was the new hairstyle and makeup or the new attitude I projected, but he was definitely caught off guard. This wasn't the Fran who screamed at him about his affair, the Fran he had walked out on a little more than two weeks ago, but a new Fran. And he obviously wasn't sure how to respond to her.

"Did you have a nice trip?" trying my best to keep my voice calm as my heart pounded and my palms began to perspire. While I might not *look* like the old Fran, there was still enough of her inside me to make it a challenge to keep control over all my warring emotions: anger, pain, and heartache all fighting for the upper hand against the admittedly fragile sense of self-esteem and awareness that my time away had birthed.

And let's not forget about love—or what I thought was love. Just the sight of John brought back those memories from so long ago: the nights in his arms, the times we had attended parties together and I had been so proud and happy to be with him, by his side....

Stop that, I told myself firmly. That wasn't *love* but sexual attraction. Real love was something else, something healthy, something you can count on to grow through the years.

"I was going to put on a pot of coffee. Would you like some?" and I walked past him on my way to the kitchen. "Sorry about the rescheduling. I know how you hate it when things don't go according to plan."

But if he heard the irony in my voice, he didn't respond. Instead, he followed me into the kitchen, coming close enough to touch my hair.

I held myself stiffly, hoping that he wouldn't try to embrace me, wondering what I would do if he did, but then he stepped back.

"I like your hair," he said. "It makes you look different, very stylish and sexy. And the color—it's wild! I would have never pictured you as a redhead, but it looks great!"

So that was how he was planning to play it, I thought as I filled the coffee basket and turned on the machine. No "I'm sorry I had an affair" or "Please forgive me" or even "Let's sit down and discuss what happened."

I could tell by his attitude that, as far as he was concerned, the unpleasant events that marked our last meeting were in the past. He had decided to ignore the whole situation and expected me to do the same.

The old Fran would have gone along with it, not brought it up, just swept it under the rug. But that Fran was gone. The new Fran was angry, but it was a different kind of anger—one that didn't trigger an outburst of screaming but a cold flame. And it was directed as much at myself as at him. I was angry with John for cheating, yes, but angrier at myself for taking it and all his other bad behaviors that had marked our time together. Angry at myself for not taking better care of Fran—for letting someone hurt her as though she deserved to be hurt.

"Not this time." I didn't realize I had spoken out loud until he repeated my words.

"'Not this time'? What do you mean?"

I poured coffee into one of my new mugs before answering him. "I've been thinking that it's time for a change."

"Well, you sure made a good start on that!" he said, a shade too heartily while he watched me warily. "What else did you have in mind? Oh, I'm sorry. I didn't ask about the book. How is it coming?"

Now that was *really* out of character and a good indication of how uncertain he was feeling. The only interest John had ever shown in my work was when it came to sales because it was my income that paid the mortgage and the real estate taxes and most of the other bills that came our way.

"Fran? How is the book coming?"

I could tell he was more than a little worried. I was too quiet. This wasn't like the old Fran he knew.

"As I was saying, I think it's time for a change." I drank my coffee and set the now empty mug in the sink before turning to face him. "This house is too big for me, too much of a burden, financially speaking. I want to downsize, get a place that doesn't have such a high overhead. Taking all that into account, I've made a decision. I'm selling the house."

"Selling the house," he repeated. "Sure, we can talk about that. Although this really is a great place and—"

But I kept on talking, cutting him off. "I don't need much, after all: an office, two bedrooms and a big space where I can entertain my friends. Somewhere closer to the coast where it will be peaceful and quiet. I always liked living by the ocean, you know."

It might have been my decisive tone or the repeated use of the first-person-singular pronoun, but whichever was responsible, John knew something was wrong, that something major had changed. He shifted from one foot to the other, looked away and then back at me, and shoved his hands into his pockets.

"If that's what you need," he said finally. "You may be right. This house does require a lot of money to maintain. I have an idea," his enthusiastic tone not quite ringing true. "Why don't we look for a place closer to my office? Or over in Oakland," perhaps suddenly realizing that being in proximity to his studio might prove to be a little inconvenient, given his extracurricular activities. "Let's talk about it—"

But I stopped him again, raising a hand as though to keep his words from coming any closer to me.

"There is nothing for *us*" emphasizing the pronoun "to talk about. Not anymore. And I really have to thank you for being so insistent in the beginning about not getting married. What was it you said? That it would be such a major legal expense to get the prenuptial paperwork drawn up? That the only people who would benefit would be the attorneys? That after all, it wasn't like we were going to have children, so it didn't matter if we were married or not?"

I paused, looked at him, and went on. "You even recommended that we put the house and mortgage in my name. For tax purposes, you said. And you were absolutely correct. That will make it all so much simpler now."

"Now?" he repeated.

"Yes, now. But I'm a reasonable person, John. I know it will take you time to get yourself packed up, so I'll give you until the end of the month to move all your belongings back to your studio. Although I'd like you to plan on staying there starting today. That was another area where you were so right: keeping your studio. Especially since it has that bedroom where you would stay when you said it was too late to make the drive all the way back here. In the meantime, I have writing to do so I'm going back to work," and I walked out of the room, trying to project the appearance of calmness while I resisted the urge to give my emotions free rein and let the old Fran—the screaming, outraged Fran—out.

There was still a part of me—a big part, I had to admit—that was angry, and that anger's source was pain. I may have entered this relationship with my eyes shut to the issues that existed, but my heart had been open. I had made lots of room for John inside it. Now, even though I knew that ending the relationship was the right thing to do, there was still the issue of that huge empty space inside me—the loss of my dream of a future together.

One foot after the other, I repeated to myself, remembering Martha's advice. Just keep moving forward because to go back to what we had, which wasn't what I *thought* it was, would be damaging and destructive.

I closed the office door behind me and debated what to do first, shutting my ears to any sounds that John would be making. I didn't want to hear him, didn't want to know if he was packing or waiting for me to come out of my office and come to my senses, at least from his point of view.

I moved some papers around, toyed with the idea of continuing to work on my book, and finally slumped in my chair, staring blindly out the window. It was all well and good to be so firm and positive regarding what I wanted, but I knew the transition, however long overdue it was, would not come without pain and fear and a host of other emotions I would have to get through until I reached the other side.

But that's the only way change happens, I reminded myself. If you want to build a better, more fulfilled and happier life, you have to dig through a lot of dirt to get the foundation solidly in place while discarding all the debris that's in your way. Otherwise, the first decent-sized earthquake that comes your way—be it money problems, health problems, or relationship problems—will shake the whole structure until it breaks into smithereens.

John opened the door and stood there as if uncertain whether to enter or stay safely out of reach.

"Fran? Can we talk? About us, I mean. We've made some mistakes in our relationship, but I'm sure we can work things out."

"Why?" I asked, turning to face him. "Not why do you think we can 'work things out' but why do we even need to discuss it? There is nothing *to* discuss—not really. We made mistakes, both of us, because of the people we were. But I'm not that person anymore, John. I've changed. And that means I want something else."

He looked at me, then frowned.

"You found someone *else*?" and the disbelief in his voice would have been irritating if his opinion of me still mattered.

"No, of course not," I answered impatiently. "Why is it that men always take it for granted that when a woman leaves them, it's because there is another man? I am leaving you," slowly, clearly, "because of *me*. Because this," and I waved my hand, the gesture encompassing more than the room or house but the whole of our life together, "just isn't working for me anymore," echoing the very words that the fictional husband in *Love in the Islands* had said to my heroine when ending their marriage.

"Fran—" he started, but I shook my head.

"Please leave, John. I need to finish my work."

And I turned away from him, back to my desk, back to my new book, back to the new life I had started to create.

I heard the office door close and for a moment was tempted to open it, to take back everything I'd said. Because as much as I knew it was the right choice, it was still a terrible thing to watch something die and not lift a finger to stop it—indeed, to be the one making the choice to let it end.

But it had to be done. Otherwise, he would continue to betray me, and I would continue to be hurt.

"And I deserve better than that," I said, my words echoing in the room.

Resolutely, I went back to the novel, deciding to forgo work on the bedroom scene in favor of the one where Cookie checks out the dance options. Since I needed to do a little in-person research on that aspect of the book, I searched online for local dance studios that offered adult classes. If a man was going to dance his way into Cookie's heart, I had to know the type of steps he would use. Would it be the oh-so-sexy tango, the dip-and-swirl of the waltz, or the get-your-pulse-racing Texas two-step?

I was sidetracked by the online videos showing couples gliding around the dance floor. They were perfectly in sync, and I found myself envying their smooth steps and perfect turns. What would it be like to have that kind of real-life relationship, I wondered, where each person knew instinctively what the other would do and was prepared to follow or lead?

"That certainly wasn't the one I had with John," I said, but realized I was back in that "what went wrong" cycle of thought that would get me nowhere. To escape, I grabbed my cell phone. I had told John I was selling the house, so I had better make good on my statement, and that meant calling Diana to start the process.

But when she answered, I could tell from all the background chatter that she wasn't in her office but at one of the many showings she scheduled for Sunday afternoons.

"Fran! How are you?" Not waiting for my response, she went on. "I'd love to talk, but I'm with a client so I have to scoot. Can I call you later?"

"Yes, but it's business. I want to sell my house."

Silence ensued, and I wondered for a moment if she had already hung up. Then her voice came back on the line.

"I'll be there at six with the contract and a bottle of wine. It will be just *you*, won't it?"

"Yes. John's gone," my emphasis on the last word answering her unspoken question.

"Great. I'll see you then. What? Yes, the appliances are included..." and Diana was gone.

Okay, the first step was done, and somehow with that one call, I felt a little bit lighter, a little more focused on my future instead of the past. I went back to my research, noting the phone numbers of different dance studios, then started drafting bits of dialogue and scene details as I took Cookie from her sofa to the dance floor. Several hours later I pushed away from the desk and stretched my stiff muscles, feeling the effects of too much time at the keyboard.

Suddenly, I realized how quiet the house was—the kind of silence that indicated the absence of another person. I backed up the files and shut off the computer. Then I opened the door and stepped back into the other part of my life.

John was gone. Not just absent but gone entirely. It was telling to realize that, in the space of a few hours, he had managed to pack up all his belongings. His clothes were missing along with the few pieces of camera equipment that he kept in the downstairs closet and the running shoes that were usually parked by the French doors.

Everything else that was left was mine—bought and paid for with my money.

I walked through the rooms, noting the bare spaces in the closets and drawers. And as if to make it even clearer, he had left his house keys on the hall table right on top of yesterday's mail. I had done the unforgiveable, from his point of view. I had told him that *I* didn't want *him*. And that was something that his ego couldn't take.

I slipped the keys into my pocket, picked up the mail, and went back into my office. I felt oddly disconnected as though I didn't know where I was or where I belonged. I looked through the envelopes, set aside the bills, and threw the advertisements in the trash. All that was left was one envelope with the name "McCallister" in the upper left-hand corner. The last name of the man who had called to tell me of John's infidelity. Why was he writing to me? What could he want now?

I opened the flap, pulled out the single sheet of paper, and read:

I want to tell you I'm sorry. My husband told me he called you and that he told you about the affair. And after a long talk, I realized whatever problems our marriage had, getting involved with John was no solution. I told John it was over. And it is—that part underlined twice—*I hope you can forgive me,* followed by her signature: *Beth McCallister.*

I stood there and for a moment wondered if my decision would have been any different had I read the letter before John came home. Would I have gone back to being the old forgive-and-forget Fran?

"No. Not now," my words coming with a determination that surprised me. "Too much has changed in me to be that woman again."

I read the letter one more time before tearing it into tiny bits and tossing it into the wastebasket. It wasn't only the note I was throwing away. It was any remnant of the old Fran that still existed.

Chapter 28

Just then, the doorbell rang. It was Diana.

"Are you okay?" I nodded. "Good. Let's go into the kitchen and we can talk. I brought the wine," she added. "The good stuff—a bottle of expensive Cabernet I got from a client who was thrilled to death that he only had to come down ten grand to sell his house. But let's get to your news. What's up?" she asked, filling our glasses.

I took a sip as I mulled over where to begin.

"John's gone," I said finally, and she nodded.

"Good. And the bad news?"

"Diana, that's cold!" I protested, but she held up her hand to stop me.

"Look, I'm not trying to be mean, but I have waited a long time to see that jerk out of your life! Tell me: Was John leaving his idea or yours?"

I took another drink, a longer one this time, while I considered her question. Whose decision *was* it? Granted, you could say that he left a long time ago when he first started seeing other women. Or maybe, to be brutally honest, it wasn't so much a case of leaving as never being here to begin with—at least, not in any meaningful way. In the years we had been together, he had kept his bags packed, metaphorically speaking—temporarily in my life but not being part of *our* life or the life I had hoped we were creating together.

But in the end, it was my decision to open the door and put him on the other side.

"Mine," I answered firmly, and she applauded.

"Good girl! I was hoping that was the case!" She started rummaging through the pantry looking for something to eat. "I'm starved," pulling out a jar of organic peanut butter. "Do you have any crackers to go with this? I haven't eaten all day."

When I didn't answer, she looked over at me and frowned. "You're not second-guessing your decision, are you?"

"No, I'm not," but my voice held less determination than I would have liked. "It's, well—what's wrong with *me*? Why did he *do* this to me?"

Diana set down the jar and came over to where I stood, suddenly overwhelmed with waves of anger and pain.

"Look, this has nothing to do with you—not really. A man like John wants the thrill of the hunt. He has to prove something to himself, that he can have anyone he wants. And once he gets her, then it's all over and the hunt starts again."

She was right. The signs were there, but I had chosen to ignore them until I received the phone call that finally started my self-realization process. I nodded and took out a half-empty box of stale saltines and handed it over to her.

"Okay. That's over with. Done. *Fini*. End of story." She smiled at me, and I couldn't help but smile back. "And these won't do," tossing the crackers back at me. "Throw them out and let's order a pizza. And while we wait, tell me about Martha and the Whale Inn. She sounds like a hoot! Where is this place anyway?"

By the time I got as far as the senior show, the pizza had long since arrived and we had made our way through most of it.

"You absolutely have to have the launch for your new book at her place, and I'll foot the bill. I insist," as I started to protest. "Besides, even though I'm not charging you commission for selling this joint, I have a few clients in mind who are looking for a place like this, so as the buyer's agent, I'll make my money there."

After wiping the pizza sauce from her fingers, she opened her briefcase and pulled out a folder. "I brought some comps to help us set the right price and get this place sold. *And* the sales contract," handing it over to me with a raised eyebrow.

Obviously, she still doubted if I would stick to my decision. But without hesitation, I took the paperwork from her and definitively signed my name on the property-owner line. And with that, I could hear the door on my past closing, firmly and emphatically, and made up my mind never to open it again.

From that point on, Diana was all business. We went through the house, room by room, with Diana making notes and pointing out selling features as well as a few places requiring minor improvements. By the time we were done, it was eleven and I was exhausted.

"I'll send someone out from my office the end of next week to take some pictures and shoot a video. Once those are ready, I'll schedule the open houses. Although I might already have someone who would be interested," Diana said as she gathered her papers, including the listing contract, now signed and dated. "In the meantime, let's set up a time this week when we can go look at some houses. Do you have any idea what you want?"

"A smaller place for sure," I said as I walked her toward the front door. "And near the ocean and by Coastside Bay if possible," thinking how good I had felt while I was there and hoping those feelings would help me adjust to the change in my circumstances.

"A Craftsman-style home," I added, recalling the pictures in the books I had bought at Barnaby's, "with lots of warm woods and soft colors."

"Hmm." She pulled out her phone to check her calendar and said, "I have a few listings that might be what you want. How does tomorrow look? I can pick you up after ten and we'll make a day of it."

"Okay," I agreed before I could reevaluate my decision.

While selling a house is usually a stressful event, in this case, it went a lot more smoothly than I had any right to expect. One of Diana's buyers was ready to close in less than a month, and with a cash offer on the table, I didn't even have to wait for loan paperwork to be approved.

But when it came to buying a home, my luck didn't hold. Every day for two weeks, Diana and I toured houses along the Pacific Coast Highway, but after fourteen days we were no closer to finding a place that was right for me in terms of price, style, and location. I had just resigned myself to having to find a rental apartment and a storage unit for those items I was taking with me when she called me late Thursday night.

"I have a dozen new listings, and I feel certain that one of these will be the right one," she said. "Be ready. I'll see you bright and early tomorrow!"

"Okay, fine, whatever," I answered halfheartedly, and she hung up, probably afraid that, given my apparent lack of enthusiasm, I might change my mind if we talked any longer.

Tomorrow, I thought, looking at the task list I had made for the following day, which included a chapter with a key pivotal point. Cookie had to decide if she should take the risk and buy the adjoining commercial space to turn it into a café. Doing so would put her financial security at risk since it would involve a mortgage and expensive renovations to turn a retail establishment into a food-service one. At the same time, she couldn't get the picture of the café out of her mind.

But when I tried to picture how Cookie's café would look, all I could think of were Craftsman-style homes and the way the sun set on the ocean and the smell of saltwater and the cries of seabirds. Cookie's decision would have to wait. I needed to deal with my own first.

Not that I was all that optimistic the next morning when Diana arrived.

"Keep an open mind," she said as she handed me a sheaf of listings to review. "Even if you don't like these, your comments will help me narrow the field when more come on the market. And don't worry," she added, "we'll find something. I promise."

Although I wasn't as positive as Diana, I flipped through the sheets, trying to boost my enthusiasm for what I was certain would be a failed expedition. But while the first eleven had strong points, none of them were what I wanted, and I was determined not to settle. I had done enough of that. This time my decision had to be the right one for me, even if it took months to find.

But as it turned out, it didn't take months—just a twenty-minute drive down a side road off the highway, midway between Coastside Bay and Moss Beach. Diana pulled up to number twelve on the list: a thousand square feet of stone-fronted charm, from the long brick driveway bordered with yarrow to the coffeeberry bushes ranging along the front of the house. Like eyes meeting across the crowded room (as romance novels go), the house and I looked at each other, and that was all it took. My heart was captured.

I got out of Diana's car and stood there drinking in the view while Diana unlocked the front door.

"Hey, don't stand there forever! We came to see the house, so let's get moving!" she said and disappeared inside, pointing out features before I even made it all the way into the home. "Check out the fireplace in the family room," she ordered before I could get my bearings. "And look at the hardwood floors: dark walnut, the perfect contrast to these creamy walls—which, by the way, have been freshly painted, so no work there for you to do. And the kitchen," leading the way down the hallway. "Look at these gorgeous cabinets with frosted glass doors! Not to mention the granite countertop and stainless appliances. You'll have to get new dishes to match this look!"

Before I could take it all in, she pulled me out of the kitchen and farther down the hall.

"And here," she said, opening the double doors, "is where you'll finish your next best seller!" standing back so I could get the full effect of the office. Another fireplace, large casement windows on two sides that reminded me of my room at Martha's, and best of all, French doors leading out to a deck.

I could see myself writing there, maybe with a dog sprawled out on a braided rug in front of a crackling fire. This was my dream office, my dream home.

But as beautiful as the interior was, it was the backyard that sealed the deal. I went out the French doors and into a veritable paradise of plants: coyote bushes holding the promise of yellow-white flowers in the fall, a bed of wood strawberries already full of fragrant white blooms, and even more yellow, this time the yellow orange of California poppies. Cypress trees mixed with vine maples and dozens of other plants and shrubs that would take a horticultural guide to identify... I sat down on the top step of the deck to catch my breath.

For once, Diana was quiet too, as entranced by the setting as I was. But her silence didn't last long.

"One more thing," and she reached down to pull me to my feet. "Follow that path," indicating the flagstones set in the grass leading away from the house. And obediently I did. There was a tall wooden post with an oil lamp hanging from the cross beam and, alongside it, a stone staircase wending its way down through yellow-flowered bush lupines, leading to a beach—*my* beach—complete with a small fire pit and two weathered but still sturdy Adirondack chairs.

I kicked off my shoes and strolled along the shoreline, letting the waves caress my toes. There was no debate. The house was meant for me.

"Yes! Yes, I want this house. I have to *have* this house. It's *exactly* the house I've been looking for! Damn it, Diana, why are you laughing at me?"

She came over to give me a hug. "Because I've never heard you so determined! And you're in luck. The owner dropped the price this morning."

That was it. I wrote the check, packed my possessions, sold the furniture, and hired movers. And less than sixty days after I returned from my stay at the Whale Inn, I found myself in my new home and more than halfway through my fourth book, *Love in the Light of Day*, the story of Cookie and her life and loves and how she made it all work in spite of, or even because of, her age and the wisdom that came from growing older.

Chapter 29

"So, tell us, Ms. Carter, where did you get your idea for *this* book?"

It was my sixth book signing in less than two weeks—this one at Barnaby's—and once again I heard the same question someone always asked during the Q&A part of the event.

Readers always want to know the facts behind the story: who are the real people that the characters are based on, what kind of research went into getting accurate background details, and where the original idea came from.

In the interest of fair play, I always offered some kind of truthful answer—half-truths really. I certainly didn't want to explain the down-and-dirty details of how I—"Fran Carter, successful romance novelist"— had had a week-long epiphany that ended with my realizing the kind of person I wanted to be and, from there, the kind of women I wanted to bring to life through my books.

Instead, as all writers do, I edited and revised until I came up with a true enough answer that would satisfy them.

"Women these days aren't waiting for a man to come rescue them from feeling unfulfilled or lonely, but are living busy, exciting lives on their own," was my usual response. "So, I wanted to create a protagonist those women could relate to, who was already in a good place but was open to sharing that space with a man who *also* had it 'all together.' A man who was happy with *his* life and wanted to share that happiness with her."

That usually satisfied them. But this time, my female inquisitor wasn't quite through with me.

"But it's so different from the other books you'd written before. Yes, of course there is a love interest and of course she ends up living happily ever after, but in this one"—and she held up her copy of *Love in the Light of Day*—"Cookie isn't sitting around crying and complaining. She's doing something with her life, and whether she ends up with or without a man, she's satisfied with the life she has created. Does that mean that your idea of life has changed as well? In your life, are you Cookie or are you like those women characters you used to write about?"

I took a long sip of water, more to gain time to collect my thoughts than because I was thirsty. I wasn't sure if my reading public knew that my fairy-tale romance was over. Maybe some had noticed that my jacket bio no longer mentioned how I "shared my home with John Robbins, noted celebrity photographer," but instead featured a photograph of me in my new garden at my new house with no reference to anyone else.

I set down my glass. "Well, as any fiction writer will tell you, there is always some part of the author in the book, and I'm no exception. You'll find a bit of me in *all* my characters, from the heroine to the hero to the villain—not that my books have villains in the sense of murderers or other evil-doers but villains in that they didn't bring out the best in my leading ladies. But in answer to your question, I like to think I'm more like Cookie than Melanie or Serena or Caroline," naming the heroines of my first three books. "Not that there is anything wrong with them, but because as we grow older and learn more and have more life experiences, we change. And I must admit that, in this case, I *have* changed, influenced, I suppose, by Cookie, strange as that may sound."

Some of the women in the audience nodded as I continued.

"That's why this book is called *Love in the Light of Day*. Since it is a romance novel, the main character has to fall in love. But sometimes the man we fall in love with amid the moonlight and roses isn't the same guy we find at our breakfast table when the sun comes up. In Cookie's case, after a few romantic missteps, she finds love and it lasts from the moonlit evening until dawn and all the way through to dinner time—that day and beyond."

"So, you do still believe in love? You don't mention anyone on the back cover—not like you did before. Do *you* have someone in your life now?"

The interest level perked up, and I knew I wouldn't be able to blame the omission as an error by the jacket designer or avoid the question entirely.

I smiled. "Yes, I still believe in love and no, I don't have anyone in my life—not unless you count Lady, my dog!" which got a chuckle from my audience. "As I said, we all change as we go through life, and these days I am in a place where I think I am doing better being by myself. It's not that I don't value love or want it in my life," I added. "I just want to take some time to get to know who this latest Fran is before I send her out to meet anyone else. I've been so busy the past few years—researching and writing my books and then traveling to meet all you wonderful people who read them—that I lost touch with myself. Do you know what I mean?"

And this time, more than a few heads nodded in assent.

"So, it's time for me to get to know who I am and what I want for this stage of my life. And if love comes knocking, well, I wouldn't exactly slam the door in its face, but I would make sure it's the right one before I asked it in for coffee!"

"And that winds up the speaking part of Ms. Carter's visit to our store," said Connie, shepherding me away from the microphone and over to the table where several tall stacks of *Love in the Light of Day* awaited my signature.

I took my seat, pulling my lucky purple pen out of my purse. Then it was on to the conversations I'd had so many times since my first book came out: "And your name is...?' "So glad you came to my book signing! It's always great to meet my fans!" and "Thanks so much, and you have a wonderful day, too!"

And this time, unlike the book events that had taken place with my last book, the line seemed to extend endlessly, past the roped-off author area, down through the row of travel guides and maps, and into the sci-fi section. Woman after woman waiting to buy *Love in the Light of Day* and hoping, perhaps, to learn something from Cookie's experience that they could use in their own lives.

As *I* did, I thought as I smiled and signed copy after copy. They say that writers write about what they most need to learn, and that was certainly true in my case. Writing Cookie's story—taking her from an in-demand bakery owner to one on the brink of bankruptcy (due to a lawsuit that was eventually thrown out of court) and back again.

Following her through several relationship possibilities, courtesy of an online dating site, until she finally met the "man of her dreams," who turned out to be the man of her waking hours, too. It was the type of story *I* needed to read when I was building a new life of my own.

Now, like Cookie, I was back where I felt most at home. And if I hadn't yet found the man for my future, I was doing better than when I was with the man who was now in my past.

"May I get you more water? Or perhaps you would like a latte?" Connie was at my side as she had been since I arrived at Barnaby's, unobtrusively making sure I had everything I needed.

"No, I'm great," I answered, looking at the size of the line and estimating that another forty minutes or so should be enough to finish.

"I wanted to tell you what a difference your book made in my life," she continued, taking the next customer's money with one hand while handing her a book with the other. "I was in a relationship—not a bad one but one that wasn't working. And I didn't realize that I needed to make a change until I read your book about Cookie. Sometimes we women can be so stupid." And she sighed.

"Well, the good thing is that we can also get smart," I responded with a smile. "Although it sometimes takes us longer than we would like!"

She smiled back and kept the line moving until I signed the last book with a flourish. I had sold all three hundred books, making this the most profitable signing yet. But it was more than just the dollar amount in sales I had generated that made me leave the store basking in a warm glow. It was the sense that I had given my readers something new to consider, had offered them a heroine who was a new kind of woman living a life they could aspire to—one where they were in control of their destiny.

As I left Barnaby's, I glanced at my reflection in the store's windows. The crimson dress from Maxwell's was the perfect shade for my auburn highlights while my makeup and shorter hairstyle made me look like a poised, self-assured woman who was ready for anything.

I smiled at the woman I saw. It had been a long, hard, and painful road, but I finally felt like I had arrived at a place where I wanted to be, a place where Fran Carter was at home, both literally and figuratively.

I tossed my handbag onto the passenger seat and pulled onto the highway in the direction of Martha's place. She had telephoned last week, asking me to come over for a post-signing wine-and-cheese celebration, and I was looking forward to having some quiet time with her amidst the woods and water.

Well, the ocean and trees were there, but the quiet time wasn't an option, I realized as I saw how many cars, including Diana's, were in the parking lot.

"Here you are!" said Martha when she caught sight of me. "Come on up and have some food!"

Not that I needed any encouragement. The aroma of fresh-baked pizza and heady scent of fresh-brewed coffee made me realize that I was ravenous and more than willing to forgo quiet in favor of food.

"I thought it was time we threw you a coming-out party to celebrate the new Fran," said Diana, coming up behind me and linking her arm in mine. "I called Martha, and we decided to have it at the inn. And we've all been waiting here, eating and drinking, until you were done being the 'successful author'! Now come on and get something to eat!"

I followed her up the steps and into the dining room, but before I could reach the food, I was surrounded by familiar faces.

"We are all so proud of you!" said Shauna, handing me a flat rectangular package. "I hope you like it!" and she waited anxiously while I carefully removed the paper to reveal a pen-and-ink drawing of a woman's smiling face with a baker's toque perched atop her curls.

"It's Cookie, your character," she explained. "I took the idea from the cover image. I never did something like this before, but I felt inspired, know what I mean?"

I nodded and hugged her. "I know *exactly* what you mean, and I love it! You captured her perfectly! I'll hang it in my office where I can see it every day."

"Now, Shauna, don't hog Fran," and there was Sadie, gently pushing Shauna out of the way before thrusting a small box at me. "Don't drop it! They're breakable!"

I opened it to find four mugs inside, each one featuring a scene from *Love in the Light of Day*: Cookie in her bakeshop kitchen wearing an oversized white apron, Cookie in Paris with the Eiffel Tower in the background, Cookie in front of her café, and last but not least, Cookie holding her very own cookbook.

"These are for you, but I can make more if you want to use them as promotional items," Sadie said, and I nodded.

"That's a great idea! Or it can be part of the raffle we're doing to benefit the food bank," Martha said, and I turned to find her right behind me. "How long will it take you to make four sets?" and she pulled Sadie away just as Diana came up.

"Come on, you'd better get something to eat before it's all gone," leading me over to the food table.

"So how did it go?" she asked as I debated between the garganelli pasta with Swiss chard or the pine nut, black olive, and sun-dried tomato pizza.

The hell with the calories, I thought and took both, adding a few crab cakes for good measure.

"It went really well," I answered, after swallowing my first bite. "When I think back to what happened with my last book and how those signings went—well, this one was so different! Back then I could see the fan base dwindling before my eyes, and I figured I'd end up as one of those has-been authors who slid right back down after getting halfway up the success hill! But this book... well, this book has really changed things around!"

"You know, it's not just your professional future it changed but your attitude as well," Diana said. "You're not the same person you used to be. And I don't mean the hair and clothes, but deep down inside. You're happier, more confident. I haven't seen you like this in years—not since your first book came out!"

I took another bite of pizza, chewing thoughtfully while I reflected on her words. It was true that I did feel better about myself, but was it just because John was no longer part of my life?

I remembered the Fran I used to be even before John and had to admit that, as much as I'd like to think his absence was why I now felt more satisfied with my life, it wouldn't be quite accurate.

John—and by extension, all those other men with whom I'd had relationships that didn't work out—wasn't the cause but the symptom of what had been wrong in my life. Had I believed in myself more, had a clearer understanding of what I wanted in life and relationships, I wouldn't have settled for the kind of man who reinforced my own poor self-image.

Had I loved myself more, I wouldn't have chosen men who, in hindsight, didn't love me at all.

"Hey, pay attention here! This is a party, not introspection time," Diana admonished, jostling my arm. "And we have a lot to celebrate! Not just your book's success but your new life!"

She waved her arm to include all the people gathered there: Martha, of course, and Shauna along with April and Donna, her coworkers from the salon. Carol from Maxwell's boutique together with Sadie and some of the members of the Bay City Bullets. And more faces I recognized from the library's book club and Martha's seniors' group.

It was hard to remember those days when I was working alone in that other house living a life that wasn't a good fit. I felt like Sleeping

Beauty, but instead of being awakened by a prince's kiss to live happily ever after in his castle, I had awakened myself—admittedly with help from Diana, Martha, and even my fictional heroine Cookie. Now I was happily residing in my own castle, surrounded by friends and looking forward to a future full of possibilities.

Maybe that future would include a love relationship. Or, like Martha, I would live out the rest of my life without a man by my side. Maybe my next book would be a success, or some other author would pass me by to claim the top spot on the best-seller list.

No matter what happened or what path my life took, I would still be okay.

"To Fran, our author and friend!" Martha said, raising her glass, and the rest of the group followed suit.

To Fran, I thought decisively. To the Fran I am today and the Fran I want to be from now on. Now that I've found her, I won't let her go.

Author's Notes

READERS FREQUENTLY ASK WHERE WRITERS GET THEIR STORY ideas. To tell the truth, sometimes we writers wish *we* knew that, too. Our writing life would be so much easier if we only had a clue behind which door the latest source of inspiration was hiding or in which box the characters were patiently waiting or under which bed the plotlines were stored.

In the case of *Finding Fran*, I can't point to any one thing but rather a compilation of random events: unexpected phone calls that brought bad news rather than good, relationships (mine and those of other women I knew) that didn't quite turn out the way one had hoped, and the unavoidable realization that the life I was living wasn't exactly the one I wanted to live anymore.

And the more women I spoke with only confirmed that my own experiences weren't unique to me. Life is, after all, a series of transitions: positive and negative. We can either ride the ups and downs like unwilling passengers or take charge of the journey, navigating through the rough spots on our way to our chosen destination.

That was the situation Fran Carter found herself in and the challenge she faced: figuring out what she wanted and then finding the courage to go after it. I hope you enjoyed her story!

About Nancy Christie

NANCY CHRISTIE HAS BEEN MAKING UP STORIES SINCE SHE learned how to print, and she plans to continue as long as her fingers can work the keyboard since she can't help herself. Writing is her addiction, and fiction her drug of choice.

Finding Fran is the second novel in her Midlife Moxie Novel Series and her eighth book. An award-winning author of both fiction and nonfiction, Nancy is a member of the American Society of Journalists and Authors, Women's Fiction Writers Association, and the Florida Writers Association.

She's also the host of the Living the Writing Life podcast and founder of the annual "Midlife Moxie" Day and "Celebrate Short Fiction" Day.

For more about Nancy and links to her social media profiles, visit her website at www.nancychristie.com.

Scan this code for more information about her current and upcoming books.